Reclaiming

THE SPOTTED DOG SERIES

CHRISTINA SOL

Reclaiming

By: Christina Sol

Published by: Sol Media LLC

Editor: Lynne Pearson, Allthatediting.com

Proofreader: MS Literary

Cover Design: LJ Anderson, Mayhem Cover Creations

ISBN: 979-8-9855935-3-2

❀ Created with Vellum

For my mom.
*From grade school Scholastic Book Fairs to now, whether you knew
it or not, you've always encouraged me to pursue this dream.
Thank you for believing in me.*

CONTENTS

CHAPTER ONE

"What are you doing with that guy?"

Kate Peterson glanced to her right, where her best friend sat. Pasting a smile on her face, she shrugged. "Scott's a really nice guy, Raven."

Her friend shot her a death glare and Kate tried not to wince. She turned her attention back to the baseball field as the Sunday afternoon crowd around her roared with laughter at the Seattle Mariners Moose's change-of-inning antics. Her smile was starting to hurt.

"He's a douchebag," Raven said, disgust dripping from every word. "A douchebag who pays more attention to his damn phone than he does you."

Kate started to shake her head but stopped and let out a breath. Dang. Raven was right. Kate leaned forward, elbows on her knees, and looked back at her friend. She tried to ignore the empty feeling that settled in her belly. "Yeah, he's pretty obnoxious."

"Obnoxious? Kate, he's a fucking idiot. Seriously. Why are you even giving him the time of day? If anything, you should be dating his friend, Dave. At least that guy is less douchey and looks you in the eye when he talks to you."

"Scott's nice," Kate repeated, glancing around to make sure he and the rest of the guys weren't back from getting drinks. She hurried on as Raven rolled her eyes. "Really. He's very sweet and, um, nice." Good lord. It took all her willpower not to groan. If that sounded half as lame out loud as it did in her head, then there was no way Raven was buying it. Heck, Kate wasn't even sure *she* was buying it. "Scott enjoys nature and—"

"No." Raven held up her hand, her expression pained. "*Hell no*, Kate. Sweet and nice and enjoys nature are qualities you want in a dog. Not—I repeat—*not* in someone you want between your legs."

"Geez, Raven." Her face heated as she looked around, thankful the seats around them were empty. "Family-friendly environment here!" She'd known Raven for close to twenty years, and one day—hopefully, one day soon—she'd stop blushing at her friend's blunt speech. Doubtful, but a girl could hope.

It wasn't that Kate was a prude. Well, not really.

Okay, maybe just a little bit.

Kate didn't have a problem with swearing and suggestive talk, she just didn't do a lot of it herself. While Raven could make a sailor blush, Kate's attempts at that kind of talk always fell short and felt awkward, like she was trying too hard. It was something she'd always envied about her friend. Raven oozed confidence and didn't care what anyone thought. Kate, on the other hand? Yeah. Polar opposite.

"By the lovely shade of pink you've turned," Raven continued, "I can see that in the last couple months you've blessed that douche with your presence—why, I have no fucking clue—ole Scott hasn't made it anywhere near your legs, let alone between 'em."

Kate couldn't help but laugh and sent Raven a glare of her own. Her friend wasn't wrong. She and Scott had messed around plenty. But whenever it started getting heavy, much to his frustration, she'd put a halt to things. And she didn't want to linger too hard on the reasons why.

Over Raven's head, she saw the rest of their group coming down the stairs, fresh drinks in hand, and was grateful for the distraction. "Behave, missy."

Raven's fiancé, Blake, and their friend, Parker, led the way. Dave, in deep conversation with the third member of Team Testosterone, Jake, followed with Scott trailing behind since—surprise, surprise—he was staring at his phone. All the men, aside from Scott, settled into seats to the right of Raven. Both women rose as Scott shuffled past them to his seat on Kate's left.

Scott sat with a beer in one hand, phone in the other. His eyes stayed glued to his phone.

Okaaay.

Kate cleared her throat. "Were they out of wine?" Nothing. Not even a hint that he'd heard her. She cleared her throat again. "Scott?"

"Huh?" He glanced at her, annoyance flickering over his handsome face. "What?"

Was his phone seriously that much more entertaining than her? "I asked if you could get me a glass of white wine when you were up. Did they not have any?" *Benefit of the doubt, Kate. Forget the fact that you* know *this baseball stadium has a fully stocked wine bar. Just give him the benefit of the freaking doubt.*

"Did you?" Scott shook his not-quite-so-handsome-anymore head. "Huh. I forgot."

"Jesus. Kick him to the curb already," Raven grumbled as she squeezed Kate's arm. "I'll be right back, sweetie. Blake wants me to meet someone."

Kate nodded an acknowledgment without taking her eyes off Scott, who, of course, was back to his phone. Unbelievable. She waited for him to say something. Anything. Perhaps a "Let me go get you that glass of wine" or even a "Sorry about that."

He chuckled at something on his phone.

Jerk.

"You look like you could use this," a deep voice to her right murmured. Her dear sweet friend, Parker Cunningham, sat in Raven's vacated seat with a beer in one hand and a glass of white wine in his other. "We picked up an extra glass for you too. Jake's got it when you're ready." He nodded his head in Scott's direction. "Seriously, Kate?"

Again, her face heated, and she gratefully took a gulp of the crisp, sweet white wine. Turning her attention fully to her friend, she grimaced. "I know, Park."

He pinned her with dark green eyes and she tried not to squirm. "Do you?"

Kate sighed. All her friends must think she was an idiot. Maybe she was. Scott *was* a nice guy. When he wasn't on his phone. Which didn't happen very often. Unless they went camping. Which wasn't her most favorite thing to do . . . but still. Scott liked camping, and the couple times they'd gone with his friends, they'd actually talked—since there was no cell reception—and had gotten to know each other.

Or so she'd thought.

She glanced back at Scott. Yup, still on his phone like a freaking teenager.

Kate met Parker's gaze and nodded, her eyes rolling. "Oh, it's getting clearer by the minute."

"Look what I found," Raven called out. She and Blake made their way to their group's two open seats, a two-man camera crew trailing behind them. "The Kiss Cam segment is coming up!"

"Oh geez," Kate groaned as the camera crew positioned themselves in front of Blake and Raven at the end of their row. "Did she hunt you guys down? Because that's the only reason she came to the game today."

"What?" the man with the camera asked. "You're telling me she has no Mariners pride?"

"Her?" Kate shook her head. "Nope. She's all exhibitionist."

"Hey," Raven called, wagging a finger at her. "Watch yourself, or I'll have them get you and Phone Boy over there on the Kiss Cam too."

Kate glanced at Scott. Phone Boy was oblivious. Perfect.

"All right, guys," the camera assistant called out. "Keep your eye on the jumbotron. When you see your exhibitionist buddies up there, make some noise and cheer them on!"

Kate laughed along with the crowd as the between-inning Kiss Cam segment began. A stream of couples popped onto the screen and gave each other obligatory smooches. Then Raven and Blake's images lit up the jumbotron. She, and everyone around them, cheered as Blake pulled Raven to her feet and dramatically dipped her before laying a giant, sloppy kiss on her lips.

"Get a room!" Jake shouted.

"Keep it clean!" Parker called out.

"There are kids present!" Dave heckled.

Kate continued to laugh as the cameras cut to more couples. Then her heart stopped.

Oh no. No, no, no, NO!

Staring back from the jumbotron was her pale, wide-eyed face. And the top of Scott's bent head.

She elbowed him. "We're on the screen, Scott!"

"Hang on," he hissed, ignoring her, his attention never wavering from his phone.

The crowd began to boo.

A wave of heat washed over her. She peeked up at the screen and her stomach rolled. She and Scott were still on display. Her mortification was complete.

The crowd's boos got louder.

Why were they still on the screen? Chewing her bottom lip, she clasped her hands tightly in her lap. Apparently, she was a loser. Now everyone at T-Mobile Park knew it.

Her heart jackhammered in her chest. Crap. She didn't know what to do. She didn't even know where to look.

She jerked as a warm hand settled on the back of her neck. Turning to her right, she met Parker's steady gaze and let out a breath. *Help,* she wanted to beg, but was too embarrassed to utter that one little word.

Before she could take her next breath, Parker tugged her closer, his free hand cradling the other side of her face. Her stomach fluttered as he pulled her close, his gaze never leaving hers. Kate held her breath as his lips met hers, vaguely aware of the cheers surrounding them.

For a split second, everything stood still. Who knew Parker's lips would be so soft, so sweet, so . . . perfect?

Her pulse thudded in her ears as he pulled slightly away. He held her gaze for a moment. A soft smile played at the edges of his mouth before he tugged her back, this time with a bit more urgency, his lips tasting hers.

Kate was breathless when his lips released hers, his hands still cradling her face.

"Hey, Kate," he whispered, tracing his thumb over her lower lip. He flashed her a lopsided grin she'd seen a thousand times, but there was something in Parker's eyes . . . something she'd never seen before.

Something that made heat pool low in her belly.

"Hey, Parker," she replied, her voice hoarse, her heart still beating wildly.

"What the hell, Kate?"

Jerking away from Parker, she turned toward her supposed date. The anger on Scott's face took her by surprise. Who'd have thought he'd actually look up from his phone?

Scott lurched toward her and she flinched away.

Kate opened her mouth to give the jerk a piece of her mind, but all that came out was a yelp. With a swiftness she didn't know Parker possessed, he'd somehow hoisted her out of her seat and moved her behind him. Now Parker stood in front of her like a guard dog.

The outrage in Scott's weaselly eyes morphed into trepidation, and she bit back a chuckle. Stupid idiot.

"Leave," Parker said, his voice edged with unfamiliar steel. Who was this guy? "Take your damn phone, lose Kate's number, and leave. Now."

She should probably say something, but words were impossible. All she could do was stare. At Parker. The guy who'd been her friend since forever. The guy who'd just kissed her, and . . . wow.

Kate shook her head in an attempt to clear it. It didn't work.

She'd always thought Parker was attractive because . . . well, she wasn't blind. Six foot two; shaggy, chestnut brown hair; amazing bottle-green eyes; and the guy knew how to rock a five-o'clock shadow. Add to that, he was a regular at the boxing gym and had the physique to prove it. And he cooked for a living. Of course he was attractive.

But this was Parker, for God's sake. Parker!

With Dave helping move the fucker along, the back of Scott's head finally disappeared from sight. Parker dropped into his seat and let out an unsteady breath. What an asshole. Kate had such shitty taste in guys, it was ridiculous. Over the years, he'd watched idiot after idiot prance through her life. Most were harmless little tools. But this Scott asshole?

Parker's fists clenched. That little shit had the audacity to get in Kate's face. Hell no. It had taken every ounce of his willpower not to lay the shithead out flat. Good riddance.

Taking a swig of his beer, he tried to calm his thoughts. Then frowned. No dice.

What the hell possessed him to kiss Kate in the first place, he hadn't a clue.

Scratch that.

He knew precisely why he'd kissed her.

Kate had been sitting there white-knuckled, her giant brown eyes filled with a mix of uncertainty and humiliation. *Humiliation.* And that asshat had just sat there and ignored her.

How could he not kiss her?

He'd meant to keep it friendly. And he had.

Until he went back for the second kiss.

The first one had been for Kate and the cameras and to appease the booing crowd. The second kiss? That one had been for him. He could still taste the hint of sweet wine on her lips and feel the way her lips had parted under his . . .

Damn. His cock twitched, and he shifted in his seat, taking another swig of beer. This was *not* the time to spring a boner.

The heat of eyes boring into his skull was like a bucket of ice-cold water. Parker fixed his gaze firmly on the field and did all he could to block out everything in his peripheral vision. Yeah, he was man enough to admit that he was a chickenshit, but he really didn't want to know which of his friends were sending him evil glares. It was probably all of them with what he'd just pulled.

A sharp elbow jabbed him in the ribs. Rubbing the slight

sting on his side, he looked over at Kate. Her eyes were focused on the field, her long, dark brown hair hanging like a silky curtain around her, but it didn't hide the soft pink flush coloring her face.

"Thanks, Park." The pink on her face deepened, and she guzzled her wine. "I don't know what I'd have done if you weren't here."

He frowned. Kate wasn't much of a drinker. Taking the empty glass from her hand, he replaced it with a bottle of water. "Not a problem, Kate. It wasn't a hardship." At all. Damn. *Keep it casual, Cunningham.* "I'm sure Jake wishes he'd sat next to you instead."

Kate chuckled and finally met his eyes. He tried not to be disappointed at the relief evident on her face. "You're so sweet, Park. Thank you for saving me."

So sweet.

Parker tried not to cringe but failed. Fantastic. *And back into the friend zone you go.*

CHAPTER TWO

"Parker Cunningham, you dirty little dog."

Parker fought a grimace. The ambush began before he'd even made it two steps out of the damn elevator.

After the M's game, he'd made up some dumbass excuse about needing to get more groceries for their small dinner party at Blake and Raven's. He knew there'd be more than enough food tonight—he'd practically made it all—but he'd needed time to collect his thoughts. He couldn't do that while making small talk with his friends, especially with Kate.

His cousin, Blake, owned the building that housed their Irish pub, The Spotted Dog, and had converted the building's entire top floor into an ultra-modern apartment that had been, until recently, Blake's bachelor pad. Now Raven leaned against the apartment's front door, a sly smile on her gorgeous face. Not a good sign.

And so it begins.

"I have no idea what you're talking about." The entryway lights flickered, followed by the distant rumble of thunder. Surely an omen of what was in store for him.

Raven stepped in front of him, blocking his way. "You're a sneaky fox, you know that?"

"Dog? Fox? Which one is it?" He held up the full grocery sacks in his hands and tried to give her his best bored expression. "Can this wait?"

Raven shook her head. "Blake," she called out. A split second later, his cousin appeared like a damn puppy. "Can you grab Parker's loot? I want to have a quick chat with him."

"Sure thing, babe," Blake replied, dropping a kiss on the top of her head. Taking the bags from Parker, he chuckled. "Good luck, buddy. She's been waiting for you to get here."

"Traitor," Parker muttered.

Raven pinned him with her indigo eyes and he tried not to squirm. She was a tiny little thing, but damn, she was formidable. Not knowing what to do with his hands, he jammed them in his jeans pockets and tried for casual. "Yes, ma'am?"

"I must say, Parker, I didn't think you had it in you."

If Raven wanted to play, he was game. "What exactly are you referring to?"

Her eyes twinkled. "Tonsil hockey."

"Uh, excuse me, we were just at a *baseball* game. And there was no tongue." He'd know. "Besides, if this situation is in any way awkward—which it is—then it's all *your* fault."

"*My* fault?"

He nodded, and at the shocked expression on his friend's face, a smug grin grew on his own. "You brought the damn Kiss Cam people over and then put it in their heads to get Kate and that dipshit on screen."

"Yeah." She winced. "But Phone Boy should have been paying attention to her. That guy's a complete tool."

There was no denying that. "All the guys Kate dates are tools."

Raven's brow rose, the corners of her lips tipping up. "Jealous?"

He paused for a moment. Was he?

Parker wouldn't deny that he'd been attracted to Kate for . . . well, a long freaking time, but it wasn't like he'd been pining after her. He fought a cringe at the thought. Okay, maybe a little. They'd always been great friends, and he'd been conscious to never cross the line. Because that would be stupid on his part.

But Parker *had* crossed the line this afternoon. Because he was stupid.

He cleared his throat and brought his focus back to the woman before him. "I don't think 'jealous' is the right word."

Raven laughed. "You know you're better than all those jokers."

It wasn't a question. God knew Raven could drive him crazy, but he adored her. "So, you gonna bust my balls or what?"

"I'm not going to lie, that was the initial plan. But I know you've been sniffing around Kate for as long as I've known you."

Parker scoffed. "Sniffing? Seriously? What's with all the dog references? I thought you liked me."

She rolled her eyes. "You know I do. I love you. However, I love Kate more. So, don't fuck it up."

He let out an exasperated sigh. "I just kissed her, Raven. Got her out of a jam. Kate and I are just friends. Nothing more."

She stared at him, her perfectly painted red mouth hanging open. "Do you really think if you keep telling yourself that, you'll actually start to believe it?"

"Trust me on this. She friend-zoned me years ago. She's always seen me as just a friend. Not only is that her prerogative, but I'm completely happy with it because Kate actually *is* one of my closest friends." He shrugged. "It is what it is." It hurt his pride to admit that out loud, but it was the truth.

"You just need to have some patience with her."

Parker shook his head. "I don't need to be patient, Rave. I don't want anything more from her than what we already have."

Raven advanced so quickly he took two hasty steps back, almost tripping. "You," she jabbed her finger in his chest and glared, "are so full of shit that I'm at a loss for words."

How his cousin could live and work with Raven, he hadn't a clue. "Oh, I'm sure you'll find some . . . choice words for me."

"Yeah. Don't be a complete fucking dumbass. And don't lie to my face."

He opened his mouth to defend himself, but she kept right on talking. Apparently, she'd found those words after all.

"I see you, Parker Cunningham. I see the way you watch her when you think no one's looking." His mouth dropped open again, then shut just as quickly. His brow furrowed. Well, shit. "Don't give me this bullshit about wanting to be just friends with Kate. You *are* friends with her. And now you've finally nutted up and you have the chance for something . . . more. But Kate's cautious; you know that about her. You've taken her by surprise."

"I took myself by surprise," he mumbled and ran a hand through his hair.

"Good." She reached up and patted his cheek. "You're a strong man, Parker. Bust the fuck out of that friend zone."

He sighed again. "Seriously, Raven, it's not like that."

It wasn't. Not really.

True, he was kind of an idiot when it came to Kate, but not *that* big of an idiot. Putting himself in line for certain rejection wasn't his idea of fun. Unless he magically got a bright green Go light from Kate, he wasn't going to do a damn thing to jeopardize their friendship. Or to get kicked in the face. No, thank you.

Hell, even if he did get that bright green Go light, he wasn't sure he'd take it, or rather *should* take it. Kate's friendship meant the world to him and his track record with relationships spoke for itself. God knew Kate deserved better than that, deserved better than him.

———

Parker was avoiding her. Kate scanned the crazy amount of food on Blake's massive kitchen island. That had to be it. Because Parker's lame excuse of needing to get more groceries was ridiculous.

She replayed everything after Scott left the baseball game; it had all been normal. Everyone just hanging out and giving each other grief like usual. Well, maybe not just like usual. There had been a subtle awkwardness hovering over everyone. And yeah, she'd probably babbled on more than necessary, but that couldn't be helped. She'd also thrown back more drinks than usual, but that couldn't be helped either.

She was so freaking embarrassed. For so many reasons. If getting caught on the Kiss Cam hadn't been mortifying enough—exhibitionist, she was not—then being completely ignored by Scott, the phone-obsessed jerk, had sealed the deal.

But her embarrassment went deeper than that.

It was more than the fact that she'd been at the stinking baseball game with the jerk in the first place. If she were being honest, what humiliated her most had nothing to do with Scott but stemmed from her own actions. That she'd misread it all so badly, misread *Parker* so badly.

The way he'd looked at her after he kissed her? Like he'd

wanted to devour her right then and there, and who cared about the twenty thousand other people in the stadium? Kate couldn't help the sigh that escaped her lips.

So. Freaking. Dreamy.

But she'd been wrong. So, so, *so* wrong!

Because it hadn't been really dreamy. Not to him, anyway. It was a pity kiss. And then she'd gone and embarrassed him. God, that just sucked on so many levels.

She'd thanked him for coming to her rescue and he'd quickly made a crack about Jake doing the same thing. Kate cringed. If that wasn't like an ice-cold drink being dumped over her overheated head, she didn't know what was.

In all honesty though, the Jake comment had made her relax. It wasn't that she was relieved, because she was . . . well, she wasn't sure what she was. What she did know was the way Parker had looked at her, or at least how she'd *thought* he'd looked at her . . . all dreamy and hot and bothered-like—had made her stomach flip.

Now Kate couldn't think about Parker or even look at him without wanting to know what it would be like to kiss him again. *Really* kiss him.

But that wasn't going to happen.

Parker's comment about Jake and how he'd winced—yes, *winced*, though the sweet man had tried to hide it—when she'd thanked him made it clear that he'd been doing her a favor. That what he'd done was something he did just as a buddy and not because he liked her or anything.

Her lips pursed. Well, of course he liked her. They were friends, for goodness' sake. But Parker didn't *like her* like her.

Kate closed her eyes and stifled a groan. Good. God. What was wrong with her? She was thirty-two. A grown freaking woman. Yet she sounded like a teenage girl. An obnoxious teenage girl. She may as well start gluing her face to her phone like Scott, a.k.a. Phone Boy. Ugh.

"Trouble in paradise, Katie?"

She groaned out loud and swiveled on the island stool to glare at her friend. "Don't call me Katie. You know I hate that."

Jake laughed. "I know. That's why I do it. And that's why you love me."

See, now Jake—

Jake Alvarez was gorgeous. Six-four and easily two hundred-plus pounds of pure, solid muscle. He looked like The Rock, but a little less beefy and with a full head of thick, black hair. He co-owned The Spotted Dog Irish Pub with Parker and Blake, was brilliant with all things tech, and also ran a wildly successful mobile gaming company—though his bookkeeping skills were absolute crap. However, as a book-keeper, Kate was admittedly biased on that point. Jake was also one of the most charming guys out there.

Good-looking, charming, and though he was a self-admitted workaholic, he was definitely the life of any party when he came out to play. And Kate had zero dreamy thoughts, ideas, or anythings about Jake.

Why couldn't Parker be like that?

Whoa. She frowned. When had Parker even changed from being exactly that?

When he pity-kissed you, idiot!

Good lord, if that was a pity kiss, she couldn't even begin to imagine what a *real* kiss would be like.

Gah! Focus, Kate! FOCUS!

Jake slung an arm over her shoulders. "Seriously, Kate. What gives?"

She really needed to work on her poker face. "I don't know what you're talking about."

"You've been looking all over this kitchen for something and I'm thinking you're not going to find him—ahem—I mean, you aren't going to find that *something* on the kitchen island." He winked at her, gave her shoulders a squeeze, then reached for a bottle of tequila. "Though I'm sure if you asked nicely, Parker would be happy to oblige if you wanted to do it on the counter."

"Oh my God, Alvarez!" She elbowed him in the ribs, her face heating. Why everyone loved to tease her, she hadn't a clue.

Jake laughed and placed a shot of tequila in front of her. "Hey! You can't fault me for that one. It's the giant-ass elephant in the room, honey." He held up his own shot, his gaze momentarily rising to the ceiling as the lights flickered, then met hers, his brows doing an exaggerated wiggle. "Cheers."

She couldn't help but laugh. "Seriously, Jake, you're getting to be just as bad as Raven." Their glasses clinked, and she tossed back the tequila. The fire that slid down her throat had her pulling in a breath between her clenched teeth.

Jake's brows rose again, this time in question, as he held up the tequila bottle.

She preferred her tequila mixed into pretty pink or blue drinks, preferably with an umbrella. A smooth fire still burned her throat, but she nodded and held out her shot glass for a refill.

"Please, Kate." Jake chuckled as he poured another round. "No one can come close to Raven."

"True. You just mentioned doing it on the counter." She touched her glass to Jake's and threw back the second shot. Probably not the wisest decision, but desperate times and all that. "Raven would have added much more detail. Positions, toys, that kind of thing. You've got a long way to go, Alvarez."

"I'm not even going to ask what you guys are talking about," Parker said, coming up behind her. He gestured toward the living room. "Can I steal you?"

Nodding, she hopped down from the stool. And wobbled.

She steadied herself and smacked Jake on the shoulder when he laughed.

Snagging her hand, Parker led her through the archway out of the kitchen. She ignored the tingles his touch shot up her arm and sent an "I'm watching you" gesture to Jake with her free hand.

With the open floor plan of Blake's kitchen and dining area, the living room was the one place that offered a small bit of privacy from the rest of the group. Not much, but it was at least something. While that second shot may not have been the greatest idea, from the serious look on Parker's face, Kate was thankful she'd taken it.

Passing the couch and seating area, they stopped in front of the giant floor-to-ceiling windows. He was still holding her hand, but his gaze was focused on something outside. He looked nervous. Kate wanted to kick herself. Parker was never nervous. Ever.

His green gaze caught hers. "Kate, we're friends, right?"

"Of course!" Her eyes widened in surprise. How could he doubt that?

"Our friendship is important to me, and I feel like I've messed it up."

"No, Park, of course you haven't." *She* was the one being weird about the whole thing.

"Things have been awkward since the game." He bit the side of his lower lip in another rare show of nerves. "You can't deny that."

What she wouldn't do to taste that tiny little spot on his lip. Dang it! Her eyes jerked away from his face. *Oh my God, this is what a horny teenage boy must feel like.*

No. More. Tequila.

"Kate, look at me."

All she'd been doing since the game was thinking of Parker. Now, the *last* thing she wanted to do was actually make eye contact. Here he was, worried about their friend-ship, and all she could think about was what that tiny spot at the edge of his lips tasted like.

You're an idiot, Kate Peterson. A mean idiot. With a heavy sigh, she met his gaze. "I'm so sorry."

Confusion had Parker's brow scrunching.

Kate could feel her face flaming. "I'm sorry I put you in the position of having to rescue me. You did me a huge favor —bigger than you know. It's just you're, um . . ."

Stop talking, stop talking, stop talking!

But that second shot of tequila told her she had to get this out. It also said she had to look Parker in the eyes when she did. "You're a very good kisser. I wasn't expecting that. And it threw me." *Why, tequila, WHY!?!* "Now I'm being really weird about it and that's all on me. You and I?" She gestured between them with her free hand. "As far as our friendship goes, we're great. I just have . . . it's just that . . ."

It was official. She hated tequila.

Kate closed her eyes and counted to ten. This was Parker, for God's sake. Her friend. She needed to get a dang grip.

His hand squeezed hers, sending more tingles up her arm, and she opened her eyes. Her brain begged her to stop talk-ing, but her mouth kept on moving. "I'm being a total dumb girl about this and I'm so sorry. Besides, it was probably a fluke."

"A fluke?"

She nodded. Yeah. That's what it was. It had to be a fluke. "The kiss. And I'm sure we can prove it. I mean, if you kissed me again—now that I *know* you're a really good kisser—I'm sure it would be like no big deal."

"No big deal?"

Her eyes narrowed. "You realize you're just repeating my last words back to me, right?"

"Right." He studied her for a moment, and she couldn't

quite read the look that flickered over his handsome features. But his hesitation and that look, which was starting to suspiciously resemble indecision, made her wish she could turn back time and erase everything she'd said.

Kill. Me. Now.

"Right," Parker repeated with a firm nod, heat and determination replacing the wariness that was just there. Her breath caught when he released her hand and framed her face with both of his. "Let's prove it's a fluke then."

Before Kate could take her next breath, his lips were against hers, not demanding, not pushing. It was a kiss of exploration that instantly heated her blood. Leaning into him, she parted her lips and let her mouth do some exploring of its own. She just wanted that tiny little taste.

"That, Kate," he growled against her lips, "might have been the best idea you've ever had."

"Agreed," she sighed against his mouth. Maybe tequila wasn't so bad after all . . .

His lips found hers again, more insistent this time. He paused to change the angle of their kiss, his tongue softly tracing her lower lip.

Kate pulled slightly away to catch her breath. "I take it back. You're not a good kisser. You're a freaking amazing kisser, Park. But it's still just a fluke."

"Agreed," he whispered, his lips but an inch away. "An absolute fluke."

She closed the distance this time. Her pulse raced as his fingers tightened in her hair, his mouth more urgent. She grabbed onto his waist and felt his hard stomach muscles jerk beneath her touch. A surge of female satisfaction shot through her. He deepened the kiss and his tongue tangled with hers. The soft moan that escaped her was pure bliss.

In the far corners of her mind, someone somewhere cleared their throat. But Kate didn't care. All that mattered was this. Hands down, the most mind-blowing kiss of her life.

"Ahem!"

They broke apart, and for a moment, all she could do was stare at the face she knew as well as her own. Yet he was different somehow. *They* were different.

Parker's hands were still tangled in her hair and her hands now gripped his shirt over his thudding heart. Okay, maybe not a fluke.

"Ahem!"

He kissed the tip of her nose and warmth bloomed in her belly. Her eyes never left him as he turned his attention over her shoulder.

Kate's stomach twisted as the color drained from Parker's face. She spun around and found Blake, beet-faced with his hands stuffed into his pockets, standing next to a woman she'd never seen before. A woman shooting daggers at her.

"Fuuuck," Parker breathed out behind her.

CHAPTER THREE

"I'm Victoria. And you are?"

Kate's brows rose at the other woman's condescending tone. "Kate." Good lord, this was fun. She glanced at Blake standing next to Victoria, and her heart gave a tug.

There was uncomfortable. And then there was Blake. The poor guy looked like he wanted to be anywhere but there. It was a feeling she understood well, and from the tension radiating off the man standing next to her, Parker did too.

"Well, Kate, I'm Parker's girlfriend and—"

"What?" Parker sputtered.

Kate glanced between the two. Victoria had the smug look of a satisfied, spoiled brat who'd just gotten her way. Parker had the panicked and confused look of a guy who'd just been informed he had a girlfriend.

She was siding with Parker on this one. However, if there was one thing Kate was, it was always polite. "Oh, Parker's girlfriend? Wow. First we've heard of that." And a little passive-aggressive as well. "Oh, and this isn't what it looks like."

"No?"

The amount of derision the woman put into that one little word made Kate want to throat-punch her. Instead, she pasted a smile on her face. "No. You see, Parker and I were just proving a point."

Victoria's over-plucked eyebrow arched in disbelief.

Well then. Apparently, she was passive-aggressive *and* catty. Kate mentally shrugged. She could live with that. "Really. We were proving that since we're just friends—"

"You were kissing my boyfriend."

"Whoa," Parker interjected from beside Kate. "I'm *not* your boyfriend, Victoria. We've been out like three times."

"Five! We've been out five times, which makes this six," Victoria hissed. "This is where you were going to introduce me to your friends. Hence, you're my boyfriend, Parker."

Wow. Hello, crazy. Kate could only stare in wonder, amazement, or horror. She wasn't quite sure which. A quick glance at Blake showed the same dumbfounded look she must be wearing. She hated to do this to Parker, but . . .

"What was that, Blake? You need me in the kitchen?" Kate grabbed Parker's hand and gave it a quick squeeze before making a hasty getaway.

Cowardly on her part? Absolutely.

But with Blake following right on her heels, she was totally fine with it.

"Holy hell, Kate," Blake said when they reached the safety of the kitchen. He stood silent for a moment, his mouth gaping like a fish. "That chick is nuts. Like certifiable, scary kind."

"Yeah, well I'm sure it didn't help her crazy when she walked in and saw what she did."

Blake chuckled. "Ya think?"

She cleared her suddenly tight throat. "So, um, how long were you guys standing there?"

He looked as if he were gagging. "Long enough where I

wanted to pour hot, boiling wax directly into my eye sockets."

She cringed. "Ah . . . that long. Sorry about that."

"Yeah. Speaking of *that*. What point were you and my cousin trying to 'prove' exactly?" He nudged her arm. "Aside from proving that you don't mind each other's tongues in your mouths."

"Ha-ha." She glared at him. "We were proving that we're still friends and that nothing changed after the whole Kiss Cam thing."

"You mean aside from the whole swapping-spit thing?"

"You've got to be kidding me right now." Good God. It was like talking to a twelve-year-old.

"Come on, Kate," he said with a laugh. "I've known you both forever. He's my cousin and best friend. You're like my little sister. I'm allowed to give you shit. It's my duty."

If she could strangle him, she would. "Parker and I are friends, Blake."

"Just friends?"

Was she talking to a brick wall? "Yes. Just. Friends."

"You and I are friends, right?"

"Well, I'm starting to rethink it, but yes."

"You and Jake are just friends, right?"

Her eyes narrowed. "What's your point?"

"My point, Kate, is that my tongue has never been in your mouth."

She smacked him on the arm, a shudder running through her. "Ewww."

"Exactly." He rubbed the spot she'd hit, then nodded across the room to where Jake and Raven were talking. "Has Jake's?"

Kate smacked him again. "Don't be gross."

The front door slammed, rattling a few picture frames,

then Parker hustled into the kitchen and made a beeline for them, annoyance and relief warring on his face.

"Jesus." He raked his hands through his already-disheveled hair. "Some friends you guys are for ditching me like that. You both seriously suck."

She wanted to say sorry, but that wasn't going to happen.

Parker slung an arm over her shoulders and pulled her tight to his side. "You ditched me."

Her smile was automatic, and her arm naturally circled his waist. "I did."

"Not only did you ditch me, but you ditched me in the most obvious, lamest way possible. And you gave Blake an out too."

Kate nodded, her grin growing. "All true. And I'd do it all again if I had to. How's the lovely Victoria?"

Blake handed Parker a beer. "Dude. That was nuts." His eyes ping-ponged between her and Parker. "All of it was nuts. But that chick? That chick is boil-your-bunny crazy."

Parker grimaced and took a long swallow of beer. "You have no idea. Apparently, she had us married and living out in the burbs in six months."

"Hey! Chef Boy," Raven called from the other side of the kitchen. "This food isn't going to cook itself."

"Yeah, yeah," he called out in reply. He squeezed Kate's shoulder before letting her go. He took a step away and then paused, turning back to her. His mouth opened and closed before he quickly turned away again.

She snagged him by the back of his shirt. "Uh-uh. Out with it, mister." Why had she never noticed how cute Parker was when he was nervous?

He met her gaze, his eyes serious. "We really weren't a thing. Me and Victoria. We'd gone out a few times, but it wasn't serious at all. Not like she said. I swear."

Kate's heart squeezed. Sweet, sweet man.

CHAPTER FOUR

The wind slammed the door shut behind her as Kate slipped into the building that housed The Spotted Dog. The weather people were predicting a big one and were already calling it the Storm of the Century. She shook her head. They always called it that, and nine times out of ten, the Storm of the Century wound up being nothing. Historically speaking, less than nothing.

In some parts of the city, the lights had gone out for a few hours overnight, but thankfully not hers, so there was at least that. Kate wasn't holding her breath for this supposed storm and judging by all the people trudging around their Upper Queen Anne neighborhood in their North Face and Patagonia raincoats, no one else was either.

Using her key fob to access the upper floors of The Spotted Dog's building, Kate rode the elevator to the second floor, which housed Jake's office for Alvarez Technologies. Her head began to pound at the mere thought of his company's books. The quick glance she'd taken last week made her want to groan. But Jake had reassured her that "the other computer" had the "better set of books." And if she were being brutally honest, the tequila from the night before wasn't doing her any favors.

Holy cripes.

The mere fact that Alvarez Technologies had multiple sets of books made her head throb harder. Could you say, "Hello, IRS audit"? It was most definitely a bookkeeping nightmare Kate wanted no part of. At all.

But it was Jake. She couldn't *not* help him.

With a sigh, she greeted Jake's new receptionist/assistant —was this the third or fourth in the last two months?—and made her way to the conference room where the magical "other computer" had been set up. As much as this sucked, Jake's books were ten billion times better than thinking about what an idiot she'd made of herself the night before.

Kate cringed, her stomach rolling. Nope. Better not think about it.

"How are you feeling, sunshine?" Jake greeted as he breezed into the conference room. "I haven't seen you drink like that in a while."

Her face flamed. "I wasn't that bad, was I?"

"You weren't obnoxious, if that's what you mean. But you definitely were more . . . outgoing than usual."

She covered her face and groaned. Jake had no idea just how *outgoing* she'd been. Epic. Disaster.

With her hands still covering her face, she shook her head. She'd never be able to face Parker Cunningham ever again.

"And why exactly is it you won't be able to face Parker ever again?"

Kate dropped her forehead down on the table. Perfect. Thinking out loud.

"I'm an idiot," she mumbled into the table.

"You're not an idiot, Kate."

She sat up and met his gaze. "Oh, trust me on this one."

He laughed. "Do tell."

Right. Like she was going to admit that when Parker had driven her home, she'd tried to kiss him again. And gotten rejected. Big time.

He'd pulled the "you've had a lot to drink tonight" card and literally pried her arms away from him. Her stomach turned.

It had been a fluke after all. A fluke and tequila. What a bad, bad combination.

Kate supposed that things between them could now get back to normal. She should be relieved. Really.

She wasn't.

The idea of going back to dating jerks like Scott, the Phone Boy, was depressing as all get-out.

"Ahem."

Her gaze shot to Jake, who smirked at her with an arched brow. "Off in la-la land? Or is it Parker-land?"

God, was she that obvious? "I don't know what you're talking about."

His smirk turned into a full-out laugh. He wasn't buying it.

She gestured to the monitor. "We need to focus, Jake. We're here to talk about your books and not me."

"You mean you and Parker."

Good lord, give her patience. "There is no me and Parker."

He chuckled. "Sure, Katie."

She stiffened; all humor left her. A wave of nausea surged through her. And it had nothing to do with tequila. "Seriously. You need to stop calling me that."

Jake's eyes widened and his jaw went slack. "Sure. Sorry. I was just messing with you. I didn't know it bothered you so much."

The hangover, lack of sleep, and overall mortification had

her off-kilter. But she needed to get a freaking grip. She strived for a calm, even voice. "Well, it does." More than he or anyone would guess. "So please stop calling me that. Now, let's focus before the IRS comes banging on your door. The last thing either of us wants is for them to haul your butt off to federal prison."

Four hours later, Kate's brain was mush. Seated at the bar of The Spotted Dog, she took a giant gulp of her gummy bear martini. A straw would have made it easier, dang it. It was barely two-thirty on a Monday afternoon and the pub was closed, but she didn't care. Jake—no, clarification—Business Jake could drive anyone to drink. Business Jake was stubborn, pompous, and an overall arrogant bastard.

A bastard who was sure to get audited by the IRS. That was the only reason he was listening to her. This time. Never mind they'd had the same conversation over his crappy books for years. But he always knew best. Jake could *always* do it better than anyone. No wonder he couldn't keep an assistant for more than a month!

"Hey, Kate." Blake greeted as he entered the bar area from the kitchen. He nodded at her drink. "A little early?"

Great. Now everyone thought she had a drinking problem. Well, if the last couple of days were any indication . . .

"I just met with Jake about his company's books."

"Yikes, you want a shot to go with that?" He winked at her. "Where's Raven?"

"She ran upstairs to get her phone charger." The flickering lights had them both glancing toward the ceiling. Kate frowned, her stomach fluttering. She hated storms, particularly ones with power outages. Her mind darted to the past, to flickering candlelight that should have been soothing but wasn't. To prayers that were supposed to be comforting but were terrifying, the monotonous chanting a sinister prelude that still, to this day, sent chills down her spine and bile up her throat.

Enough! Her gaze snapped forward and settled on Blake, hints of worry and confusion etched on his face. *Focus, Kate.* She reached for her drink, proud her hand remained steady. "I thought you had a generator?"

"I do, though our third-floor one is getting repaired. It takes a few seconds to kick in once the power is out, though." His eyes narrowed, the groove between them deepening. "You okay?"

"Are you guys opening tomorrow?" She waved off his concern and sipped her drink, savoring the sweet candy explosion on her taste buds. It was better to focus on Raven's epic drinks than her fear of thunder and lightning and all the memories it stirred up. "You know, with the Storm of the Century and all?"

He studied her for another moment, then shrugged. "Probably not. The wind is getting crazy already, and it's only going to get worse. By the way, Raven and I are heading to Parker's this evening. He put in a generator at his place when he remodeled, so he's cooking tonight. He said you should come too."

"Oh? Did he?" It took all her willpower to not cringe. She'd hoped those three little words had come out casually, but unfortunately, she had ears. They were more squeak than natural. Between the mortifying evening before with Parker and the unexpected memories the flickering lights conjured, memories that should have been long forgotten, her nerves were shot.

"Yeah. He was supposed to text you, but he probably forgot. After our morning scheduling meeting, he ran over to Bellevue for another meeting. He said the wind was nuts and power lines and trees were coming down everywhere. Who knew the weather guys would actually be right?"

"So, safety in numbers tonight?"

He nodded. "You know it. We'll see you later then?"

Kate finished her drink and grabbed her purse and laptop. As much as she didn't want to see Parker and face her humiliation, the idea of being stuck home alone during a big storm had less appeal. Who knew, maybe between now and then, Parker would get bonked in the head—not seriously injured, of course—and suffer some sort of short-term memory loss. One could only hope. "Yup. See you tonight."

***

A steady stream of heavy rain hit the windows while Uncle Tupelo's mellow harmonica and acoustic guitar played over the kitchen speakers. The scents of spicy ground beef, garlic, cumin, and oregano filled Parker's kitchen. With the chili simmering, he mixed together buttermilk, eggs, and butter to add to his cornmeal mixture. He should have made a more complicated dinner, like boeuf bourguignon or paella or something equally tedious that required his undivided attention. Because chili and cornbread were too easy, and his mind kept wandering back to the night before.

To Kate.

She'd been so cute and funny when he'd driven her home. And gorgeous and tempting. Then, when they'd reached her front porch, she'd surprised the shit out of him when she'd kissed him. His heart thunked hard at the memory. It had taken every ounce of willpower he had to put the brakes on.

Kate had had more to drink than usual, but she hadn't been drunk. Buzzed for sure, but not drunk. Still . . .

Parker wanted to be sure she had a clear head. He wanted to be sure she wasn't kissing him out of some misguided gratitude for rescuing her from that asshat, Scott. He wanted to make sure she wouldn't regret it the next day.

Hell, he wanted to be sure *he* had a clear head. He wanted to be sure that kissing that beautiful woman was the right thing to do. Sure, one of his heads said it was a fantastic fucking idea. However, his other head—the one attached to his neck that he should be listening to—wasn't so sure. Because what was happening between them wasn't a fluke. If it were, he wouldn't still be remembering exactly how soft Kate's lips were or how she smelled perfectly rich and spicy, yet warm and sweet.

The problem was, while it wasn't a fluke, Parker didn't know what the hell it was. He did know that it made him more nervous than he could ever recall being. Another thing he knew without a doubt? He sucked at relationships. And Kate mattered. The last thing he wanted was to fuck everything up.

A bang had him pausing. Lowering the volume on *Moonshiner*, the banging sounded again. Front door. Checking to make sure the stove temperature was at low, he glanced at the clock and chuckled. His cousin was early for the first time ever. Thank God for Raven's influence.

Parker's recently renovated home filled him with pride. He'd purchased the massive old house a couple years prior, and while he hadn't done all the renovation work personally, he'd designed every inch of the remodel—a leftover talent from his former life as an architect—and tackled some of the smaller projects. He'd modernized the historic Seattle home while staying true to the house's bones.

Unlike Blake's sleek contemporary home, his style was classic craftsman. He loved having distinct rooms, but the kitchen was his favorite. It helped that it was enormous and included an informal dining area. He'd dropped a ridiculous amount of money on it and it had every piece of technology and restaurant-grade equipment imaginable; it was the heart of his home.

As the windowed front door came into view, he caught sight of long, dark brown hair and smiled. While Parker had spent the majority of the day thinking of Kate, he realized at that exact moment he'd forgotten to actually text her about dinner. Thankfully, Blake must've relayed the invite.

Opening the door wide, the fluttering of nerves in his stomach froze, and ice shot down his spine. Not Kate.

Courtney.

His ex-wife.

"Hi, Parker! Thank goodness you're home! I hope you don't mind." She took advantage of his shocked paralysis to step past him into the entryway, rubbing her hands together for warmth.

What. The. Fuck?

"What are you doing here, Courtney?" He closed the door, his annoyance immediate as he turned toward her, scowling. She was soaked to the bone, her long-sleeved shirt plastered against her skin.

"I was out running a few blocks from here and the skies just opened up!" She glanced out the door's side windows. "Who would have thought the weather people would be right, huh?"

"You were just in the area?" Right. Suspicion flared. Courtney lived in West Seattle, which was easily a twenty-minute drive, in no traffic, from his Upper Queen Anne neighborhood. And there was always traffic in Seattle. Always. But Courtney was soaked to the bone and shivering, her lips turning blue. She couldn't fake that.

"I'm actually parked down by the Space Needle. I'm training hills for an upcoming race and figured this was the best spot. The torrential downpour caught me off guard."

As far as excuses went, Courtney's was fairly believable.

This was Courtney, though. The wariness in her eyes made it clear that she knew he wasn't buying it. She attempted a smile, but her teeth began to chatter.

Damn it. Guilt kicked in.

"Come on in," he grumbled, unable to hide the exasperation in his tone. Pulling a sweatshirt from the entryway coat stand, he draped it over her shoulders. She may be his ex-wife, but he wasn't a complete asshole. "If you want, I'll get you a change of clothes and toss what you're wearing in the dryer."

"That would be great," she said, pulling her arms through his sweatshirt. "If I could steal your shower while my clothes dry, I'd really appreciate it, Parky."

He cringed. Parky. He hated that fucking nickname. From the first moment she'd uttered it, thinking it was so cute—holy shit, it wasn't—he'd hated it. Had even flat-out told her so. Multiple times. Did she stop using it when he'd asked her to, again, multiple times? Of course not.

Now Courtney wanted to use his shower like they were old friends? The words *I don't think so* hovered on his lips. Then a shiver wracked her slight frame. Shit. He sighed and headed to the stairs. "Sure. Follow me."

The sound of the upstairs shower shutting off had Parker's head throbbing, a knot pulsed viciously behind his eye socket. Ten minutes earlier, he'd hung up with his sister, Carmen, but his head still ached from the blistering earful he'd received. Carmen was in no way amused that Courtney had shown up uninvited. His older sister was the epitome of calm and cool. Usually. But Carm had never liked Courtney and let him know, quite descriptively, all her thoughts on the current matter.

Carmen could creatively string curse words together

almost as well as Raven. It was terrifying. Impressive. But terrifying. The next time his sister asked, "What's new?" he'd have to choose his words with more care.

The upside of the last half hour was that the cornbread was in the oven and its sweet, buttery fragrance now mixed with the savory chili simmering on the stovetop. His kitchen was tidy; the dishes he'd used for dinner prep were in the dishwasher. On any other day, all these things would have soothed him. But today, they didn't. Because he was officially in hell.

A glance at the clock told him that Blake and Raven would be showing up any minute. Courtney was still upstairs in his guest shower.

He shuddered.

His sister wasn't a fan of Courtney. At all. But Blake took it to a whole new level. To say his cousin didn't like Courtney was like saying Muhammad Ali was a decent boxer. On Parker's wedding day, Blake had pulled him aside and said it wasn't too late, that he'd happily cover for him and make the excuses if Parker wanted to ditch Courtney and the entire "wedding bullshit."

He should have taken Blake up on his offer.

But he hadn't. And now, here he was. In hell.

Parker didn't trust Courtney. Not one bit. If he were being honest, he'd never fully trusted her, even when they were married. Hence, she was his ex for a reason. But he couldn't let her freeze to death on his front porch, damn it. He wiped down the quartz countertop for the twentieth time and cursed himself. He really was a fucking dumbass.

He'd been running into her a lot lately. She'd not only come into the pub more over the last few months, but he'd been seeing her at random places. Restaurants, the park, even his local grocery store, though she lived in a completely different neighborhood. He'd ignored his gut and figured he was just being paranoid. But now? There was no question. The woman was up to something.

But what? There was no way in hell they were getting back together. They were a crap couple when they were together, and time had proved to him that he'd married her for all the wrong reasons. It wasn't because they were madly in love. Hell, he hadn't even been a little bit in love.

He'd gone through with it because it was expected; it's what he was supposed to do at that stage in his life. Date for a year or so, settle into his career, get married, then pop out a kid or two while moving up the corporate ladder. He'd only gotten to the first three steps and had hated every moment of it. He couldn't blame her entirely for their lackluster marriage. They were more like two good acquaintances who lived with each other and occasionally had okay sex. Once he'd realized that he didn't harbor any real, deep feelings for her whatsoever, he'd stopped trying. That was all on him. He'd been a shitty husband.

Parker hadn't blamed Courtney when she'd demanded a divorce after he was laid off from the architectural firm. And when she'd admitted that she'd cheated on him, he knew he should have cared more than he did. But he didn't care. Not really.

Her hysterics had bothered him the most—the yelling, the accusing, the blaming. How could he provide for her now that he was unemployed? How could he possibly want to become a cook, of all things? Not a prestigious chef with a fancy culinary school pedigree, but a cook? How dare he use their money to open a pub with his man-whore cousin and his asshole, workaholic friend?

When it was revealed during their divorce hearings that the company had needed to downsize and he'd volunteered to be laid off in exchange for a decent severance, Courtney had been enraged. Should he have told her about the voluntary layoff? Yeah. But he wasn't purposely being a dick by not telling her; he just didn't think she'd care. He hadn't been happy at his job for months, and while Courtney knew that, he knew she'd care more about the severance package he'd negotiated.

She'd never understood the pull of the kitchen. He'd tried to explain it to her countless times—how he loved cooking and creating, how it reminded him of his family. She didn't get it; she was a fan of dining out, of being seen and waited on.

When the opportunity arose to leave the company and start the pub with his two best friends, he'd jumped at the chance. And yes, it hadn't hurt that he knew Courtney wouldn't bother him at the new venture.

She'd despised him for leaving his comfortable architecture job to cook at the pub. She thought it was beneath a couple of their station. Whatever the hell that meant.

She'd also hated that the pub involved Blake. She detested his cousin but did her best to bite her tongue about him. Because Blake was loaded. So was Jake. As far as Courtney was concerned, *cooking* at the pub while Blake and Jake *managed* the place was beneath him, like he was their poor little worker bee.

Then another nugget was revealed during their divorce proceedings. Well, nugget to him, but a bombshell to her. Parker had a trust fund. A very sizable trust fund.

And Courtney was quick to change her tune.

Suddenly, she wanted to call off the divorce and try to work everything out. She loved him more than ever, was so proud of him for leaving a job he wasn't passionate about and opening a pub with his friends, wanted to have his children, blah, blah, fucking blah.

Bullshit was what it was. She wanted the two million a year the trust provided.

Yes, it wasn't fair of him to not tell her that he'd volunteered for the layoff. And it wasn't right that he'd never mentioned the trust fund before or after they were married. He'd fully intended to, but whenever he'd opened his mouth to do so, the words just wouldn't come.

The way Courtney had acted when she found out about the money had disgusted him—hell, it still disgusted him—and made him grateful he'd never said a word. And equally grateful his grandparents had had the foresight to make his trust ironclad.

The doorbell jarred him from his brooding. Making his way to the door, dread soured his stomach. His cousin and Courtney in the same room always ended in disaster. Add Raven to the mix and they might have to call the cops tonight.

He reached for the doorknob just as his cell phone in his pocket dinged with an incoming text.

Swinging the door open, his greeting to Blake froze on his lips.

Not Blake and Raven.

Kate.

All prior thoughts left his brain. That's what Kate did to him. Even in a simple, black hooded raincoat, she looked beautiful. A bright, emerald-green scarf was wrapped around her neck, her long, dark brown hair windswept and gorgeous, a soft pink flush across her cheeks. Yeah, she sure as hell did that to him, all right.

"Hey, thanks for having me over," she said with a sunny smile, stepping into the entryway. "You know I'm a storm wimp, so I really appreciate it. Man, Parker, it smells great in here. Chili?"

"Of course. It's the best storm food." So what if it also just happened to be one of Kate's favorites?

Both of their phones dinged.

Closing the door behind her, he checked his messages as she fished out her phone from her pocket.

Blake: *Power lines down around the pub. R & I are staying put.*

Blake: *Will catch up with you both later*

Kate glanced up from her phone and caught his gaze. "Looks like it's just the two of us tonight. You good with that?"

Parker nearly swallowed his tongue at the shy smile tipping her lips. Damn, she was beautiful. "Absolu—"

"Parker? Is someone here?"

His stomach dropped and chills raced down his back as Kate's face went pale.

"Oh hi, Kate," Courtney called out as she came down the stairs wearing nothing but one of his old T-shirts. "It's nice to see you. Parky didn't mention you were coming over."

For fuck's sake! Where the hell were the sweatpants he'd given her? He should have let Courtney freeze to death outside.

Parker thought he'd been in hell before? Whatever was worse than hell . . . he'd just fucking entered it.

CHAPTER FIVE

Wow. Kate had no words. None.

It was safe to say that the very last person she'd expected to walk down Parker's stairs half *naked* was Courtney.

Well, Kate had *some* words, but she really tried to not be such a swearer. To think she'd changed her outfit three times before coming over. Three! It had taken her over thirty minutes to settle on a casual-but-not-frumpy-and-fingers-crossed-not-trying-too-hard look of a crisp white sheer blouse with a Peter Pan collar—with a tank because she wasn't gutsy enough to just wear a bra underneath, her fancy new light heather gray cashmere sweater, and dark skinny jeans with tall black riding boots. She'd even put on eye makeup!

Criminy. It was official. She was an idiot.

Parker cleared his throat. "Courtney was just leaving."

Kate shot a glance at the woman wearing nothing but Parker's—oh, sorry, *Parky's*—T-shirt. Her stomach did a nauseating somersault. Yeah right. Courtney wasn't going anywhere.

A flash of lightning, immediately followed by a crack of thunder, made Kate jump. She really hated storms. The memories they stirred up sucked. But memories, she could deal with, she could squash. This Courtney and *Parky* situation? This sucked more.

She couldn't bring herself to look Parker in the eyes, so she kept her gaze fixed on his chest. A chest she now knew was solid and muscled and . . . *stop!*

This was why Kate didn't—heck, *shouldn't*—date. She was awful at reading people. She always did this, always got herself worked up thinking some guy liked her when, in reality, he didn't. Then on the off chance some guy did ask her out, he'd inevitably end up being a winner like Scott, the Phone Boy.

Mortification had her pulse racing, and she fumbled for words. "You know, I forgot that I have this . . . um, thing . . . and I should probably get home anyway." She spun toward the door and ignored the sting of disappointment that squeezed her heart. This day needed to end. Now. "I'm sorry, Park," she said under her breath. "I didn't mean to impose."

Her hand settled on the doorknob, and she flinched when his hand covered hers. "Wait." He pulled her hand away from the door and stepped close, his fingers lacing with hers. "Please, Kate," he whispered. "Just wait."

She wanted to go home, wanted to get as far away from this awkward situation as possible. But when he asked like that . . . how could she say no?

First and foremost, Parker was her friend. One of her best friends. Kate fought back a cringe. The fact that she needed to remind herself of that made her an ass. This wasn't a random guy she kinda sorta had a crush on. Okay, fine, she kinda sorta did have a crush on him, but this was *Parker*. Her friend.

She gave him a slight nod, her gaze now locked on the hardwood floors.

"Courtney, your clothes are in the dryer. Get them on and leave."

Kate's head shot up at the ice in Parker's tone.

Courtney stared back at him in disbelief. "But the storm! Am I just supposed to walk? I thought you and I . . . we were going to have—"

"What the hell are you talking about? There is no *we*. I'll give you a goddamn raincoat. Just get the fu—" Parker's mouth slammed shut and he inhaled sharply.

Kate had never seen him like this. Frustration and anger had him vibrating, and it hurt her heart. His eyes darted to hers and she squeezed his hand, trying to give him some sort of reassurance.

He held her gaze. The annoyance in his green eyes calmed, and he let out a breath. The tension from his body eased, and he faced Courtney. "I need you to leave."

Parker closed the door with a weary sigh and leaned back against it, thunking his head hard on the dark mahogany wood.

Kate couldn't hold back a smile. When Courtney had gone upstairs to change, he'd hastily explained the situation. Now, with his ex-wife out the door, the guy looked exhausted and frustrated and . . . so stinking cute. There was no *kinda sorta*. She most definitely had a crush on this man. "Women just come out of the woodwork with you, don't they, Cunningham?"

"I swear, it's not like that, Kate." He straightened and ran a hand through his chestnut locks, leaving his hair in tousled disarray.

Her mouth went dry. In general, she wasn't a fan of the

longish-hair surfer guy look. But on post-kiss Parker? With his worn, faded jeans, a blue checkered button-down shirt with the sleeves rolled to his elbows, and bare feet? Holy. Moly.

Gah! Focus, Kate!

She cleared her throat and turned all her attention to unwinding the scarf from her neck and hanging it on an entryway hook. Basically, looking anywhere but at him. "Sure, Park. Whatever you say."

He helped her out of her jacket and mumbled under his breath. She couldn't quite make out all the words, but she did catch a creative combination of curse words directed at the storm and Courtney.

Kate snuck a peek at Parker and didn't know whether to chuckle or grimace. The guy looked miserable. What he needed was light and casual. If anyone knew how to do that, it was her. Ole reliable Kate.

"Chili and cornbread?" She started toward the kitchen and came to an abrupt halt, slamming her hand across his chest to stop him. "Wait! Any ex-girlfriends or former wives in the kitchen I need to be aware of?"

She'd keep things light and casual, but that didn't mean he'd be immune from some teasing. It was Parker, after all.

His eyes narrowed and the corner of his lips quirked. He hooked his thumbs in his jeans pockets and eyed her up and down, slowly nodding as if assessing her. "Funny."

"Right?" She couldn't help but laugh. "It's a serious question, though. You know, with Victoria the Crazy and Courtney the Evil Ex. A girl's gotta be prepared, you know?"

"Oh my God," he chuckled. "Have you always been this much of a smartass?" He stepped toward her, slung an arm over her shoulders, and squeezed, leading her through the living area. "I need a freaking drink."

"No kidding," Kate murmured as she tried to still the

jitters in her stomach. He'd put his arm around her. And it was still there. So what? He'd done that a million times before. This time was no different. Really.

She mentally kicked herself. Right.

As they reached the kitchen, Kate focused on the enticing aromas of the savory chili and sweet, buttery cornbread. Moving away from Parker and taking a deep inhale, Kate settled on a backless leather stool at the edge of the kitchen island. "In light of recent events, you probably need a drink more than me."

"There it is. Smartass shining through."

She gasped in mock horror. "Smartass? *Moi?*"

"Exactly." He placed an empty wineglass in front of her.

"I'm not nearly as bad as Raven." Parker held up a bottle of wine, showing her the label, and she nodded. "But can anyone be?"

"Uh, no. The world can only handle one Raven. But you, Kate?" He took a moment to uncork the bottle and pour the deep red wine into their glasses. "You have a special talent all your own."

Kate sipped her wine and smiled. The spicy and tart flavors of this particular malbec were her favorite. "Do tell."

"You're so nice."

She cringed. Good God. Because that's exactly what every woman wanted to hear. Particularly from a gorgeous man she was crushing on. Next, he was going to tell her she had a great personality.

"That's not a bad thing, you know." Parker clinked his glass to hers and took a drink. "What I mean is that when you're a smartass—which, when I really think about it, is more often than not—most people don't even realize it. Ditto for when you're being sarcastic."

"You should hear it when I actually insult someone."

"That, I have yet to experience. But let me guess, you have

the talent to tell someone to go fuc—ahem—to go to hell, and they don't even realize they've been insulted. That sweet smile on your face and all."

"I don't know if I'd call that a talent." More like a passive-aggressive, people-pleaser trait. But whatever. "And it's okay to swear in front of me, you know. I'm not going to crumble at curse words."

"I know. It's just . . ." Parker lifted the lid of the chili pot and stirred, shifting on his feet. "I don't like to talk to you the way I talk to the guys."

She fought the frown that wanted to settle over her face and just stared at him. He was stirring the chili to death and seemed to be avoiding eye contact at all costs. Did everyone think she was this fragile little flower who needed sheltering and protecting?

"So, I'm not your friend now?" She cringed. Okay, that was a little dramatic. Even for her.

He finally met her gaze and rolled his eyes. "Of course you're my friend. You're just not a dude," he said with a wink.

"And Raven is? Because, Parker, I hate to break it to you, but you swear in front of Raven all the time."

"Raven doesn't count."

"And why is that?"

He shrugged. "She's Blake's."

Her eyes widened. *So that made me . . . ?* A soft blush of heat crept over her face.

"I know it doesn't make sense to you, and trust me, I know Raven would kick my ass if she heard me call her Blake's. It's just . . ." He grabbed a fresh teaspoon and dipped it into the pot. With his hand cupped under the spoon, he blew on it and rounded the island toward her. "You're most definitely not just one of the guys, Kate. You're more than that. Here, taste."

She ignored the flutter in her belly. Wait. So Parker didn't think that she was a pansy? Did he mean that he thought of her as more than just a friend? Or did he mean something else entirely?

Holy moly, her brain was mush. She swiveled toward Parker and yelped as she knocked her wineglass over. Hopping off the stool, she cupped her hands and tried to catch the wine before it hit the ground.

Parker was next to her in seconds. "Whoa—don't worry about it." He tossed a kitchen towel to her and laid another on the island to sop up the mess. He dropped a third towel on the ground and used one foot to wipe up the wine. "This kitchen has seen its fair share of spills." He nodded toward her. "Your sweater has seen better days, though."

She glanced down at her sweater and groaned. Her beautiful new light gray cashmere sweater now had a dark crimson stain across her stomach. Like someone had gutted her with a butcher knife. She groaned again. That's what she got for splurging on full-price cashmere.

Kate blotted the towel against her midsection and winced as it seemed to make the wine stain spread more. It was no use. Her one fancy purchase in forever was ruined.

From here on out, it was only clothes from Target.

Pulling her arms from the sleeves, she shimmied out of her sweater and prayed the blouse beneath had been spared. Balling the sweater, she let out a sigh of relief when she didn't spot a stain. At least something had been saved.

"Here," Parker said, taking the balled-up sweater from her. "Let me soak that. Maybe it will help with the stain."

Her brows rose. "You know how to take wine stains out of cashmere? I'm impressed."

"Don't be. I have no clue if it will do any good." He shrugged. "For all I know, it could make it worse."

She glanced at the ruined sweater and frowned. "I wouldn't worry about that."

Parker nodded and headed out of the kitchen. "Make sure you try the chili," he called over his shoulder.

—⬥—

Standing in his second-floor laundry room, a quick Google search proved he wasn't totally full of shit. Filling the utility sink with cold water and shampoo, he soaked Kate's sweater. Minutes ticked by and all he could do was stare at the damn sweater floating in the reddening, sudsy water. When she'd shimmied out of it, her shirts beneath had ridden up and he'd caught a glimpse of the smooth, pale skin of her abs. And he'd almost swallowed his fucking tongue. It had taken all his willpower to remind himself why a relationship with her would be a bad idea.

His brow furrowed as a memory flashed in his mind, one from earlier in the evening of Kate and Courtney staring at each other. Seeing them in the same room was a harsh reminder that relationships were not his forte. Kate deserved better than him. If he got involved with her, when it ended—because it always ended—it would ruin their friendship.

Parker wasn't being overly dramatic. It was a simple fact. Sure, they'd continue to be cordial and polite, but that would be a pale comparison to what they had now. They were friends. Solid friends. Amazing friends. So what if he'd had more fantasies about her than he'd ever admit? He was a grown man who could keep those damn fantasies where they belonged. Out of reality.

He needed to eighty-six all thoughts of any kind of romantic or physical relationship with Kate. And fast. He *never* should have kissed her. Now that he knew that she tasted like sweet wine and—

"Damn it," he murmured, scrubbing his hands over his

face. He could do this. He could bring things back to normal. He had to.

Parker made his way back downstairs and froze in the kitchen's entry.

Nope. He couldn't do it. Hell, he couldn't do anything but stare.

Kate was going to be the death of him. She sat at the island, a bowl of steaming chili in front of her. And she was wearing a tiny, strappy white tank top that fit her like a second skin. Her long, dark brown hair cascaded over her shoulders.

"Sorry," she mumbled when she caught his eye, her mouth full of chili. She flashed a sheepish grin.

He gulped. Damn. How was it possible for a woman to be both smoking hot and adorable at the same time?

"In my haste to eat this delicious chili, I spilled some on my shirt." She gestured toward the table with her spoon. Her sheer white blouse hung on the back of one chair, the front obviously wet. "The good news is I was able to get the stain out." She nodded to the second bowl in front of her. "By some miracle, I was able to scoop a bowl for you without further damage."

Parker managed to move his leaden legs toward her, images of him peeling the tiny tank top off Kate flashing in his mind. Then, as if in slow motion, he reached for the bowl of chili at the same time she pushed it toward him. The bowl tipped, and with more force than he thought chili could travel, the contents splattered against his shirt.

Awesome.

"Oh my God!" Kate gasped, her mouth hanging open, shock clear in her big brown eyes. Her face flushed a pretty pink. "I'm so sorry, Parker."

Damn, she was gorgeous.

After a few seconds of silence, she was beside him,

scooping the chili remnants from his shirt back into the bowl. With strength he didn't know she had, she shoved him toward the sink and began wiping down his shirt with a wet towel.

Holy. Hell.

He clenched his jaw, trying to block out the fire that shot through him at her touch, that had his cock twitching. She was seriously going to be the end of him. He had no idea what to do, so he did the only thing that made sense. He laughed.

"Well, I'm glad you think this is funny." Her chuckle had a nervous quality to it. He didn't like that. Not one bit.

He covered her frantic hands and stilled them by pressing them against his chest. Shit. Not the smartest move he'd ever made. "It's just a shirt, Kate."

"I know . . ."

With his free hand, he tipped her chin up to see her face. "But?"

The flush over her face deepened. She took a deep inhale and let it out in a rush of words. "I'm just so mortified and now I don't know how to act in front of you and it's making me crazy."

He was so close to her. He still had one of her hands and her forearm caged against his chest. Her lips were so damn close. All he had to do was lean down just a few inches and he could taste those sweet lips . . .

"And since I'm being honest—shoot me now, Parker—I'm so, *so* sorry about last night."

That caught his attention. His brow arched in question. "What about last night?"

His breath seized as she dropped the crown of her head to his chest. "I'd thought that maybe you were interested," she mumbled into his shirt. "But the tequila . . . I don't know . . .

I'm sorry I misread everything and made you uncomfortable."

Again, he tipped her chin up to meet his gaze. He hadn't thought her face could get more flushed, but there it was.

Parker opened his mouth, but no words came. He had no idea what to say. He wanted to tell her that she'd been right and he sure as shit was interested in her. He wanted to hoist her onto the counter and taste every single inch of her, show her just how interested he was. But he couldn't. He had nothing to give her. She deserved so much more than a quick fuck or even a short-term affair. An affair that would destroy their friendship.

She pulled slightly away from him, her eyes averted, and he reluctantly let her go. As she stepped fully away, she began rambling on about the pros and cons of tequila. He couldn't quite keep up. He'd known Kate for a long time and knew that when she was nervous-talking, there was no point in trying to follow.

Parker listened with half an ear. Her nervous ramblings were better than what he could provide at the moment. Awkward silence.

He grimaced as he pulled his damp shirt from his chest. Unbuttoning it, he tried to collect his thoughts. She thought he wasn't interested? She thought she'd made him uncomfortable? Guilt coursed through him. He felt like an ass for making her doubt herself.

After he undid the last button, he grabbed a fresh washcloth and quickly ran it over his damp chest. He paused when he realized the room was silent. When he glanced up, Kate was staring at him. Just staring.

The look in her eyes was hungry and carnal, one he'd only dreamed he'd ever see aimed at him. In a split second, his pulse was racing and his blood rushed south. It took everything he had to keep his feet planted. He cleared his throat. "Sorry, what did you say?"

"I have no clue," she murmured, her voice breathy, her lips slightly parted.

Kate's gaze traveled slowly up and down his body, and his cock went rock-hard. Holy fuck. If she made one move toward him, he'd chuck the just friends bullshit out the window.

The doorbell rang, but he couldn't tear his gaze away from her. The bell rang again, but he didn't care. All that mattered was the woman in front of him.

Yelling penetrated his Kate-induced fog. Pounding at the door cleared it fully, and he recognized Blake's voice. A chill ran through him at the sheer panic in his cousin's voice, killing any and all sexual thoughts.

Rushing to the door, Parker yanked it open and Blake barged past him. "Where is she, Park? Where is she? Tell me Kate's here!"

Before Parker could reply, Raven sprinted past them. "Kate! Kate, are you here?"

Kate rushed in from the kitchen, concern etched on her face. "Raven, what—"

Raven smothered her in a fierce hug. Less than a heartbeat later, Blake was next to the women, enveloping them both in his arms. "Thank God you're okay."

Through the mass of bodies, Parker caught Kate's eye. The confusion on her face must have been reflected on his own. He cleared his throat, patting Blake and Raven on their backs. "All right, guys. Let's give her some breathing room."

Blake and Raven spoke at once, hovering over Kate, as Parker steered the group into the kitchen. Once there, Blake and Raven's incessant fussing continued. Both kept mentioning something about a tree and the storm? Jesus. They made zero sense.

Parker stuck two fingers in his mouth and let out a sharp whistle.

Silence.

He caught his cousin's gaze. "What's going on?"

"We got a call from Aunt Anna, who got a call from Janine who—"

He held up his hand. "Wait. Who's Janine?"

"She owns the house I'm renting," Kate answered, confusion tingeing her words. "She's my next-door neighbor and an old friend of Anna's."

"So," Blake continued, his focus back on Kate. "Janine called Aunt Anna and . . . well . . . I don't know how to say this, Kate—"

"Holy hell, Sullivan." Rolling her eyes, Raven pushed Blake aside and took Kate's hands in her own, squeezing. "Sweetie, we're going to do this like a Band-Aid, okay? I'm really sorry, but your house has been completely destroyed."

CHAPTER SIX

Kate's chest squeezed, her breath catching. She must have heard Raven wrong.

"I'm really sorry, Kate," Raven repeated. "You know that giant tree on the side of your house?"

Her mouth gaped like a fish, but for the life of her, Kate couldn't form a single word. She could only nod.

"It pretty much crashed through the entire house. That, with the rain . . . well, you'll be lucky if you can salvage anything."

"Jesus, Raven," Blake groaned. "A little tact?"

Raven held her gaze, ignoring her fiancé, and gave Kate's hands another squeeze. Kate took a deep breath and found comfort in those familiar violet eyes.

"It's just stuff," Raven murmured. "Don't forget that."

True. But it was *her* stuff. She didn't have a lot, but it was all hers. She'd spent her teenage years with Anna and Henry and had never wanted for anything. They had provided her everything—emotionally, physically, and financially. When she'd graduated from the University of Washington and moved out of their home, Kate had worked her ass off to make them proud of her, to prove to them that they hadn't made a mistake in taking her in and adopting her all those years ago. That tiny little house that was just destroyed? It may not have been the biggest or fanciest house, but it had been hers. The rent and everything in it fully paid for by her.

"Wait." Parker's low and steady voice cut through the replay of hazy memories of her little house. "How the hell do you know Kate's place is demolished? Maybe this Janine person is wrong on the extent of the damage. Maybe it's not as bad as she thinks."

Kate's spirit lifted.

Blake shook his head. "No. Janine took pictures and sent them to Aunt Anna, who sent them to us."

The breath Kate didn't know she'd been holding escaped in a whoosh.

Parker's eyes narrowed. "Hold on. You're saying a tree falls on Kate's place, and this Janine character takes pictures and texts them to Aunt Anna? Didn't she call for help? What the fuck?"

"Whoa there, crazy." With one last hand squeeze, Raven stepped away from Kate and toward Parker, pulling her phone from her back pocket. "Before you call out the mob to burn poor Janine at the stake, get your facts straight. One, a giant tree fell on Kate's place and demolished it into itty-bitty pieces."

Kate flinched.

"Jesus, Raven," Blake groaned again.

She knew what Raven was trying to do. The more she heard it in blunt terms, the more it would sink in, and the faster Kate could move on. But still . . .

"Two," Raven continued as if Blake had never spoken, her irritation focused solely on Parker. "Janine did call 911 because she didn't know if Kate was in there. Janine wanted to run over, but the tree also took out a power line. 911 told her to stay put since there was now a live wire flopping on the ground between their houses."

"You know, I don't think downed wires actually flop around like they do in the movies." Parker shrugged, all mock innocence, as Raven's eyes narrowed into a death glare. "What?"

"Three, Janine called Anna to see if she knew where Kate was. Anna wanted to see how bad the damage was, so Janine snapped some photos from her window. That leads us to point four. Anna couldn't reach Kate, so she called Blake. And since you two dumbasses don't answer your goddamn phones, here we are."

"Fine," Parker grumbled, crossing his arms over his chest. "I'll hold off on rallying the mob."

"Idiot," Raven murmured, turning back to Kate. "Anna sent us the photos. The damage is extensive."

As entertaining as her friends' exchange had been, Kate's heart still thudded hard in her chest. "Show me."

Raven hesitated. "It's just stuff, Kate."

"It's *my* stuff, Rave." She held out her hand and hated how it trembled. "Give. Me. Your. Damn. Phone."

Seconds ticked by in silence as Kate pulled up Raven's text messages.

Her breath caught in her throat. The blood drained from her face at the images on the screen.

Demolished was an understatement. The tree had crashed right into her second-story bedroom.

Correction.

Through her bedroom. The entire tree was in what used to be the ground-floor kitchen. What would have happened if she'd been home?

"Oh my God," she whispered. The beginnings of panic stirred in her belly. She swayed and took a deep breath, trying to steady herself.

Before she could exhale, Parker was next to her. His familiar, woodsy scent surrounded her. He took the phone from her with one hand while his other rubbed small circles along her back.

"Everything will be okay," he murmured. "I promise."

"You have renters insurance, right?" Raven asked.

Kate nodded. Every time she blinked, images of her destroyed home flashed in her mind. Clothes and furniture mixed with tree branches and drywall debris. She knew in her head that all those things could be replaced. But her photos? The souvenirs and little keepsakes she'd picked up along the way? Her heart squeezed, and she swallowed past the lump lodged in her throat. That wasn't just stuff.

Not to mention her laptop and—

Nausea rushed through her. Holy crap. Her home office! Her work!

Full-blown panic had her turning and bolting toward the front door. "I have to get over there—my client files!"

Parker snagged Kate by the waist before she made it through the kitchen archway. She was quicker than he'd anticipated. But he was faster.

"Parker! Seriously," she hissed over her shoulder, her eyes a mix of shock, annoyance, and dismay. "All my client files are there and—"

"And they'll all be there tomorrow, sweetheart." He tightened his hold around her waist and easily picked her up, ignoring her surprised yelp, and carried her deeper into the kitchen. "It's dark and raining sideways. It's stupid to go out there. You'll probably electrocute yourself if you try to—"

"I need to, Park," she protested, her face flashing with irritation. She smacked him on the shoulder as he set her down. "I need to go . . . home."

Her breath caught on the last word and his heart squeezed. She went deathly pale as all the anger left her face. She was fighting to keep it together. As the seconds ticked by, Parker could see her starting to crumble. As much as he wanted to wrap her in a bubble, he knew Raven had the right idea. Kate didn't need coddling. He needed to be firm. She wasn't going to crumble. Not on his watch, damn it.

Parker turned her to face him and framed her face in his hands. "You can't go back tonight, Kate. It's not safe."

"He's right," Blake interjected. "The storm's not dying down any time soon. It would be crazy."

She nodded, her gaze never leaving Parker's. "But I work from home," she replied, her voice barely above a whisper. "Everything's in my home office. My computer, all my work, my client files. My things."

The panic and sadness warring in her brown eyes slayed him. Fuck being firm. He yanked her close, wrapping his arms around her, and kissed the top of her head. "We'll get you new things, baby."

"Yeah, I know," she said, her head resting against his chest. She let out a long sigh and gave his waist a squeeze before stepping away. "But all my client files, my computer?"

"You scan all your files and your laptop is backed up to a cloud, right?"

Kate nodded. "Almost everything has been scanned, and yeah, I have a backup subscription thing."

"I have an extra laptop. We can upload all your files to it and you'll be good to go."

"See, Kate," Raven chimed in, linking arms with her. "Easy fuckin' peasy. Not only is the man great eye candy, but he's smart too. By the way, nice six-pack, Park."

It took him a second to remember that his shirt was still unbuttoned. Damn.

As his fingers worked the buttons, Raven chuckled. "Don't button back up on my account. I don't mind the view."

"Come on, Rave," Blake grumbled. "I'm standing right here."

She blew him a kiss. "And you know I love you best."

Raven was doing everything she could to distract Kate, and Parker was grateful. The panic had left her eyes, but the sadness remained. It was less than it had been thanks to Raven, but it still lingered.

Parker caught Kate's gaze and she mouthed a silent "thank you." He swore, right then and there, that he'd do everything he could to make the sadness go away for good.

Raven picked up Kate's blouse from the back of the dining table chair and wagged her brows at them. "Missing something?"

Kate's face flamed, but she chuckled, though her smile didn't quite reach her eyes. "You just don't stop, do you?"

"Nope." Raven gave Kate another hug. "I'm sorry we interrupted."

"Oh my God," Kate groaned while hugging Raven tight. "Nothing—"

"I know, I know . . . *nothing's going on.* Whatever." Raven rolled her eyes, then quickly sobered. "I'm really not sorry we barged in here because we had to know you were okay."

"My turn. Move, woman," Blake said, nudging Raven out of the way and enveloping Kate in a hug.

As they headed toward the entryway, lightning flashed close. An immediate boom of thunder shook the house. Everything went black and car alarms went off. The electricity in the air had the hair on Parker's arms raising.

A split second later, the crack of a nearby tree crashing into metal set off more car alarms.

"Holy shit," Blake whispered into the silence.

Moments later, a loud click sounded and Parker's lights flickered back on, indicating the generator had kicked in.

"Yeah, you guys aren't going anywhere tonight," Parker said.

He glanced at Kate and his insides tensed. She'd gone eerily still. He wrapped an arm around her shoulders, her slight frame trembling against him. He pulled her closer, and when her arms wrapped around his waist, he pressed a kiss to the top of her head. "I've got you, sweetheart."

Over her head, he caught Blake and Raven's gazes and nodded toward the kitchen. "I've got chili, cornbread, and alcohol if anyone's interested."

CHAPTER SEVEN

It was Friday afternoon, a mere four days after the Storm of the Century had hit the Puget Sound area, and Kate's headache had reached astronomical heights. Cradling the phone between her ear and shoulder, she lowered the volume on the hold music blaring from the landline.

Kate yanked out her ponytail's hair tie and massaged her head, staring blindly out the second-story office window. The past few days had been a madhouse.

Her little two-bedroom house was indeed demolished, though she hadn't quite wrapped her head around that fact yet. Her whole life, she'd been good at shoving difficult situations out of her mind. This time was no different. Thank you, chaos.

Along with the house, almost all her personal belongings had been destroyed. The good news was that when the tree hit, it had somehow managed to only collapse half of her closet, so she could salvage some of her clothes. Not all of them, but enough to get her through the next week or two before her renters insurance paid out.

But that was it. Between the tree, the rain, and the house turning to rubble, that was all she had left.

To add salt to an already gaping wound, when Parker's neighbor had called a tree removal company to hoist a fallen tree from their garage, the company had managed to drop the tree into the street. And onto her car.

Her ancient, trusty Honda was officially totaled.

Kate was homeless, carless, and the only personal possessions she had left fit into a small duffle bag.

She wrinkled her nose. Okay, maybe that was laying it on a bit thick.

She shouldn't complain. Really. It wasn't like she was living on the streets and destitute. She was staying with Parker, so technically, she wasn't homeless. And since her home office had been demolished, Parker had not only arranged for her to set up shop in the small conference room of Clean Water Campaign—the non-profit founded by Parker's parents that shared the second floor with Jake's Alvarez Technologies—but he'd also cleared out half of his own home office so she could use it if she didn't want to get out of her pajamas.

The sweet man had an amazing home four times bigger than her tiny house, and he'd welcomed her into it with open arms, for which she was grateful. It just wasn't *her* home.

Being carless wasn't that big of a deal either, since Parker had two vehicles and his house was in a walkable neighborhood. She grimaced. Well, it *shouldn't* be that big of a deal.

But all her salvageable possessions really did fit into one small duffle bag. And that hurt her heart. She knew they were just things . . . but still.

Ugh!

She switched the phone call to speaker, replaced the handset, and slouched in the conference room chair, dropping her head back. Pity parties sucked. Kate took in a deep breath and blinked away the ever-present tears.

Things, she reminded herself. *Just things.*

Enough.

Taking another fortifying breath, she sat up and focused on the scattered papers on the table. As she busied herself with organizing everything into various piles—complete, ongoing, follow-up, to-do—her nerves settled.

She cringed. How freaking OCD was that?

Though power had just been restored to their Queen Anne neighborhood overnight—thank goodness Parker had installed a generator at his home—Kate had been nonstop busy since the storm hit. The pandemonium had left her head throbbing multiple times, but she'd embraced it because things could have been worse.

Things could always be worse.

She was lucky, really. Straightening an already-even stack of papers, Kate repeated those words over and over in her head. Repetition would make them sink in.

Eventually.

A glance at the clock reminded her she needed to be down at the pub soon, and she mentally kicked herself. While she was sitting in her tidy, make-shift office having a pity party, Parker and Blake were busting their butts, and had been for the past few days.

With so many people out of power in their neighborhood, Parker and Blake had decided to open the pub to everyone. Even though Blake and Raven's residence on the building's third floor didn't have power since their generator was being repaired, the generators for The Spotted Dog and the offices on the second floor were working. Parker had determined that since they had a fully stocked kitchen and the food needed to be eaten, they may as well feed everyone they could. So they had. And over Blake's initial protests, they'd also installed two flat-screen televisions behind the bar so people could keep up with the local news.

Kate had spent hours on the phone dealing with tree issues for herself and Janine. Because she was a sucker and couldn't say no when her landlord had asked for help. When she wasn't on the phone or waiting on hold, she pitched in at the pub where she could. That is, when she wasn't busy throwing herself the world's most pathetic pity party.

The guys had closed the actual bar area and turned it into an amazing, cafeteria-style buffet, free of charge. She and Raven served the food while Parker and Blake manned the kitchen. The four of them were the only ones who lived close enough to the pub to make it into work; the storm had knocked down so many trees and power lines that the rest of the pub staff were stuck in their various Seattle neighborhoods.

Kate took another sip of her lukewarm coffee and groaned as the muffled strands of an '80s power ballad—instrumental, of course—filled the conference room. Insurance company hold music was going to be the death of her.

One thing all the calls to the insurance companies had made clear was that she was screwed. When the insurance eventually paid out, the money she'd receive would cover some things, but nowhere near all of it. She needed to either pick up more bookkeeping clients or pick up more shifts at the pub.

With a click of her mouse, she brought up her personal QuickBooks file on her borrowed laptop and sighed. Both. She'd have to do both.

She blew out a breath as the *St. Elmo's Fire* theme song played for the third time. Kate stood, disconnecting the call. There was only so much instrumental hold music one person could take.

Downing the last of her coffee, she prayed the caffeine

would kick in and get her through what was sure to be a long evening. With a final glance at her meticulously organized desk, her shoulders drooped. She'd better get used to long hours if she wanted to dig herself out of this financial mess.

"Stop being a pansy," she muttered, turning to the wall mirror to redo her hair. "So many more people have it worse than you."

With a final adjustment to her ponytail, Kate squared her shoulders. *This is nothing. You can do this.*

Sleep was overrated anyhow.

Three hours later, a good-sized crowd remained at The Spotted Dog. With power restored to most of the city, the pub was back to its usual operation. Since they were still down two servers, Kate picked up a tray and got to work.

The first hour passed in a blur. Even with power back on, it seemed as if no one in their neighborhood was eating at home tonight. There were also a large number of folks who'd come in for drinks and dinner as a way of thanking the guys for opening their doors during the storm.

It warmed her heart to know that Parker and Blake's kindness hadn't gone unnoticed. Even though her feet were starting to ache.

Kate headed toward the bar and caught a glimpse of Ali, the lone server who'd been able to make it in, as the young, gorgeous woman glided through the pub, a full tray of loaded dinner plates balanced on one hand and three baskets of bread in her other. All the while sporting five-inch heels.

Kate didn't need to look at Raven behind the bar to know her friend was wearing similarly heeled footwear. She glanced down at her sensible Dansko clogs and frowned. Granted, she owned her fair share of stilettos—before they'd been waterlogged by the storm, of course—but they'd only been donned when Kate knew she didn't have to actually move too much.

Reaching the bar's service station, she unloaded her tray of empties. All this wallowing in negativity wasn't her. She really needed to suck it up because she was starting to annoy herself.

"These flat screens were a great idea," Raven said, adding three cocktails to the drink rail.

Kate smiled at her friend. "Of course you'd say that. Weren't they your idea?"

"Yeah, but don't tell Blake. He didn't want them at first, but he eventually came around. I like to let him think it was all his idea. It helps his ego."

Kate scoffed. "Right. Like he has any deficiencies in that department."

"You'd be surprised. He may have put this pretty sparkler on my finger, but I'm still a ball-buster. His balls especially. But yin and yang, right? For every ten times I take his ego down a notch, I throw one or two 'attaboys' his way. And the TVs were it. Sweet of me, right?"

Kate chuckled. "So gracious of you."

Raven worked her bartender magic and nodded toward the screen playing the local news. "They're about to replay the *In Lighter News* segment. You should check it out."

Kate wiped her tray and readied it for another round, glancing up. "Why would I want to ch—" Her breath caught, the words lodging in her throat. Heat rushed over her face. "Oh my God."

Staring back from the sixty-inch display was her face. And Parker's. Kissing!

Someone in the pub let out a whoop and a cheer. Then there was clapping—*clapping!*—and all Kate could do was stare at the Kiss Cam footage being replayed on the screen. Her face was on fire and she was sure she was redder than red, but for the life of her . . . she couldn't tear her eyes away from the television.

No. Correction. Kate couldn't tear her eyes away from Parker.

She had always thought Parker was a good-looking guy, but seeing him on the screen with all his attention on *her*, being all smoldery and all . . . well . . . crazy freaking hot, left her breathless. And then some. His shaggy hair, the kind that any red-blooded woman would want to run her fingers through, and that chiseled jaw with its sexy five-o'clock shadow . . .

Holy moly.

"He's a face-holder," Raven said.

The screen cut back to the news anchors and a video of a dancing cat. Not nearly as captivating as Parker.

"What?" Kate murmured, turning her attention back to her friend. "Sorry, what was that?"

Raven smirked. "Parker. When he kisses, he's a face-holder."

"Oh man, trust me—I noticed." She leaned against the bar and sighed, part dreamy, part . . . something else. She should not—repeat, *not*—be getting all whatever-it-was-she-was-getting about Parker, but Kate couldn't help it. "I love that. Guys don't do that enough."

"No, they don't."

"And when they hold your face just right? Then wrap their arms around you so perfectly?" Kate sighed again. "Amazing."

She could still feel Parker's arms around her, the way he had filled all her senses. Tingles danced down her spine at the memory. And then when he had—

Raven cleared her throat.

Kate jerked to attention. Crap. "Well, um, what I actually meant was that I, uh . . ."

Amusement was written all over Raven's face. "Seeing as there was no wrapping of arms in that Kiss Cam clip, I assume that reference was from your make-out session with Parker after the M's game?"

Kate's jaw dropped.

Raven rolled her eyes. "Please, sweetie. Did you think Blake would hold back that juicy little nugget? When a crazy chick comes crashing into our home and stakes a claim on Parker, you better believe Blake is going to let me know about it. Besides, I think you and Parker and all your tongue action scarred my sweet man for life. Or is there another make-out incident I don't know about?"

Kate's mind flashed to that mortifying moment she practically threw herself at Parker. Well, there was no *practically* about it. She had thrown herself at the poor guy. And Parker had politely declined. She supposed it was more like a non-make-out incident.

And yeah, they'd had a couple highly charged moments since then—particularly the night of the storm. But nothing had actually happened. She opened her mouth to say so, but slammed it shut. Her ego couldn't take another hit, particularly with Raven, who'd just been voted "Seattle's Hottest Bartender" in the local paper. "Nope, that was it."

"Hmmm . . . don't forget that I know you, Kate." A giant smile split Raven's face. "You're holding out on me, *baby*."

Kate's eyes narrowed in confusion at the endearment. Sure, her friend used a lot of nicknames, but baby wasn't one of them. At least not with her. "What?"

"Oh, sorry, do you prefer *sweetheart*?"

She could only stare at her friend. "What are you talking about?"

Raven laughed. "Parker called you both on storm night, remember?"

Her face flushed. What? "I have no clue what you're talking about."

"Well," Raven mused, her lips pursed. "You *were* stressed with the whole tree-demolishing-your-home thing. But he did. It was super cute. Blake and I both thought so."

"Oh my God, you're nuts." Had he called her those names? The thought had butterflies erupting in her stomach. If he had, it was only because he was being a good friend. Right?

Kate shook her head—she needed to focus!—and added a martini and two lemon drops to her tray. She pointed to the final two drinks. "What are these?"

"Gin and tonic with the lime and a vodka soda with both the lime and lemon. And after you drop those off, come right back here, missy, because I'm not done with you."

"Promises, promises," Kate called over her shoulder as she hustled off to deliver drinks.

Moments later, she was back at the service station and keying in a new round of drinks.

"As I was saying," Raven said in a sing-song voice, all the while mixing drinks. "You and Parker, huh?"

"Seriously, I'm not sure how many more times I have to say it, but there is no me and Parker."

"Well, you are *staying* with Parker." Kate didn't miss the suggestive emphasis her friend added. "How's that going? You and the cook getting cozy?"

Kate didn't know whether to groan or laugh. "Stop it. You know it's not like that. Staying with Park made sense. Besides, it's been so busy we've barely seen each other."

Which was the absolute truth. She was up and hunkered down at her temporary office at CWC before Parker was even awake. She could have worked out of his home office, but she didn't want to impose.

Besides, on the first morning at Parker's, she'd tried to

figure out his fancy coffee maker and had accidentally woken him up banging around in the kitchen. Apparently, she needed a master's degree to operate the thing. Either that or she needed someone less . . . Parker . . . showing her how to operate it. Because sleep-rumpled hair, a bare chest, and washboard abs on display in low-slung sweatpants? Yeah. Ridiculous. There was zero coffee-making knowledge retention to be had.

All in all, she was better off working at CWC or else she'd never get anything done. And would be suffering from severe caffeine withdrawal.

"Made sense? You could've stayed with me and Blake. We have extra rooms too, you know."

"You didn't have power." Kate wanted to pat herself on the back when Raven frowned.

"I'll give you that. *But* you could have stayed with Anna and Henry. They had power in that giant house of theirs. You know, the home you spent the better part, literally, of your childhood in."

She chuckled at Raven's play on words. It was true. When she'd been adopted by Anna and Henry, life had gotten a million times better. Everything about her childhood prior to that had sucked. "They're over in Magnolia, and last I checked, the two exits out of that neighborhood are *still* blocked."

"Okay, fine. I'll give you that one too." Raven placed more drinks onto the service station. "You'd think that with all the money in Magnolia, they'd have more than two options out of the damn place. Have Anna and Henry just been sitting at home counting their money?"

"Raven Magenta Wagner, you—"

"Tsk-tsk," Raven interrupted with a wag of her sparkly ring finger. "That's Raven Magenta soon-to-be-Sullivan to you."

Kate reached for another drink to load on her tray and

paused, fighting a smile. "You are a thousand percent ridiculous and you know it. Henry's actually been going to work like usual."

Raven's brow furrowed. "Just how does the good doctor—excuse me, *surgeon*—get to work if the exits are blocked?"

"He catches a ride out of Magnolia with his neighbor, Stan." Raven's brow arched in question and Kate chuckled. "On Stan's really fancy boat."

"What?" Raven asked. "No helicopter?"

Kate laughed. "Stan's helicopter was damaged in the storm."

"Oh, fancy people." Raven brought the back of her hand to her forehead in a perfect southern belle imitation. "Life must be so hard."

"Uh, Raven? You do realize who you're marrying, right? Blake's not exactly a pauper." More like a multimillionaire.

Raven let out a sigh, glancing around them, then leaned closer toward her. "I know. It's just a little intimidating, you know? I mean, you understand. All this," she waved her hand in the air, "is so different from how you and I grew up. I mean, you pre-Anna-and-Henry."

Kate did know. Living with Parker in his amazing house was like when she lived with Anna and Henry in their equally amazing house. She just hated feeling like a charity case. She knew none of them thought of her that way, not Parker, Anna, or Henry. But she couldn't help how she felt. How she'd always felt.

Since day one in this upper-crust world, she'd never quite felt like she belonged. What killed her was that she knew Anna and Henry loved her and thought of her as their daughter. And she loved them with everything she was. Hell, she was who she was because of them. However, no matter their love, there was always that tiny part of her that nagged at her, that told her she wasn't truly one of them.

And that made her an asshole. Worse. It made her an ungrateful asshole.

She reached over the counter and gave Raven's hand a quick squeeze. "Believe me. I get you. Like I said, I haven't seen a lot of Parker this week, but it's kinda the same. My tiny little house was what, barely a thousand square feet?"

Raven nodded, placing two more drinks on the service station. "You loved every inch of it."

"I really did." She added the new drinks to her tray and couldn't help but smile at the memories of her cozy former home. "Parker's place is easily four times the size. Probably more. Like you said, it's a little intimidating. I mean, his freaking stove is worth more than my car."

Raven chuckled. "Not to mention the cost of his actual car."

"You mean *cars*."

"True. Those boys and their crazy ridiculous toys. Guys are strange, strange beings." Raven's nose wrinkled. "Don't worry, babe. I know you'll bounce back from this and wherever you land will be even better than before."

Kate carefully hoisted her tray and blew her friend a kiss. God, she loved that girl.

She wove her way through the tables, slowing as a man stepped in front of her. She startled but managed to keep her tray upright. The man faced her, a sheepish smile on his face.

"Hey, Kate."

"Scott." Her mind scrambled to find some sort of polite thing to say. "Can I get you something to drink?"

Not quite polite, but it would have to do.

"When you have a minute, can we talk?"

She'd never been so thankful to be holding a tray full of drinks. "We're super busy."

Kate wanted to kick herself. *No.* That's what she should

have said. Perhaps even, *No, Scott, I have nothing to say to you. Ever. Now go away.*

"Maybe later?" she asked.

Idiot! If she could bash her own head in, she would.

"Great," Scott replied, his puppy dog eyes brightening. "That would be perfect."

The urge to roll her eyes was strong, but she resisted. Instead, she gestured to her tray. "It may be a while. Like hours."

Scott stepped out of her path, motioning her to pass. "Not a problem. I don't have any plans tonight. I'll just hang at the bar until you have a moment."

Lovely. Just lovely.

As Kate passed him, she cringed when she caught a whiff of his douchey, too-strong cologne. She really, really needed to grow a pair.

Kate loaded yet another round of drinks onto her tray and tried not to grimace. Her feet were on fire. How Raven and Ali strutted around night after night in stilettos was beyond her. She was wearing clogs, for crying out loud.

"You keep making that face and it'll stay like that forever," Raven called out.

So much for hiding her grimace.

"Don't worry. Your feet will get used to it." Raven rose on her tiptoes to peek over the bar and tsked. "Since your feet will hurt like hell no matter what you wear, at least have the decency to ditch the Amish shoes."

Her jaw dropped and she took the opportunity to rest the tray back on the bar. "Excuse me, but clogs are Dutch. Not Amish." Raven stared at her with that devious smirk she knew so well. Yeah, so they weren't the cutest in footwear. But still. "And nurses wear them."

Kate cringed. Not the best comeback.

Raven's smirk grew. "The only nurses here are trying to hook up with that table of soccer jersey-clad bros in the corner. And none of those ladies are wearing Amish footwear."

She should probably concede this round.

"Hey, guys!"

"Oh, thank God," Kate murmured as she turned toward the chipper greeting. She smiled as her friend, Amanda, hopped onto a barstool. She hugged Amanda and chuckled at Raven's groan.

Kate knew Raven and Amanda weren't each other's biggest fans, but the two had developed a more cordial relationship over the last few months. The side effect of being at so many of the same functions.

Kate and Amanda had known each other for years. Amanda's parents were not only longtime friends of Anna and Henry's, but friends of Blake and Parker's families as well.

"Don't let me interrupt," Amanda said, hanging her purse on the under-bar hook. "What are you talking about?"

"The Amish, the storm, this and that," Raven replied, placing a coaster in front of Amanda. "The usual?"

Amanda nodded.

"Footwear and stuff." Kate added another drink to her tray and glanced at Amanda's strappy four-inch-heeled pumps. It was a losing battle. "But mostly about Parker's house. My place got demolished in the storm, so I'm crashing at his."

"Sorry about your place, my mom told me. But on the bright side, lucky you! Parker's house is amazing."

"Yeah. We were talking earlier about how it's like four times the size of mine." A heaviness settled in her belly. Kate hoped she sounded happier than she felt. She didn't want to talk about her destroyed home. Not with Amanda, anyway.

"Right?" Amanda's blue eyes lit up. "It's like Parker installed every high-end finish you could imagine. It's like *Architectural Digest* meets *Wired*. I guess when you have that kind of money, it isn't a big deal. I mean, there's money. Then there's *money* money, you know?"

Kate frowned. Amanda made it sound as if Parker was a materialistic and shallow prick. Nothing could be further from the truth. Yes, he had a crazy amount of money from his trust, but he wasn't irresponsibly frivolous. He reinvested and gave back to the community. And it's not like it was any of Amanda's freaking business anyway. "You know, he put a lot of work into that house. He designed every inch of it and hand-picked all the contractors himself. He worked closely with everyone who had a hand in it. It's not like he just threw money at some cookie-cutter builder and—"

"So, Amanda," Raven interrupted, placing an Ultimate Lemon Drop in front of her. "Kate claims that nothing is going on between her and Parker."

"You don't say?" Amanda sipped her drink, her attention on Raven. "I saw the Kiss Cam video. No way in hell they're just friends."

Seriously? Kate crossed her arms over her chest. "I'm right here, you guys."

"Sorry," Raven said in a sweet sing-song voice. "You always deny everything, so I figured Amanda and I would have this conversation without you."

Oh. My. God. "For the last time, there is—"

"The lady doth protest too much," Amanda chimed in, using that same obnoxious sing-song voice.

She ground her teeth together. "It's not protesting too much if you guys keep asking me the same damn thing."

"Damn. She said damn." Amanda's mouth dropped in

mock horror. "She's swearing now. Raven, look what you've done."

Kate glared at both women. "You guys aren't even friends, and now you're ganging up on me?"

Raven shrugged. "We're growing on each other."

"Like a boil," Amanda added with a snicker.

Raven snorted. "A nasty, unpreventable abscess. Good one."

Kate hoisted her full tray up and couldn't help the chuckle that escaped. "Why are we friends again?"

Raven chuckled. "Because you love us."

"I do." Kate air-kissed them both and turned on her own sing-song voice. "Even though you're both assholes."

Ten minutes later, Kate's tray was empty and the new orders had been entered into the pub's system. She scanned the tables for any sign of Scott. Call her a passive-aggressive chicken, but she really didn't want to deal with him tonight. Not seeing him, she started toward the bar.

A hand settled on the small of her back and she jumped, quickly stepping away.

"Hey, Kate."

Her heart raced as Scott's cologne permeated her senses, making her want to gag. It had been at least a couple hours; how had the smell not dissipated? "Geez, Scott. You gave me a heart attack," she said, taking another small step away. Dang, she should have smelled him coming. Over his shoulder, she saw Scott's friend, Dave, and gave him a slight nod as he raised his pint glass to her in greeting. She bit back a grin when he grimaced and mouthed, "I'm so sorry," his eyes darting to Scott.

"Look, I know you're busy, but since you didn't return my calls or texts, I wanted to come see you and apologize."

Calls and texts? She supposed blocking his number would be why she'd never received them. She tried to stamp down the guilt that was beginning to percolate. And failed.

She wanted to kick herself. *He'd* been the jackass. *He* was the one who should feel guilty. Not her.

Wait, what? Was Scott actually apologizing?

"I'm really sorry, Kate. The whole baseball game thing was my fault. Actually, all of it was my fault. I was an idiot."

Her mind couldn't keep up. "I'm sorry, what?"

He looked sheepish. "I'm an idiot. I'm stupid because it took my friends hounding me and that dumb video playing over and over again for me to realize that I was paying more attention to my phone than to you. It went viral, you know." His eyes brightened, but he shook his head and stepped closer. "Sorry, that doesn't matter. Can we start over? Can I take you out to dinner?"

Her mouth opened, but nothing came out. Of all the words that could have come out of Scott's mouth, those were the last she would have imagined. "Wow, Scott."

In her peripheral vision, she caught a glimpse of Parker leaning against the archway that separated the kitchen from the rest of the bar, a glass of ice water in his hand. And a gorgeous blonde fluttering her lashes at him. The blonde's hand was on his arm, and he didn't look like he was in any rush to get back to the kitchen.

She ignored the disappointment and turned her attention back to Scott. "Sure." The guilt she'd felt earlier from inadvertently ignoring him eased at his growing smile. A tingling in her gut told her this wasn't the best idea, but screw it. "Dinner would be nice."

His face lit up with a full-blown grin, the handsome smile that had attracted her to him in the first place. "How about tomorrow night?"

Wow. Okay. He was serious. "Oh, um, I can't tomorrow.

I'll be working here. The guys are short-staffed with the storm and all."

"Are you working Sunday?"

Her first instinct was to lie and say yes. But she couldn't. "No. The pub's closed on Sundays and my bookkeeping clients are regular weekday types."

"Sunday then."

She nodded. She could still be attracted to him. Scott was a good-looking guy. Heck, she *should* be attracted to him.

"Great. I'll pick you up at six?"

In her peripheral vision, she caught sight of the blonde's hand moving to rest on Parker's chest. Stupid Parker.

She started. "Oh, wait. I'm actually staying at Parker's."

Scott's brows rose. "You're living with Parker?"

"Yeah, the storm really messed up my place and I needed a place to stay, and he lives really close, so it made sense to move in with him." *Stop talking, stop talking, stop talking.* "We're friends and all, and then my car was totaled and his place is close to here, so it made sense, but I already said that . . ."

"Okaaay." Scott nodded slowly. "I'll pick you up at Parker's then. Text me his address."

She cleared her throat and felt heat rush over her face. "I should get back to work." She shifted on her feet. "Um, thanks for coming in, Scott. That was really sweet of you."

His grin was back, and he leaned toward her.

Surprised, she jerked back, but not before he managed to land a kiss on her cheek.

"See you Sunday, Kate."

She watched him head back to Dave, letting out an unsteady breath, then headed back to the bar to pick up more drinks. What just happened?

"Please tell me you didn't give that fucker the time of day."

Raven.

"I did."

"Why?"

Kate shrugged and set down her tray on the bar. "He wanted to apologize."

"Bullshit."

Kate scanned the customers at the bar. "Where's Amanda?"

"Bathroom and don't change the subject."

"No really, Raven. Scott said he was sorry for the way he paid more attention to his phone and that the whole Kiss Cam thing was his fault. He wants to go to dinner and maybe start over."

"He waited until now? Convenient."

"No." Kate squirmed, guilt stirring. "I'd blocked his number, so I didn't get any of his messages."

Raven's brow arched. "Yet you're still going out with him."

"I never said I was," she hedged as Raven's brow arched higher.

"I repeat," her friend began, "you blocked this jackass's number and yet you're *still* going out with him."

Fine. Raven had a point there. "It's no big deal. Besides, Scott's sweet."

"Like a dog."

She glared at her friend. "Seriously?"

"What?" Raven added a couple more drinks to the mat in front of her. "And Parker?"

Kate rolled her eyes. "What about him?"

It was Raven's turn to glare.

Kate let out a sigh. "We're friends. That's it."

"That's it?"

The edge of Kate's lips tipped up. "No, we're roommates too. But that's it."

She groaned as Raven's brow arched higher. How that was even possible, Kate had no clue. She nodded toward the kitchen. "Rave, he's been hanging with Blondie over there for the last ten minutes. That flirting thing happening over there?" She waved her hand in their direction. "That doesn't happen between me and him."

"If you ask me, all that flirting looks a bit one-sided—"

"Sorry," she interrupted, loading her tray with drinks. "No one's asking you, Raven. But I appreciate the concern." Sort of.

She turned with her full tray. Nope. No more listening to Raven and her crazy talk about her and Parker.

Hoisting the tray up, she glanced over at Parker and Blondie. Her breath hitched and the tray wobbled as she caught Parker's eye. With Blondie still plastered to his side, he nodded at her and raised his glass in a silent toast.

Yup. Her and Parker? Crazy talk.

CHAPTER EIGHT

Parker had been working up a healthy sweat shoveling rocks in his front yard in the post-storm Sunday sunshine. It was the start of fall and the days were still long, so he'd been taking full advantage and adding more mid-sized rocks to the landscaping edging his home.

That was ten minutes ago.

Now, he could only stare at the woman before him. Disbelief ricocheting in his head, his hand fisted tight on the handle of the shovel he'd been using. "I'm sorry. I don't think I heard you correctly."

"We should give our marriage another shot," Courtney repeated, an innocent smile on her perfectly made-up face.

Shit, that's what he thought she'd said. "Look, no offense, but that's probably the most horrendous idea I've ever heard." There was no *probably* about it. No way in hell.

"Come on, now," she chuckled, and gave him that coy grin he'd once thought was sexy. "It wasn't all bad, Parky."

"It was definitely more bad than good, and seriously, enough with the *Parky* shit already." He shook his head. Unfortunately, it didn't make anything clearer. She opened her mouth, but he held up a hand. "I don't know where this is coming from, but we're not getting back together."

"You must admit that seeing each other these past few months has been nice."

His jaw dropped. Fucking hell. "We've barely spoken over the last few months. How the hell does that count as 'seeing each other'?"

"*Parker*, we were good together, and I miss you."

She stepped toward him. He stepped away. Hell no.

"Did you forget that when we were married, you fucked another guy?"

Her eyes narrowed. "You know that he meant nothing to—"

"No, Courtney, see—"

"I'm sorry I cheated, but I thought of you the whole time." He cringed. Good freaking God. How were they having this conversation? "I swear to you, Parker. He meant nothing. I was only trying to make you jealous."

"Well, it didn't work." He scrubbed his free hand over his face, then rested it on his hip. His other hand still held the shovel handle in a death grip. It was either that, or he would bash his own head in with it. "Which, when you think about it, basically sums up our entire marriage. I didn't particularly care who you fucked then, and I especially don't care now."

Courtney was silent for a moment, studying him. All hope that she'd get a clue and leave fled when her face softened, like she'd just witnessed puppies and kittens frolicking in a field of flowers. "Awww. You don't see it."

Frustration clawed at him like an alien trying to escape his chest. "What are you talking about?"

"This whole Kiss Cam thing with Kate."

He jerked, repulsed at hearing Kate's name pass through Courtney's lips. "What about Kate?"

"You don't see it. God, you're so sweet, Parky." She shook

her head, the sappy grin growing on her face. "You've never noticed how she has long brown hair like me? Dark brown eyes like mine?"

Holy shit, this conversation needed to end ten minutes ago. What the hell was Courtney even getting at?

"How she's a few inches shorter and definitely has more pounds on her, but has a similar overall build as me?"

Similar overall build? Sure, if Courtney meant a head, two arms, and two legs. And shit—did she just call Kate fat? The fuck? Kate was perfection. Courtney needed to eat some goddamn cheeseburgers.

In his stupefaction, he didn't notice Courtney had stepped closer until she laid a hand on his bicep, startling him.

"I think you miss me too, Parky. And I think subconsciously, you want me back. Hence, that whole Kate Kiss Cam thing." Before he knew what was what, she rose to her tiptoes and laid a quick kiss on his cheek. "I'll see you soon," she called over her shoulder as she made her way to her car.

Parker stood motionless for a full thirty seconds. He knew his mouth was hanging open and was pretty sure his face showed a mixture of confusion, revulsion, and shock. What the fuck just happened? Did Courtney seriously believe that Kate was some kind of substitute for *her*? Yeah, they both had brown hair and brown eyes, but so did millions of other people.

As far as similarities, that was it; that's where it all ended.

"Dude." Blake walked up the drive, a scowl on his face as he glared at the bright red BMW pulling away from the curb. "Was that your ex-wife?"

Blake considered Courtney on par with He Who Must Not Be Named.

"Yeah." Parker was dumbfounded. "She wants to get back

together and suggested I do too because I kissed Kate at the M's game."

"Bro, that makes absolutely zero sense."

"She implied that I'm only attracted to Kate because Kate physically resembles her."

Blake opened his mouth but snapped it shut; his face scrunched as if he was trying to find the right words. After a few moments of silence, he shook his head and snorted. "I knew that bitch was crazy, but I didn't realize how fucking delusional she was. She thinks that *Kate* resembles *her*? And *that's* the explanation for why you're attracted to Kate?"

Parker nodded, glad he wasn't the only one thunderstruck.

"Kate?" Blake continued. "The woman who's currently living with you? The one that basically screams 'girl next door' and who everyone but me thinks is totally hot?"

The corners of Parker's lips twitched. "That's the one." He dropped his shovel onto the rocks and headed toward the garage, certain his cousin would follow. He made a beeline to the garage fridge and retrieved two beers. Opening both bottles with the opener mounted to the wall, he took a pull from his beer while handing Blake the second.

"What are you going to do about that deranged woman?" Blake asked as they entered the family room.

"Fuck if I know." Parker sank into his favorite leather recliner. "The night of the storm, I wasn't exactly polite when I kicked Courtney out. You'd think she would have gotten the hint."

"You'd think the divorce would have been a big clue." Blake rose from the couch and disappeared into the kitchen. Seconds later he was back, a bottle of Parker's best whiskey tucked under his arm and two lowball glasses in his hands.

"She's been showing up more and more the last few months, and for the life of me, I have no clue where this is all coming from." He accepted the glass of whiskey with a nod of thanks. "We've been divorced for almost three freaking years."

Blake poured himself a drink, then leaned back on the couch. "If you need Raven to run interference, you know she'd *love* to go toe-to-toe with you-know-who."

Parker chuckled, savoring the slow burn of the Macallan. Courtney wouldn't stand a chance against his fiery friend. He held his glass out for a refill as the doorbell chimed.

"Hope you don't have any plans tonight," Parker said as he stood. "Courtney broke my brain and I'm thinking whiskey-drinking sounds better than laying rock. You game? I can see if Jake can break away from work too."

Blake laughed. "Count me in, cuz. I'll text my boss and let her know I'll be out late."

"Do that. That is, if she'll give you permission," he chuck-led. Whipped. That's what his cousin was. But thank God, Blake was whipped by an awesome woman.

Parker opened the door, and all humor fled. The very last person on earth he expected to see stood on his doorstep.

What. The. Fuck?

"Hey, Parker. Good to see you again. It's Scott. We met last week at the Mariners game."

The asshole held out his hand for a shake. Parker ignored him.

Scott shifted on his feet and stuffed his outstretched hand into his pocket. "Is Kate ready? We have a date tonight."

Blake slapped Parker on the shoulder as he walked by. "Yeah, I'll let the boss lady know I'm crashing here tonight."

Holy fuck, really? Kate had been staying with him for close to a week, but aside from showing her how to use the damn coffee maker, they'd barely seen each other. Things had been so hectic they hadn't had the chance to talk about . . . well . . . anything. But she was seriously going out with this fucking asshat again?

Shit. It looked like his evening had just turned into a pathetic, drown-your-sorrows-in-beer-and-whiskey kinda night. If he had a pickup truck and a dog, he'd be a damn country song.

CHAPTER NINE

Kate scanned the iconic Seattle restaurant and tried to relax against the soft velvet booth. The Metropolitan Grill's upscale mix of dark wood, brass, velvet, and marble was luxurious, yet the staff wasn't overly pretentious.

She didn't come here as often as she'd like since she wasn't swimming in money, but she always enjoyed herself when she did. One of her favorite restaurants, it offered to-die-for food and an equally fantastic atmosphere. And the bartenders' healthy pours didn't hurt.

Yet tonight, she couldn't get comfortable.

She glanced across the table at her date and fidgeted in her seat. She stifled a sigh as he scanned his menu with a pinched look. It wasn't the good kind of sigh.

What was wrong with her?

Scott was a handsome guy, sharply dressed in a button-down and slacks, not too formal and not too casual. He was freshly shaved, with no sign of a five-o'clock shadow. If she were here with Parker, his five-o'clock shadow would be—

Whoa. *Focus, Kate!*

Concentrating on Scott, she pushed all thoughts of Parker

out of her mind. He was probably going out with the blonde from the other night anyway. Not that she cared. Besides, Parker had been unusually grumpy when she'd left the house earlier. Not that she was worried about whether he was okay. She was here with *Scott*, for crying out loud.

Kate appreciated how Scott was impeccably groomed. Not that Parker was a slob by any stretch of the imagination, but Scott was meticulous with his appearance.

She fought a cringe.

It wasn't like she was comparing the two. At all. Parker was her friend. It was just a simple observation that Scott's haircut, undoubtedly, cost more than hers. Sure, he also wore too much cologne, but that wasn't the worst thing ever. He'd placed his phone on the table next to his silverware, but to his credit, he hadn't checked it once.

Scott closed his menu and smiled at her. A calculated and condescending smile. It was probably just her imagination, but nonetheless, a queasy feeling rolled in her belly. "The food here is excellent, Kate. The steak is divine, but you'll probably want chicken. I can order for you if you'd like."

She ground her teeth together. "I'm actually a big fan of their porterhouse." She swirled the red wine in her glass. It was either that or punch him.

"Well, that's surprising."

She held back a scoff. Barely. "How?" In the couple months they'd dated, whenever they went out for dinner, if steak was on the menu, she chose it. Every. Single. Time.

"I figured by now you'd be more of a salad kind of girl."

Her lips pursed. She couldn't figure out if that was a compliment or a dig.

"Thank you again for agreeing to come out with me," he said while scanning the room. It would have been more believable if he were actually looking at her. "Holy shit, Kate! Check out who's sitting at the table in the corner!"

The excitement in his voice surprised her. She didn't recognize the foursome at the corner table and sipped her wine. "Do you work with them?"

His eyes bugged out of his head. "Work with them? I wish. Those two guys are pitchers for the Seattle Mariners."

She chuckled at his sheer giddiness. Okay, fine. Maybe Scott wasn't so . . . disagreeable, annoying, obnoxious . . . after all.

"I'm going to get a selfie with them," he whispered, placing his napkin on the table.

"Hey." She reached across the table and placed her hand on his arm, stilling him. "They just got their food. You shouldn't interrupt them."

"You're right." He settled back in his seat. "I should buy them a round of drinks."

She shook her head. "Both of the women they're with are pregnant." Like obviously, about-to-pop pregnant. Observant, Scott wasn't.

"Well, the drinks aren't for them. They're for the players."

"Wait." She held up a hand, her lips pinching together. "You're going to buy a round of drinks, but for only the guys? Not the whole table?"

Confusion filled his face. "Yeah. The guys are the important ones."

Wow. Scratch what she'd thought earlier. How had she not noticed what a chauvinistic idiot he was?

His phone vibrated. He ignored it.

That was something.

It vibrated again. His eyes darted to his phone and swung back to her. He looked pained.

The urge to roll her eyes was strong, but she held back. "Go ahead and check your texts."

The absolute relief on his face would have been comical had they not been on a date. Not that she really cared. The longer they sat there, the more ridiculous the whole evening became. They hadn't even ordered dinner yet.

While he checked his texts, she glanced around. Tables of people actually talking to one another surrounded them. "Are you ready to order?" The sooner they got through this dinner, the better.

"Hang on," he murmured, his thumbs flying over his phone. "Dave and the guys are over at the W Hotel bar and just sent a pic of this table of hot chicks . . ." After a long moment, he put his phone down, that sheepish grin back on his face. "Sorry about that. You have my undivided attention now."

Yay. Lucky me.

"Where's our server?" he muttered, glancing around. "Ah, there he is." With an aggravated sigh, he raised his arm and snapped his fingers in the direction of their waiter.

Kate's jaw dropped. Holy. Crap.

Too much cologne, she could handle. Dumb, chauvinistic, trying-to-be-the-alpha-male behavior, she could deal with. But snapping your fingers at the waitstaff?

Hell. No.

Jason, their waiter, approached, and as he neared the table, Scott squared his shoulders. "I'll have the porterhouse, well done, with the garlic mashed potatoes. The lady will have the steakhouse chicken with a salad, no dressing."

Kate frowned, not only at his curt tone but his entire attitude. Not to mention his crappy order. Who ordered a porterhouse well done? While she was sure The Met's chicken was tasty, she'd specifically just raved about their steak. And salad, no dressing? Really? She turned her attention to the waiter. "I apologize for my dinner companion."

The baffled look was back on Scott's face. "What are you apologizing for?"

She glared at him. How could she have thought there was something wrong with *her*?

Scott was a jackass. The fact that he was so oblivious to his appalling behavior made it even worse.

Grow a pair. That was her new mantra, wasn't it? What would Raven do?

A smile tipped her lips. Geez, what *wouldn't* Raven do?

She turned her attention to the waiter. "I'll stick with just wine, Jason. It's going to be a short evening for me. I'm sure you understand."

"Oh," Jason chuckled. "I do, miss."

"What are you talking about, Kate?" Scott asked. "Aren't you hungry?"

She drained her wine in three swallows. It would be a shame to waste such fantastic wine, after all.

Being polite had been drilled into her at birth, but where had that gotten her?

Sitting across from a narcissistic douche, that was where.

Now or never.

She placed her napkin on the table and stood. The waiter pulled her chair out for her. All while Scott looked at her in confusion.

"I shouldn't have agreed to go out with you again, but I didn't want to be rude." She placed her purse strap over her shoulder.

"Wait. You're just going to leave? You can't do that," he hissed, an angry flush blooming over his face.

"Yes, I can. And I am." She waited for the guilt, ready to squash it down. After a moment's pause, it didn't come.

Would you look at that?

Progress.

"Thanks for the drink, Scott." A smile tipped her lips. "And lose my number. Please."

The waiter led her toward the front door.

"Good call on making a clean getaway," the waiter said under his breath, his eyes dancing with laughter.

Her face heated.

He held the door open for her. "No shame, my dear. The guy's an idiot."

"Thanks, Jason. Have a good night."

With a final wave, she fled the restaurant. As luck would have it, a taxi pulled up and let its passengers out. She hopped in, gave the driver the address to Parker's house, and settled back against the seat.

A sigh of pure relief escaped her.

Her phone dinged. She pulled it from her purse and prayed it wasn't a text from Scott.

A glance at her phone had her smiling.

Raven: *Apparently the drunkards ran out of whiskey.*

Raven: *I've taken the two idiot cousins & the idiot workaholic back to my place. I'll be watering down their drinks from here on out. I'll keep Parker for the night however they may all die from strangulation. Have I mentioned they're idiots!?!?!? At least they won't die from alcohol poisoning.*

Raven: *These fuckers owe me.*

With a chuckle, Kate texted back a thumbs-up and kissy-face emoji.

The taxi wound through Seattle's business district toward her and Parker's Queen Anne neighborhood, and Kate couldn't wipe the smile off her face as she thought back on her What Would Raven Do? moment.

She'd actually walked out on her dinner with Scott. Holy moly, who would have thought?

Parker, Blake, and Jake weren't the only ones who owed Raven.

CHAPTER TEN

Parker startled when a pint of beer thunked down in front of him. Glancing up, his eyes landed on his cousin across the bar top. He couldn't recall how long he'd been sitting there, his gaze unfocused, his mind far away. He reached for the cold beer and took a sip. "Thanks, man."

It was late afternoon and the bar was closed for the day, but as they did each Monday, he, Blake, and Raven were at the pub pushing paper. At least, that's what he was supposed to be doing. His focus was complete shit.

"Something on your mind?" Blake asked.

Aside from the fact that his ex-wife was on a mission to get them back together? Or that there was a jackhammer currently trying to make its way out of his damn skull? Or that every time Parker closed his freaking eyes, he could see that fuck-you grin the dickwad, Scott, had given him when he'd picked up Kate last night? "No, not really."

Blake snorted. "Please. You've been staring at your order sheet for the last five minutes."

He sat up straight and stretched, groaning when the

throbbing in his head intensified. "Jesus, Blake. Why do we always think whiskey's a good idea?"

"Whiskey *is* a good idea," Raven interjected, carrying in a rack of clean pint glasses. "Just not in the amounts you idiots downed last night. I assume you guys skipped the boxing gym this morning?"

Parker blanched, his stomach rolling at the mere thought of sparring. It was already afternoon, and he still felt like shit. There was no way in hell he and Blake were making their standard Monday morning session. He scrubbed a hand down his face. "We drank top-shelf whiskey. I don't know why I still feel like crap."

"Again," Raven said, "top-shelf or not, the amount you guys put down last night would have a drunk hurting today. Besides, I'm sure it doesn't help that you two aren't exactly spring chickens anymore."

Parker chuckled at Blake's offended look and took a bigger gulp of beer. Hair of the dog was helping. It had been a long time since he'd tied one on like that. He hadn't meant to. His plan had been to lay some rock with Blake and have a couple of beers post-yard work. But when Courtney had showed up and dropped her delusional bombshell, he'd known it was going to be a drinking kind of night. That fucker from the M's game arriving to pick up Kate had pushed him over the damn edge. His fun, drinking-with-the-boys night had turned into a drown-your-sorrows-and-deep-talk-into-oblivion night.

It was probably a good thing he'd gotten shit-faced and spent last night at Blake and Raven's place. If he'd been at his own place and Kate had brought that tool home, he didn't know what he would have done. He'd yet to go home for just that reason. Sure, it was a pansy-ass move, but the last thing he wanted to do was walk in his front door and see that shit sitting in his home.

Kate wasn't an idiot. She wouldn't fall for whatever lame excuses Scott had for her. She was smart and she . . .

Damn. She was the nicest person he'd ever met. And would easily give the dickwad a second chance. Hell, probably even a third.

Fuck.

Raven let out a low whistle. "Yowza. What's that grumpy face for?"

His first instinct was to go into denial mode, but he knew Raven. She'd call bullshit and wouldn't let up. "Flashback to that fucker who took Kate out last night."

"And?" Raven prodded, her hand moving in a circular get-on-with-it motion.

"And nothing." He shrugged. "I have no idea why the hell she'd go out with that guy again. He's a dick."

"True," Blake said, slinging an arm around his fiancée's shoulder. "But he asked her out."

"So?"

A dippy grin spread across his cousin's face. "Since you and Kate are just friends, why do you even care?"

"Because she *is* my friend. He's an asshole, and she can do better."

"Give her some credit." Raven rolled her eyes. She stepped away from Blake and began organizing the bar.

"I do," Parker said. "But you both have to agree that Kate's seriously the nicest person. She always gives people the benefit of the doubt. Even the assholes. He'll feed her all this suave bullshit and—"

"Kate's got a pretty good bullshit radar," Raven interrupted. "It's just hidden under a very polite and very sweet smile."

"True," he conceded, then turned his attention to the beer in front of him. He cleared his throat. "She, uh, must have said something to you about him today."

He snuck a peek at his friend. She shook her head and looked to be fighting a smile. Damn.

"I haven't talked to Kate today. We were going to meet for breakfast, but she had to head over to Hudson Island for a last-minute client meeting." A small smile tipped her lips. "Why don't you call her and see how her date went?"

His heart stuttered at the thought. "Why would I do that?"

"It would be a friendly thing to do."

He thought about it for a few seconds, then nodded. It would be like small talk, a just-checking-in kind of thing. "You're right. I mean, we're roommates and all."

"Exactly. I mean, why get yourself in a tizzy, Park?"

"A *tizzy*, Rave?" His brow furrowed. He was not in a fucking tizzy. He opened his mouth to say so, but Blake, standing behind Raven, caught his attention. His cousin's eyes were wide, his hand moving in a slashing motion across his neck. Fine.

"I mean," Raven continued. "For all you know, their date could have been a total bust."

True. Parker nodded and took another drink of his beer.

"Or not, and they ended up bumpin' uglies all night long."

He choked, spraying beer over the papers sitting in front of him. "Jesus, Raven," he coughed.

"Harsh, babe," Blake chuckled as he dropped a kiss on the top of her head.

Bastards.

"Look," Raven said as she wiped up his mess. "The fact is, Phone Boy asked her out. Now you have two options. One—"

"Jesus," he groaned, his eyes seeking out his cousin. "How the hell do you deal with the counting thing?"

Blake shrugged. "She's hot." Then quickly sidestepped as Raven turned and tried to whip him with the bar rag.

"Asshole," she chuckled. "You'll pay for that, Mr. Sullivan."

Blake laughed. "I hope so, babe."

Parker shuddered and scrubbed his hands over his face. He loved them, he really did, but they were too damn much sometimes.

"As I was saying," Raven said. "Option one. Picture in your mind our beautiful Kate."

Not a hardship.

"With Phone Boy."

He frowned.

"Fucking."

"Come on," Parker growled. "Seriously?"

"In your house."

Holy shit. The visual was now seared in his brain. Parker thunked his head down onto the bar top and heard both of his so-called friends laughing.

Raven ruffled the hair on the back of his head. Like a dog. He sat up and glared.

She laughed harder, crossing her arms over her chest, smug satisfaction on her face. "Or there's option two. You grow a fucking pair, Parker Cunningham, and ask the damn girl out." He opened his mouth to reply but didn't have the chance to speak. "Kate doesn't initiate anything. She went out with that dipshit because the fucker asked and she's too polite to say no."

"Great." Parker couldn't help but roll his eyes. "I ask her out, and she says yes because she's polite? Or even worse— out of pity? No thanks."

Raven's brow arched and she turned to Blake. "Is he always this dramatic?"

"Surprising, right?" Blake turned his attention back to Parker. "You're not an asshole, dipshit. A dumbass for sure, but not an asshole. Besides, if you don't ask her out, she sure as hell is never going to ask you. The woman doesn't make moves. We all know that."

Parker's mind flashed to the night of the baseball game when that hadn't been the case. Kate had kissed him—thrown her arms around him, smashed her body flush against his, and kissed him.

And he'd pushed her away.

Fuck.

At the time, it had seemed like the right thing to do. Now? Not so much. Especially with Scott back in the picture. "I'll think about it."

"Think about her fucking Scott," Raven grumbled. "*That's* what you need to think about. Man the fuck up already, Park."

He bit back a chuckle. Raven was something else. All attitude, that one. But behind the swagger, he knew she was a big softie who meant well. "Look, I just don't know if me asking her out is the best idea because—"

"I don't want to ruin our friendship," Blake interrupted, his voice mimicking a small child, exasperation written all over his face. "Christ, we know. But seriously? You ask Kate out on a date. What's the worst thing that could happen?"

She could laugh in his face. She could be seeing someone else. Hell, she could say that there was no way on God's green earth that she was interested in him in *that* way. Countless scenarios swirled in his mind, things going wrong, things blowing up in his face. He wanted no part of any of them. "She could say no."

"Exactly." Blake pointed his finger at him. "If that happens, you play it off with your laid-back Parker charm and you'll be in the same spot you are now. Not dating Kate. But at least you'll know where you stand with her."

Damn.

He hated being wrong. But what was even worse?

When Raven and Blake were right.

CHAPTER ELEVEN

"So, how was Phone Boy?" Raven asked.

Kate groaned and keyed in a new drink order.

Raven chuckled as she filled a cocktail shaker with fresh mint. "I take it that douche canoe isn't as reformed as you'd hoped?"

"It was enlightening, that's for sure. He's a chauvinistic prick. But you know what's worse?"

"Than being a chauvinistic prick?"

She nodded, her mouth pursing into an irritated line. "He snaps his fingers at the waitstaff."

Raven let out a low whistle. "That must have been quite the painful dinner."

"Nope." A satisfied smile lifted her lips. "I left."

Raven paused mid-shake. "What do you mean, you left?"

Something akin to pride bloomed in Kate's gut. "After he ordered, I asked myself what *you* would do. Then I walked out."

Raven laughed as she resumed shaking the drink, then poured the concoction into a chilled glass. "Holy shit, babe. Color me impressed."

Once Raven garnished the cocktail, Kate loaded the Irish Mojito onto her tray, its sweet, minty fragrance tickling her nose. "I can forgive many things, but snapping your fingers at the waitstaff?"

"Narcissistic asshole move."

"Exactly." Kate nodded, adjusting the weight of the glasses on her tray.

"Well, congratulations, sweetie," Raven clapped. "I'm glad you got on the schedule tonight so I can celebrate this momentous occasion with you."

Her brow arched. "Momentous?"

Raven gave her the are-you-a-fucking-moron look. "You walked out on him after orders had been placed. That's fucking huge!"

The smile on Kate's face grew wider. "It is, isn't it?"

With a hop in her step, she dropped off the drinks at various tables. She hadn't planned on working at The Spotted Dog this week—things were crazy busy with her bookkeeping clients—but a couple of storm damage bills had come in. Large bills. So, she'd called Blake late last night and practically begged to get on the schedule.

As luck would have it, both Ali and Becca were on vacation, which left her and Melody holding down the fort. It was looking like a slow Tuesday night. The post-dinner lull was in full swing, and the band scheduled to play had canceled last minute, the second time this month. Which was fine by her.

Kate's primary role at The Spotted Dog was being the pub's bookkeeper, which she loved, and over the past year she'd gotten in the habit of picking up the occasional server shift to help out. However, serving still made her nervous. Taking orders wasn't the problem. Balancing whole trays of food and drinks? Yeah. That was another thing entirely.

"Taxes," Raven stated when Kate returned to the bar.

She frowned, her concentration focused on adding two full pitchers and a stack of glasses to her tray. "What?"

Raven nodded toward the muted television, its closed captioning flashing on the bottom of the screen. "Taxes. It seems that's what always ends up taking down the scumbags of the world."

Kate glanced at the television and froze. A man's face filled the display; his familiar hazel eyes stared back at her. Underneath, the words "Eastern Washington Cult Leader Arrested for Tax Fraud" scrolled by.

A chill wracked her body and Kate forgot to breathe. She knew that face. It had haunted her dreams for years. It was older now, but she knew that face.

Her eyes watered when her mother's hand cracked against her cheek.

"Katie Rose Westerly! How dare you?"

The anger and disgust in her mother's voice surprised her. It shouldn't have, but it did. She'd hoped her mother would believe her, even though deep down, she knew she wouldn't. But she'd still hoped.

Her mother's hand rose again, and Katie turned to run, but she froze when she saw him in the doorway. Her stomach dropped.

There was no hope.

She winced when her mother pinched her side.

"Katie," her mother hissed.

Katie's eyes locked with his and she saw the evil glimmer. Why was she the only one who saw it?

His brow arched and his lips pressed into a thin, angry line. Her mother's fingers dug deeper into her side.

Katie dropped to one knee and bowed her head. "Master Sebastian," she said, puke rising in her throat. "How may I serve you?"

· · ·

A crash brought Kate back to the present.

"Oh my God." She'd dropped her tray of drinks.

Grabbing a bar rag, she crouched and attempted to wipe up the mess around her feet. Broken pint glasses and pitchers littered the floor. Her hands shook as she collected the largest shards and placed them on her tray. Using the beer-soaked rag, she gathered up the remaining glass fragments and willed her hands to stop shaking.

A hand settled on her shoulder and she jerked away with a yelp, slapping at the hand.

"Whoa." Parker straightened, his hands up, his brow furrowed.

She needed to get a grip but couldn't catch her breath. Her heart raced and her hands wouldn't stop trembling.

"Kate," a quiet voice spoke behind her.

Raven.

"Leave the glasses. Come on."

She shook her head. "I got it."

"No, you don't," Raven replied. "You're bleeding."

Her breath caught. She stared at her still-shaking hands in wonder. Sure enough, blood oozed from both hands.

Kate felt nothing.

Glancing down, the sopping-wet bar rag had only spread a mixture of beer and blood over the floor. When Raven pulled her up by her shoulders, she rose. Even though her heart threatened to gallop out of her chest, like her hands, her mind was numb.

She vaguely heard Raven ask, "You got this, Park?" as her friend steered her toward the back office. She wanted to protest, wanted to say she could clean up the mess she'd made. But her mouth, her brain wouldn't work.

Memories of long ago swirled in her mind, flashing like a horrid slide show. Her entire body trembled.

· · ·

Kate stood in silence in the employee bathroom as Raven bandaged her hands. She focused on her breathing, on her jittery inhales and shaky exhales. It was either that or throw up all over her friend.

"Want to talk about it?"

Kate wasn't fooled by the casual tone. Raven was worried about her. That wouldn't do. She shrugged and tried to set her friend at ease. Keeping her eyes glued to the bandages, she prayed her voice was steadier than she felt. "Rookie mistake, I guess. The pitchers always give me a hard time. I shouldn't have put so much on the tray."

Silence.

She peeked into the mirror and fought a cringe when she met Raven's gaze.

"Are you really going to make me call bullshit, Kate?"

She straightened her shoulders. *Pull. It. Together!* "I don't know what you're talking about."

"Right," Raven scoffed. "Like I didn't see you turn white as a ghost when you saw that cult guy on TV. Like you didn't jump a mile when Parker touched your shoulder. You damn near clobbered him."

The cringe she'd been fighting won. "Holy crap, Rave," she said on an exhale. "I didn't mean to. I didn't think I'd react like that. I just . . ."

"I know, sweetie," Raven murmured, her voice soft as she secured the final bandage over Kate's left wrist. "Memories can be a nasty, nasty bitch. I get it. Old habits rear their ugly heads when you go into autopilot."

Kate let out another breath. She should know by now that Raven could read her like an open book. And Raven never judged. Not once. That was one of the things she loved about her.

Her friend knew the most about her past, even more than Anna and Henry, but Raven didn't know all of it. No one did.

Except her birth parents. And *him.*

Nothing good could come of seeing his face again. A shiver wracked her body and dread filled her.

A quiet knock on the bathroom door made her jump.

"Rave?" Parker called through the door. "We need you back out. A large group just came in."

Raven met her gaze. "You okay?"

She wasn't, but Kate nodded anyway and hugged her. "Thanks," she whispered before opening the door. Focusing on the ground, she followed Raven out of the bathroom.

She jerked when Parker's hand settled on her arm. He quickly pulled it back, and she wanted to kick herself.

"Hey," he said, that one little word conveying so much apprehension.

She wrapped her arms around her waist and studied her shoes. "Sorry."

"Why don't you go ahead and clock out tonight?"

Surprise had her meeting his gaze. "You just said a large party came in."

"I did." He nodded at her hands. "You aren't lifting trays any time soon."

She couldn't read his expression. It wasn't exactly annoyance, and it wasn't quite anger. Whatever it was, Parker was upset. At her. Because she was an idiot who couldn't hold her shit together. "You're right, Park. I'm sorry. I'll make sure to take the cost of all the stuff I broke out of my check."

Disbelief flashed across his face and his jaw tensed. Worry swirled in her stomach. He really was mad at her. She rushed on, "I'm really sorry about the mess I made. I should have been the one to clean it up. Not you."

"Stop. I don't care if you break every glass in this damn place. They're fucking glasses. We can order more." His hands lifted like he was going to reach for her, but he quickly stuffed them in his jeans pockets and turned his attention to the ceiling.

After a couple deep breaths, he focused on her. Frustration radiated from him, and she shifted on her feet. She didn't know what to say. "I'm sorry, Park."

"Please, stop apologizing," he grumbled as he scrubbed his fists over his face. Bracing his hands atop his head, he sighed and looked at her. "You sliced up your hands, Kate. You can't carry trays tonight. Clock out and go home."

No. She needed to stay here. Stay busy. Surrounded by people who could keep her mind off . . . everything.

She took in a deep breath and squared her shoulders. "Don't be crazy. It's just a scratch." Never mind that her left hand and wrist felt like someone was holding a blowtorch to it.

His lips pinched into a thin line. "Go home."

"I'm fine."

"You're not."

"I'm *fine*, Parker," she repeated, fear beginning to bubble deep in her belly.

He shook his head. "Your hands and wrist are all cut up. You're paler than a ghost and look like you're about to drop. You do books all day and then waitress all night. Kate, you're running on fumes."

"Parker!" Blake's muffled voice called from the kitchen. "Get your ass back over here!"

"I'm serious." Parker held her gaze as he walked backward toward the kitchen. He pulled out his phone from his back pocket and waved it at her. "I'm calling you a ride. Go home and get some rest."

Her stomach dropped as he disappeared into the kitchen. The last thing she wanted was to go home. Alone.

———————◆———————

Parker slammed down a plate of crunchy soda bread and a bowl of steaming beef stew onto the pickup window with enough force to send the bowl's contents sloshing over the rim. The last half hour had been a blur of orders. Why was it that everything had to pick up at the most inconvenient fucking time?

He'd sent Vince home earlier in the evening and was now the only one left cooking. So, when a shitload of customers had hit the bar, he couldn't leave. He couldn't make sure Kate was okay.

He'd called an Uber. Her hands had been bleeding, she was obviously shaken, and instead of driving her home and making sure she was okay, he'd called her a goddamn Uber. He was an asshole.

"You okay?" Blake stood beside him at the plating counter.

"Fuck if I know, man."

"Kate?"

He nodded while adding finishing touches to the next order. "Something's wrong. But she's like a goddamn vault. Everything's 'I'm fine.' And she's clearly fucking not. She's not even telling Raven what's wrong."

Blake paused and glanced up from the dish he was plating, concern evident on his face. "Really?"

Parker nodded again and added another two plates to the pickup window, glancing at the ticket. "Melody!"

"If Kate's not confiding in Raven, something's definitely wrong," Blake muttered.

Parker wiped his hands on a rag and let out a breath. He groaned as the POS system spit out another round of orders. "This damn night can't end soon enough."

He continued cooking and slamming together orders

while Blake helped and plated where he could. His mind kept flashing back to Kate. Before he'd called her that goddamn Uber.

The woman who'd stood in front of him in the hallway had looked like Kate, but she wasn't the Kate he knew. That Kate was sweet, somewhat sassy, a little shy, and had a backbone of steel. The Kate who'd stood before him earlier had looked so fucking lost.

She'd stood there with her arms wrapped so tightly around her middle he had feared she would snap in two. He was sure she hadn't even realized her body was shaking like a leaf in the wind. Thinking of how her whole body had trembled in . . . fear? . . . made him crazy.

He hadn't been able to do anything.

Fuck. He shook his head as he handed off a plate of food to his cousin. With another deep breath, he snagged the next order ticket.

He had no clue what to do. Hell, he had no clue what had thrown Kate in the first place. All he knew was that in all the years he'd known her, he'd never seen her like that.

Shy? Yes. Nervous? Yes. Worried? Yes.

Terrified? Hell no.

He'd gone out to the bar for a break. One moment she was loading drinks, then a split second later, she'd gone deathly pale, her tray tumbling to the ground. He'd raced to her, but she'd slapped him away. His stomach turned as he recalled the confusion and terror in her eyes.

She'd recoiled at his touch.

That killed him. Absolutely gutted him.

His back pocket buzzed. Eager for the distraction, he fished out his phone. Seeing Kate's name on the display, his muscles tensed further. "Kate?"

"Parker?"

His scalp prickled at the hesitancy in her voice. "What's wrong?"

"Can you come get me?" Her voice shook, and she sniffed. His heart stopped. "I think I need to go to the hospital."

"I'll be right there." Fear shot up his spine as he rushed out of the kitchen. He vaguely heard Blake yell his name, but he didn't stop.

Kate. That was all that mattered.

CHAPTER TWELVE

I t wasn't just a scratch.

It took less than five minutes for Kate to get to Parker's house from The Spotted Dog. By the time she walked through the front door, the bandages on her left hand and wrist were soaked with blood. Rummaging through Parker's master bathroom, she found gauze and tape. She replaced the soggy bandage, wrapping it as tightly as she could.

Half an hour later, blood had completely soaked through the gauze and dressing again. Her head was pounding as she rose from the couch to go back upstairs to Parker's bathroom.

The room swayed. Worry morphed into the first stirrings of panic.

Easing back onto the couch, she glanced down at her hand and her vision wavered. Not good.

Reaching for her phone, she pulled up a rideshare app. Then paused. Criminy, what if she passed out in the back of the car? She closed the app and pulled up the phone function, then dialed 91—

Nope.

She deleted the two numbers. She was *not* going to pay for a freaking ambulance ride for a measly cut. Her next exhale was part groan, part whimper. If only her trusty little Honda hadn't been smooshed to smithereens.

Her hand throbbed, and when she glanced down again, blood dripped from her fingers.

Her stomach rolled. Okay, maybe not quite so measly.

She rose slowly and tucked her phone into her back pocket, willing the room to stop swaying. Careful not to get blood on Parker's couch, she made her way to the bathroom upstairs.

Kate turned the faucet on cold and unwrapped her hand. Blood gushed from the wound, running from her palm to the outside of her wrist. Her stomach turned. When had it gotten so wide? She flexed and stretched her fingers, her hand burning as if she were holding a sparkler too close.

The cut widened. Bile rose in her throat, but she managed to tamp it down.

Bracing for the sting, she shoved her hand under the running water.

Fire bolted up her left arm. "Fuck!" Tears filled her eyes and she fought to catch her breath.

With tears slipping down her face, she pulled out her phone with her free hand. With unsteady fingers, she dialed Parker.

Parker burst through his front door. "Kate!"

Silence. He held still, his heartbeat thudding in his ears. Where the hell—

His eyes narrowed. A faucet was running upstairs.

Racing up the stairs and down the hallway, he came to an abrupt halt in his bathroom doorway.

Kate leaned over one of the sinks, her elbows on the counter, one hand under the running water, the other propping up her head.

"Kate," he said on an exhale.

She glanced up and met his eyes in the mirror. His heart stopped. Her face was deathly pale, her eyes glassy. Tear streaks marred her cheeks. "It won't stop bleeding," she murmured, her voice barely audible above the rush of running water.

He hurried over, grabbing a towel along the way. The sink was filled with reddened water, and he turned off the tap. The wound on her hand oozed blood.

What the hell?

He helped her straighten, and with her hand over the sink, he wrapped it tightly in the towel. His stomach twisted as the blood seeped through the cotton.

Motherfucker. Why was she bleeding so much?

"Press down," he said. "I'll be right back."

Her glassy brown eyes widened and her breath caught. "Please don't go."

Those three words damn near gutted him. "I swear I'll be right back, sweetheart." He laid a quick kiss to her forehead. "I promise. Now press down."

He raced to the kitchen, nearly killing himself on the stairs, and grabbed his first aid kit and a stack of clean kitchen towels. Within seconds, he was back upstairs with her.

"I'm really sorry, baby, but this is gonna hurt like a bitch." After tearing open the first aid kit, he braced her arm against his chest and packed her wound with gauze. She cried out in pain and jerked away from him, but he held her arm firm. "I'm so damn sorry, Kate," he murmured, his full concentration on applying as much pressure to the wound as possible. No matter how much pain he caused her. "Hang on, baby."

He wound the bandage around her hand and wrist as tight as he could, hating himself for hurting her, but knowing the tighter he got it, the better. When the bandage was secure, he straightened, keeping his arm around her. "Can you walk?"

"Yeah."

With the way she swayed, he didn't buy it. "Here, hold these," he said, shoving the stack of kitchen towels at her. "Keep your fingers pointed to the sky."

Her brow furrowed in confusion, and she let out a tiny yelp as he scooped her up and carried her out of the bathroom.

Taking more care on the stairs with Kate in his arms, he snagged his keys and was out the door.

Breaking every speed law, Parker tore through Seattle's streets and made the four-mile trek to the Ballard neighborhood's Swedish Hospital ER in under eight minutes. He'd never been so grateful for the late hour's lack of horrific Seattle traffic.

Screeching to a stop in the ER bay, he killed the engine and hustled to Kate's door. His tough girl was struggling to climb out of his car. He scooped her into his arms again and rushed her through the ER's main doors.

Parker raced toward the front desk, careful not to jar her. "Help, please!"

The kitchen towels she still clutched in her hand were crimson.

The man behind the glass nodded and stood, motioning to the left.

Parker moved toward a set of double doors, and after a split second, a loud buzz sounded and the doors opened.

Numerous people in scrubs approached, one with a stretcher.

"What happened, sir?"

As he placed Kate onto the stretcher, he explained everything he knew about her injury, which, sadly, wasn't much. "It won't stop bleeding."

"Parker?" Kate called out, her voice weak. Her eyes were closed, as if it were too much effort to keep them open.

"I'm right here, sweetheart." He took her right hand in his as the nurses wheeled them to a curtained-off area.

More people entered; more people left.

In seconds, Kate's pallor went from deathly pale to ashen. He hoped to hell it was just the ER's shit fluorescent lighting.

"I'm Dr. Gonzales," a woman in green scrubs said as she unwrapped Kate's bandage. She glanced at him. "You pack this?"

"Yeah," he replied, taking in the coordinated chaos surrounding them.

"Good job," she said, her focus remaining on Kate.

Parker's stomach rolled as the woman prodded the wound, the flesh of Kate's hand gaping open.

She whimpered in pain, and he squeezed her hand. "You're okay, baby," he murmured close to her ear. "I'm right here."

"Kate? Can you hear me?" Dr. Gonzales asked, pitching her no-nonsense voice louder. "I know you're tired, but I need you to open your eyes and look at me."

Parker let out a breath of relief when Kate complied. He stroked her hair with his free hand, unsure if it was a reassuring gesture for her or himself.

"Kate, your boyfriend did a great job bandaging your wound, but it looks like multiple pieces of glass are still inside your hand. That's what's causing the continued bleeding. We have to get those pieces out. No surgery or anything. We can do it all right here. Okay?"

Kate nodded and leaned her cheek into his hand.

"We'll put some topical anesthetic on it to help with the pain, okay?"

Again, Kate nodded.

"We'll also need to take your right hand back from your boyfriend so we can check that one out and start an IV. Okay?"

"No!" Kate shook her head, terror scrambling in her eyes. "I need him here."

Parker brought her right hand to his lips. "Baby, look at me," he said, his voice firm. He waited until she met his gaze. "You need to get some fluids, sweetheart. You need the IV." He ran the back of his fingers along the side of her cheek. "I'm not going anywhere. I'm not leaving you. They'd have to drag me out of this room."

The fear in her eyes faded. "Promise?"

"Promise." He squeezed her hand before letting go. Moving fully to the top of the gurney, he kissed her forehead and resumed stroking her hair. "Now be a good patient so we can get the hell out of here and go home."

After the longest four hours of Parker's life, he lay a sleeping Kate on her bed. The chaos, the mayhem . . . the goddamn blood. He had no idea how nurses and doctors did it. Just watching Dr. Gonzales fish the glass fragments out of Kate's hand had made him want to barf. Hell, just thinking about it now made him queasy.

With the soft hallway light spilling into Kate's dark room, Parker watched her sleep.

Exhaustion and relief coursed through him. He couldn't remember the last time he'd ever been that scared. All the blood—*Kate's* blood—and how weak, how gray she'd been. . .

He sighed and pulled a blanket over her, pressing a kiss to her forehead.

She jerked awake, her eyes flying open. Her good hand gripped his arm like a vise. "Are you leaving?"

Damn if she didn't just take another five years off his life. He willed his pulse to return to normal. He sure as hell didn't think his heart could take any more surprises tonight. "You're home, Kate."

Parker saw the moment she recognized where she was. Her breathing evened, her body relaxed, and her eyes cleared. Her death grip on his arm loosened but remained.

"You're okay, sweetheart. The doctors were able to stitch up your hand. Now you need to rest."

She met his gaze in the dim light. "Stay with me? Please?"

Parker's chest squeezed hard as he stared into her brown doe eyes. He could never say no to her.

"Of course," he murmured, scooting onto the bed beside her.

His heart pinched when she curled against him, resting her head on his chest. He pulled her close and kissed the top of her head. "Get some rest, sweetheart."

"Thank you, Park," she said, her voice groggy. "Thank you for being there for me."

His arms tightened around her, and he pressed his lips to the top of her head again.

Always, Kate. Always.

CHAPTER THIRTEEN

Sighing softly, Kate snuggled deeper into her bed. Warmth enveloped her and hints of soap and sandalwood tickled her senses. The scents were comforting and familiar, a couple of her favorites, but she couldn't pinpoint them in her hazy slumber. It was more masculine than her body wash. It reminded her of Parker.

Her eyes flew open.

Oh. My. God.

"Morning." Parker's voice was gravelly. His breath tickled that hidden spot behind her ear, sending goosebumps racing down her arm.

She tensed. The only sound in the room came from the howling wind outside. And her heart thudding in her chest.

"I know you're awake, Kate." There was laughter in his quiet voice, and the strong, solid arms that cocooned her tightened ever so slightly.

Her mind scrambled to find something to say. Anything. And came up blank.

Holy crap. She'd just spent the night with Parker. In his arms.

He shifted away, causing her to roll onto her back. He adjusted his position so he lay next to her on his side, one arm propping up his head, the other draped over her middle.

Her body instantly missed the heat of him spooning her, and she leaned into him. The hairs on his solid chest tickled her arm and sent tingles through her.

Stupid body.

He gazed down at her. A half-smile played on his lips, and she forgot to breathe. Parker had lost his shirt sometime during the night. Her mouth watered.

Watered.

Absolutely, one hundred percent, completely inappropriate.

Regardless, she wanted to touch. She wanted to reach up and feel just how scratchy the stubble was along his jaw. She wanted to run her fingers through the dusting of hair on his chest, over his flat nipples, and trace the hard ripples of his stomach.

Every single part of her wanted to touch every single part of him.

His sleepy green eyes darkened. "Hi."

Every thought in her brain fled. That gravelly voice and the way he gazed down at her with a look that was slightly amused, slightly . . . something else . . . sent heat rushing through her.

She was so close. His head hovered only inches away. She could see flecks of gold in his bottle-green eyes. How had she never noticed those flecks before?

She swallowed. Hard. "Hi."

She needed to get a grip. Her inappropriate thoughts immediately strayed to the hard length pressing against her hip. She wouldn't mind getting a grip on that . . .

Heat washed over her face. Good lord, what was she doing? Being this close to Parker was turning her brain to mush and kicking other parts of her into overdrive. The thoughts of what she wanted to do to him were a bad idea. If she acted on them, she had no doubt the experience would be out of this freaking world, but it would be a bad, bad, *bad* idea. And complicated. Way, way, *way* too complicated.

She could not—repeat, *not*—go there.

"Don't overthink this, Kate."

The flush from her face spread over her body. Holy crap, was she that transparent? "Overthink what?" Her voice cracked. Dang it.

The arm over her middle pulled her closer.

"You know exactly what, sweetheart."

She did. If she didn't, the hardness pressing against her would have told her what.

She really, really, *really* should not be thinking about how good Parker's hard cock felt against her hip, how good it would feel other places.

Holy hell. Her heartbeat thumped loudly in her ears, and she didn't think it was possible to blush more, but there it was.

"Killin' me," he murmured. With a chuckle, he dropped a quick kiss to her forehead. "Omelet or waffles this morning?"

While her body wanted to snuggle closer to him, she held herself still and cleared her throat. "It's okay, Park. I'm not hungry."

Her stomach chose that exact moment to growl. Stupid stomach.

Parker's chuckle turned into a full-out laugh. "Breakfast will be ready in thirty." He dropped another kiss to her forehead and rolled off the bed. "Take your time, sweets."

Kate remained motionless. Not a single muscle in her body dared twitch. Her gaze never left Parker as he exited her room. His broad, sculpted shoulders and muscled back, which flexed with each movement, tapered to a narrow waist, and his unbuttoned jeans hung low on his hips.

The click of her door closing sounded loud in her near-silent room. She flipped to her stomach and buried her face in her pillow. She didn't know whether to groan in mortification or squeal like a middle school girl.

After a split-second pause, she settled on middle school girl.

Holy crap, the man was delicious!

Rolling onto her back, she raised her hand to push the tangled mess of her hair from her face. A sharp sting shot up her forearm. She winced at the reminder of the night before. Settling back against the pillows, hazy recollections of the chaotic night flashed in her mind. Everything was a blur.

Except for three things.

Her stomach pitched as she recalled the panic of seeing the basin water turn red and the terror of being alone in Parker's bathroom when the sink looked to hold more blood than water.

The sheer relief she'd felt when Parker showed up.

And then the abject fear of him leaving her alone, not only at the hospital, but once they were home.

A part of her, the logical part, said that he'd stayed only to comfort her, to make sure she was safe through the night, to appease her. To be the wonderful friend that she knew he was.

But the other part of her, the *more* logical part, reminded her that the erection pressed against her hip this morning had had nothing to do with friendship.

She had no idea what to do. Except lie there, staring up at the ceiling, over-analyzing everything. Overthinking.

"Not exactly productive," she muttered, irritated with herself.

Her stomach growled again. She caught the hints of coffee in the air. And something else . . . something bacony.

She sat up in bed, taking care not to jostle her hand.

Her new mantra popped into her brain. *Grow a pair.*

Fine. She could do this. Hell, she *had* to do this.

The wishy-washy back and forth in her mind was getting old. Moreover, she was giving herself a freaking headache. Her lips pursed. That could be due to blood loss and hunger. She shook her head. Regardless, she needed to lay her cards on the table.

Yeah, that's what she needed to do.

Her stomach growled again.

Food first. Then she'd grow a pair and talk to Parker.

She stilled. The thought kind of scared her to death. Erase that. There was no *kind of*. It *did* scare her.

What if Parker laughed in her face? What if what she'd felt that morning had nothing to do with *her*, but was a simple, biological, all-guys-get-erections-in-the-morning kind of thing?

She sighed, disappointment and embarrassment washing over her. What if it was like the last time she'd made a move?

They pulled up in front of her house and Parker cut the engine.

"You don't have to walk me to the door," Kate said as she got out of the car, the tequila making her steps a bit unsteady.

Parker smiled, pocketing his keys. "You realize you say that every single time I take you home, right?"

As they made their way up her driveway, he took her hand and placed it in the crook of his arm. She leaned into him. "True."

He stopped at the base of her front steps. Like he always did.

All she had to do was go up those four little steps to the front door and say goodnight. Just like always.

She stepped up onto the first step, but the tequila had her turning to face him.

What are you doing? *The liquored part of her brain overrode the sane part.* Stop being a fuddy-duddy! You're thirty-two, not ninety-two!

The step up had her closer to eye level with Parker; liquid courage had her draping her arms over his shoulders. He stilled, his gaze moving to her lips.

That tiny movement of his eyes sent heat tearing through her body. She wanted to kiss him again. She had to.

So she did.

Her heart raced as she pressed her body tight against his, delighting in the warmth when his arms came around her, holding her tight. His mouth fused to hers and she tangled her tongue with his.

Someone moaned. She didn't know if it was her or him. She didn't care.

Then it was over.

Parker's breath was as ragged as hers, but his hands were on her hips, gently pushing her away. Then they moved to her arms, unhooking them from around his neck. He squeezed her hands before letting go and taking a step back. "You should go inside."

Her body went cold. She must have heard wrong. The tequila gave her courage, though her voice was barely a whisper. "Do you want to come in?"

Please say yes, please say yes, please say yes.

Her breath caught at the slight shake of his head. It was like a sucker punch in the gut.

Oh my God. Kate, what the hell did you just do?

He cleared his throat and shifted on his feet, his hands jammed into his jeans pockets. "You've had a lot to drink tonight, Kate. I don't think that's a good idea."

She'd thought that being publicly rejected on the Kiss Cam had been mortifying.

Nope.
This was a million times worse.
Idiot. Tequila or not, she was a complete freaking idiot.

Kate's face flushed at the memory. With hindsight, she understood why he'd put the brakes on that night. She'd been drinking more than usual, and he wasn't a jerk who took advantage. She got that. She really did. But illogical as it was, it still stung. It still embarrassed her.

Never mind. Talking to Parker was out of the question.

Her mind flashed to that sweet, shirtless man and the way he'd held her . . . not once leaving her side . . . and warmth filled her.

What if it wasn't like last time? What if he didn't laugh in her face? What if his physical reaction was because of *her* and not just a morning-wood thing?

Her stomach fluttered, part nerves, part anticipation.

Fine.

Pride be damned. She was going to grow a pair and talk to him. She had to.

Parker flipped the thick-cut bacon. It sizzled and spit, and its smoky, salty perfection filled the kitchen. He took a gulp of his bitter coffee and kept an eye on the waffle iron.

He ran a hand through his damp hair—nothing like an ice-cold shower to start your day—and all thoughts turned to the woman upstairs.

Kate.

Parker wasn't much of a cuddler; he'd always been more of a hug-and-roll practitioner. But with Kate? Lying in bed with her had been unbelievable. The way she'd curled into him, the way she fit snugly in his arms, the way her body nestled into his. It was damn near perfection.

He'd known the moment she'd woken up. Her breath had hitched; her body had tensed. For a split second, he hadn't known what to do. There was no way he could have hidden the effects of being so close to her, the effects of having her wrapped in his arms, her perfect ass snug against his groin.

He'd been nervous as hell. Because if his hard-on had freaked her out, there was no way he would have been able to talk his way out of that.

Thank Christ she hadn't pulled away.

Then he'd just about died when she'd taken in his body, fire shimmering in her eyes as she'd skimmed his chest like she wanted to touch . . .

Electricity zinged through him. "Damn," he muttered. He was going to need another cold shower. He let out an unsteady exhale and adjusted himself.

However, along with the heat in her gorgeous brown eyes, he'd also seen a flicker of doubt. So, he'd done what he always did when things were a little intense.

He'd lightened the mood, keeping it as normal as possible. Though he wasn't sure if he'd done that for her benefit or his own.

And then he cooked. Because bacon and waffles made everything better.

Hell, cooking made everything better.

Growing up, Sunday family dinners were sacred. His parents had traveled a lot with their foundation, particularly when he and Carmen were in their final high school years, but they'd always made sure that at least one of them was home for Sunday dinner.

Those dinners hadn't just encompassed their immediate family; more often than not, they'd included a mishmash of relatives and friends. And it'd never been a "women cook the meal, men relax" kind of deal. It was all hands on deck. Always.

As soon as he and Carmen could navigate a step stool, they'd been put to work. He'd forever be grateful to his parents for not only teaching him the life skill, but for showing him the joy of cooking for others. It was his own little way of bringing people together, of making people happy.

Sunday dinners had dwindled when Carmen went off to college, with him following her to the University of Washington a year later. Though the UW was close to home, their parents had ramped up their international travels, and their weekly Sunday dinners morphed into monthly gatherings, which eventually morphed into every other month.

After graduation, Parker had enjoyed his architect job, but as he'd moved up the career ladder, something had left him antsy—something missing. And at the same time, his marriage had been floundering. So, he'd retreated to what he knew. He'd reestablished monthly Sunday dinners with his family and friends and rediscovered the satisfaction of being in the kitchen. It was where he'd always found comfort.

Feeding people fed his soul. If he wanted to get sappy, he'd say it was his love language.

And after the crazy night Kate had, he needed to give her that comfort. Hell, he needed some of that comfort for himself as well.

"Holy moly, Parker," Kate said, entering the kitchen. "It smells amazing in here." She made a beeline for the coffeemaker, then the fridge to retrieve the flavored creamer she loved.

Her hair was damp, her face makeup-free, and she was dressed in black yoga pants—man, he loved yoga pants—and a simple pink shirt that highlighted her flushed cheeks. He wasn't sure if the flush was from her shower or waking up with him.

He hoped it was the latter.

"How's your hand?" he asked as she busied herself with stirring her coffee. It didn't escape his notice that she'd yet to make eye contact with him.

"Good," she replied, opening the drawer beneath the coffeemaker and retrieving a bottle of Tylenol. "Still a little sore and throbby, and it was a pain to keep the bandage dry, but it's good."

She peeked up at him and quickly looked away, a deeper flush stealing across her face.

Damn, she was cute.

He bit back a smile and moved the cooked bacon onto a paper towel. "You should take the day off in light of your late-night ER trip."

"Yeah, probably," she murmured, seemingly distracted. She sat at the kitchen table, her focus still glued to her coffee. After a moment's pause, her shoulders squared and her gaze swung to his. She blew out a quick breath, as if coming to some sort of decision.

What that decision was? He hadn't a clue.

"I was scheduled to do the pub's books today," she said, her voice wavering.

"Good thing I know the owners," he teased, and placed a giant plate of bacon and an equally giant plate of mini waffles on the table in front of her. "They're a bunch of jerks, but I'm sure they'll give you a pass today."

A smile tugged at the corners of her lips. "By jerks, I'm sure you mean really, really sweet jerks, right?"

He fought a cringe at the "really, really sweet" description. And failed.

She chuckled and rose. Parker stilled as she stood close,

settling her hand on his chest. "Sweet isn't a bad thing, you know."

He remembered to breathe only after she stepped away. Seating himself at the table, he snagged a piece of bacon and watched her gather plates and forks. He didn't want to think too hard about why the sight of her making herself at home in his kitchen, the sound of her bare feet padding around his house, warmed him.

"Speaking of bookkeeping," she continued, returning to his side and setting the table for them. "How much do you want for rent each month?"

He paused mid-chew, his eyes narrowing. She had to be joking. "Don't even think about giving me rent money."

Shaking her head, Kate sat and pointed a piece of bacon at him. "I'm serious. How much do you want?"

Christ, she wasn't joking. "I don't want your money." He held up his hand when she opened her mouth. "Save your money, Kate."

Her lips pinched together. "I will not be a freeloader, Parker Cunningham."

He didn't bother trying to hide his eye roll. "If Raven needed a place to stay and you had an extra room, would you charge her rent?"

She scoffed. "Of course not."

He lifted his brows.

"But that's different," she huffed.

He took a bite of his waffle and spoke around it. "How?"

"She's my fri—"

Parker leaned back in his chair, crossing his arms over his chest. He knew the smile growing on his face was smug. "I'm sorry, baby—what was that? She's your . . . what?"

She bit her lower lip as if trying to hold back a smile. "Fine. You win."

"I usually do, sweetheart," he said with a wink, enjoying the soft flush that washed over her.

After a moment of silence and toying with her food, she cleared her throat and met his gaze. "Speaking of amazing friends . . . thank you." He tilted his head in question. "Thank you for coming to my rescue, Park. Yet again."

He shook his head. Christ. If she told him what a great friend he was one more time . . .

It wasn't that being a great friend was a bad thing, but right now, Parker wasn't sure it was necessarily a good thing. At least, not for him. "There's nothing to thank me for." There really wasn't. He was the one who'd put her in that damn Uber in the first place when, instead, he should have taken her home himself and made sure she was okay. "You'd have done the same for me."

"Of course. But *you* came to *my* rescue." She pushed her plate aside and leaned her elbows on the table, her chin resting on her good hand. "You know, I never considered myself a squeamish kind of person. But last night, there was so much blood . . . and it wouldn't stop." A shiver coursed through her body, and it took all his willpower to refrain from pulling her close. "I kinda freaked out a little. I mean, how does a hand even bleed that much? Then I got so woozy, I was scared I was going to pass out. Then I had this picture in my mind of you coming home from work and finding me bleeding out all over your gorgeous hardwoods."

"Jesus, Kate." His stomach turned at the image.

All thoughts of how she saw him as a friend, or possibly more, didn't matter. All that mattered was her. That she was okay.

Kate's injured hand rested on the table next to him, and as gently as he could, he placed her hand in his. Avoiding her bandages, he drew small circles on her fingers.

She tensed, but he didn't let go. He couldn't. Even though

she sat right in front of him, he had to touch her. He needed to reassure himself that she was real. That she was okay and not, as she'd said, bleeding out on his goddamn hardwood floors.

Parker would take her any way he could, as long as it meant she was safe and in his life. Because that's what mattered.

He brought her hand to his lips and placed a kiss on her bandaged palm—how could he not?—before meeting her gaze. "I work the dinner shift later tonight, but do you want to catch a movie this afternoon?"

Her eyes widened and she blinked twice. "Excuse me?"

He liked that he'd caught her off guard. Hell, he'd just caught himself off guard. "A movie? This afternoon? Just you and me?"

"Um . . ." Her mouth opened and closed. Then, with a small laugh, she shook her head as if trying to clear it, the corners of her mouth lifting. "An afternoon date?" Her brows rose in question.

He nodded and held his breath.

A smile grew on her lips. "Yeah, that sounds fun. What did you have in mind?"

Elation like he hadn't felt in years coursed through him. It was like he was a high school kid who'd just asked his crush to prom—and she'd said yes! He wanted to pump his fist in the air, but instead tried for a casual shrug. And probably failed miserably, but he didn't care. "You pick."

Her smile turned into a smirk and her face sparkled with mischief. "How about that new Nicholas Sparks movie? It's supposed to be like a three-hour epic romance."

He held back a groan. Barely. "If you like your romances pointlessly drawn out and where everyone dies at the end, sure. I'm game."

"You're sweet. And that's a good thing, Park." She laughed,

the sound warming him. "Okay, I don't want to subject myself to that kind of depression, so how about the one with The Rock instead? You can't ever go wrong with The Rock, can you?"

"No, you can't," he chuckled.

Then his heart nearly popped out of his chest when she turned her hand to intertwine her fingers with his. She gave him a smile that was part shy, part nervous.

Goddamn, she was gorgeous.

"I swear, Kate," he murmured, his voice sounding like he'd swallowed a shit ton of gravel. He brought her fingers back to his lips. "You're damn near perfect."

She flushed a pretty pink but never broke eye contact, her fingers still tangled with his. "You're pretty damn perfect too, Park."

Time stood still.

The laughter in her eyes heated. When she glanced down at his lips, hers parted ever so slightly. His heart jumped. She met his gaze, and the fire, the raw desire in her eyes, had all his blood rushing south.

"Come here," she whispered, tugging on his hand.

Parker didn't need a second invitation.

His lips met hers, and the kiss he'd intended to be soft and gentle was anything but. She tasted sweet and salty and all Kate. Her tongue sought his, and the only thing he knew was that he needed her closer.

The damn table was in the way.

He pulled away from her with a groan, his chest heaving, the beautiful woman in front of him flushed, dazed, and just as out of breath as him. He pushed his chair back from the table, the legs scraping loudly against the floor.

"Come here," he growled, gently tugging her to him. Satisfaction coursed through him when she settled across his lap, her hands roaming over his chest and snaking into his hair. He thought he would die when she pulled away, but then she adjusted her position to sit astride him, her groin snug against his cock, and he was in fucking heaven.

A loud clatter had her drawing away. Her eyes narrowed and focused on the windows over his shoulder. "The bar stools outside tipped over in the wind."

"I don't care." He brought her kiss-swollen lips back to his. "Do you?"

He swallowed her laugh. Then her laughter turned into moans. His tongue explored her neck, and he slipped his hands under her shirt to do their own exploring. If he weren't already sitting, her silky soft skin would have brought him to his knees.

His phone rang.

"Ignore it," she murmured. Her hands clutched his shoulders as he feasted on her neck. Her fingernails dug into his skin, and he growled when her hips rocked hard against his erection.

Moments later, his phone rang again.

And again.

"Goddamn," he groaned, resting his forehead against hers. His ringing phone, the howling wind outside, and their gasps filled the air. "Sorry."

Her hands framed his face and she kissed him. That small gesture grabbed his heart. "Don't be." She patted him softly on the cheek, rising from his lap. "It's fine. Whoever it is will just keep calling."

Parker sat back. His heart galloped in his chest and he tried to catch his breath.

Holy shit. Kate climbing on top of him was hands down the hottest fucking thing that had ever happened to him in his entire goddamn life.

She chuckled, her smile going a little shy. "I'm glad you think so."

It didn't even occur to him to be embarrassed that he'd spoken his thoughts out loud. It was all one hundred percent true.

She snagged his ringing phone from the island. "Jake," she said, glancing at the display before holding it out to him.

He didn't bother glancing at the phone. Not when Kate stood before him, hair rumpled, cheeks flushed, a slight beard burn lingering on her neck. "Screw Jake."

A mischievous grin flashed. "I'd rather not."

Goddamn, he wanted this woman. "Someone else you have in mind, sweetheart?"

Her sly grin turned downright carnal. "Maybe."

His eyes closed and he groaned out loud.

She laughed, slapping his ringing phone to his chest. "Answer already . . . and maybe you'll find out."

***

So, this is what happens when you grow a pair?

In general, she wasn't a giggly kind of girl. But hooolyyy crap!

Yeah, she wanted to giggle like a high schooler—or at least how she imagined a not-shy, non-introverted high school girl would giggle—but she held back. She was an adult, dang it!

But she couldn't wipe the smile off her face. Not that she wanted to.

Her heart rate had yet to return to normal, and her entire body buzzed. She. Felt. Freaking. Amazing.

When Parker's phone rang, she'd been worried it would be awkward with them, that it would be weird. She'd practically jumped the guy, and she didn't do that kind of thing. Ever.

But she hadn't had time to be embarrassed. Because the

way Parker had looked at her—like he'd wanted. To. Devour. Her—

The memory had her body humming all over again.

Holy crap.

She fanned herself, but it did nothing to calm her racing heart.

A crash sounded from the backyard again, and she peeked out the window. Three of the four patio bar stools rolled on the ground, and the lone remaining stool wobbled, its back acting like a sail in the wind.

She could hear Parker in the other room, where he'd gone to take the call from Jake. His deep voice was animated and laughing at whatever Jake had to say.

A smile pulled at her lips. Her body still tingled from Parker's touch. Her mind? It was a bit scrambled. Part of her wanted to savor the giddy feeling, while the other part had a hard time wrapping itself around the fact that, moments earlier, her body had been tangled with Parker's. Rubbing against him, her tongue in his mouth, his hands on her skin.

Heat rushed through her again, and she couldn't help the smile that formed and stuck on her lips.

With a loud exhale, she unlocked the French doors to fix the outside chairs. Once she cracked the door, the cold wind whipped through her hair, though it did little to cool her down. Her scalp tingled as if Parker still had his hands in her hair.

Criminy! The man was going to be the end of—

All thoughts skidded to a halt.

Kate's bare foot froze as something wet squelched beneath her toes. She stared at her foot for a long moment, her brain not registering what it was seeing.

Then it did.

She stumbled back and smacked hard against the door.

"Parker!" Her stomach threatened to expel its contents.

She shook her leg, frantic to get the fleshy bits off her foot. Fleshy bits that had once belonged to a cat.

Correction.

Fleshy bits that had once belonged *inside* a cat. The little fuzzball was there in front of her, its poor little gut split open, all its innards spilled over the patio rug. And her foot.

"Parker!"

CHAPTER FOURTEEN

Their lunch-and-a-movie-before-work date turned into them taking the day off to figure out what to do with the dead cat. She didn't even like cats, was definitely more of a dog person, but her heart hurt for the little fella. The poor thing looked like it had been mauled by some larger animal, its innards spread out on Parker's patio doormat.

They'd called animal control, as neither of them knew the protocol for dealing with a dead cat, let alone a mauled one, and waited a couple hours for someone to come out to take care of Jonesy's body. The little ginger tom needed a name, after all.

"Jonesy?" Parker had asked. "Like Ripley's cat in *Alien*?"

Kate had spread her arms out, indicating the gruesome scene before them. "I'll admit that it's a bit on the morbid side, though quite apropos, don't you think?"

He'd laughed but agreed. Morbid or not, the name fit.

Once Jonesy had been taken care of and they'd scrubbed the back patio clean, instead of mindlessly watching The Rock blow stuff up, catch the bad guys, and bed the chick, they'd gone door to door in the howling wind and typical

Seattle sputter—not quite rain, not quite mist—asking every neighbor if they were missing their cat.

Nothing.

After trekking all over their Upper Queen Anne neighborhood looking unsuccessfully for Jonesy's family, they'd grabbed an early dinner at a local Asian fusion food truck, whose chef was a friend of Parker's and a pub regular, before returning home.

They'd spent hours together. And Kate had enjoyed every moment.

It was a lot of time walking, a lot of time talking. About everything. From the mundane to the bizarre.

Parker had mentioned how Courtney had come by wanting to get back together. He was adamant that wouldn't happen, but Kate couldn't help the slight twinge of insecurity from flaring. Especially remembering Courtney standing on the stairs wearing his shirt. She believed Parker when he said he wasn't interested, but after spending today with him, after making out like teenagers at the kitchen table and then going door to door on cat duty with him, she couldn't help but wonder what lengths Courtney would go to in order to get him back. Because simply put, Parker Cunningham was one freaking amazing man.

She had never been a fan of the other woman. Now she was even more convinced that Courtney was a downright idiot to have let Parker get away. His little touches, the stolen glances, and his sly smiles had kept Kate's stomach flipping all day. Geez, even the way he'd held her hand, how he'd laced their fingers together and softly traced the inside of her wrist with his thumb just so, had made her swoon.

Now that she knew what he kissed like, what he tasted like, what it felt like to have his hands touch her? She wanted to crowd his space. She wanted her hands on him. She wanted to take.

She usually held back, let the man take the lead. But there was something about him . . .

Maybe it was because they were already friends. Maybe it was because when Parker looked at her, he dang near set her on fire. Maybe it was because he never left her. In the chaos of the night before, he'd stayed and been her rock.

Whatever it was, the man was bona fide swoon-worthy.

Now, with a bottle of wine cracked open, they sat beside each other, snuggled down on the two-man chaise, staring at the outdoor fireplace, a light throw spread over their legs. The day's earlier wind had dwindled down to a perfect, cool breeze.

"I feel kind of bad not giving Jonesy a funeral," she said, her head resting against Parker's shoulder.

"I thought you didn't like cats."

"I don't. But I stepped on the little guy's insides." She shuddered. She could still feel the pet's cold, gooey guts squishing between her toes. "I will never eat Jell-O again," she mumbled. "A funeral would have been the least I could do."

"Admit it." Kate heard the smile in his voice. "You like cats."

She shook her head. "I'm allergic."

"Which means cats love you."

She nodded, a smile crawling on her lips. It was true. Like cats had a sixth sense about that kind of thing. *Oh, you're allergic to me? Great, let me be your best friend!*

She straightened and raised her glass. "To Jonesy. Poor little guy. May there be tons of catnip for him in kitty heaven."

Parker clinked his glass to hers, laughter dancing in his eyes. "To Jonesy. God speed, little fella."

After sipping her wine, she settled back against the

chaise. "Are you sure the pub will be okay without you manning the kitchen tonight?"

Grabbing his cell phone off the end table, Parker waved it in his hand, then tossed it onto the chaise by their feet. "We'll find out soon enough."

She chuckled and took another drink of wine, the malbec's blackberry and plum notes dancing on her tongue. She sighed in appreciation. "This is my favorite wine."

"I know," he said, topping off her glass.

The two words made her pause.

She studied him as he returned the bottle to the end table, realization dawning. Of course Parker knew what her favorite wine was. And of course he'd have it in stock for her at his house. Warmth bloomed in her belly.

Because Parker was the sweetest and most thoughtful man.

And he was smoking hot. He had the magical ability to melt her panties with just one look.

Lordy, she was about two seconds from jumping the man again.

She cleared her throat and tried to fight the blush she felt creeping up her neck. "This is Vince's first night flying solo in the kitchen?"

"Yeah. Blake will be there to help out, and Adam will be floating around in case they need an extra hand. It's Pub Trivia night, so it shouldn't be too crazy."

She frowned. "But it's always busy on Pub Trivia night."

"True, but more for the bar. Vince just has to get through that first wave of dinner. After that, tables aren't turning over, and the only thing getting reordered are drinks and fries."

"How is this the first personal day you've taken off since you guys opened the pub?"

"What can I say?" He shrugged, that charming grin lighting up his face. "I have an amazing immune system."

She couldn't stop her eyes from rolling or the groan that escaped. "Aside from your stellar immune system—"

"*Amazing* immune system."

She held her hands up. "Oh, excuse me. *Amazing* immune system. You've never just taken a day off?"

His shoulders lifted again. "Why would I? I get two full days off a week. When I do work, I don't start until—what?—one or two in the afternoon, sometimes later, so there's plenty of time to get all my crap done. I get to see all my favorite people while I'm at work." He nudged her shoulder. "Present company included, of course."

A smile bloomed, and she nudged back. "Of course."

"We run a fun place where our friends hang out and I get to cook for a living. No complaints here."

"Easy peasy," she teased.

He smiled and sipped his wine. "For the most part, yeah. I can probably count on one hand the times when I didn't want to be at the pub but was stuck there because there was no one else to cook." A shadow flickered over his face. "Last night was one."

"Last night?"

"I still feel like an absolute ass for dumping you in an Uber when I should have taken you home." The self-loathing in his voice shocked her. She opened her mouth to protest, but he talked right over her. "And then when you called . . ."

Holy crap. It hadn't even occurred to her that he'd left the pub in the middle of a shift with no one else on staff who could take over the kitchen. "Oh my God, Parker. I'm so sorry! Was Blake pissed that you left?"

His brow arched in a get-real look. "All that matters is that you're okay. As much of a pain in the ass as Blake can be, he's not completely inept in the kitchen. He was fine last night. And tonight, if Vince and Adam don't make it in for some reason, Blake will be fine. Cussing up a storm, but fine. However . . ." he pulled back slightly and turned narrowed eyes her way, pointing a finger at her.

She chuckled. She knew what he was getting at. "My lips are sealed."

"Promise?"

"The only thing Blake will ever hear from me is the part where you said he's a pain in the ass."

He clinked his glass with hers again. "And that's why you're my favorite."

The grin on her face grew. This was one of the things she treasured about Parker. Their easy friendship, their cama-raderie. As she held his gaze, the humor and laughter in his eyes warming her, her mind flashed to earlier in the day. When other parts of him had been warming her, heck, setting her on fire. His gaze heated as if he could read her thoughts, making her flush.

"Don't overthink this, sweets." He motioned between them with his hand. "It's just us. It's *still* us."

"I know," she murmured, and shifted her focus to swirling the contents of her glass. She inhaled deeply and took a long sip before meeting his gaze. "It's just kinda hard to wrap my head around this whole . . . now-I-get-to-kiss-you thing. I mean, don't get me wrong, I like it. I'm a huge fan, in fact."

"But?" he prodded.

She couldn't help but smile at him. "But it's all a little surreal."

"Believe me," he said, laughter in his voice. "I'm right there with you." He took her bandaged hand, brought it to his lips, and placed the gentlest kiss on her palm. A kiss she felt all the way down to her toes. "But it's still just us."

Yup, the man knew how to make her melt. She sighed and leaned into him, laying her head against his shoulder, turning her hand so she could lace her fingers with his. "Thank you for being there for me last night."

"You've already thanked me."

Her heart squeezed when she felt his lips on the top of her head. "I know. I just want you to know that it really meant a lot to me. That you didn't leave."

Parker was silent for a moment. "What spooked you?"

Her wineglass paused on the way to her lips. "Nothing."

"Please, Kate. I know you. You're tough."

"Right," she scoffed and drank her wine. *Tough* was not a word she'd ever use to describe herself.

"You are. You're sweet and kind and tough as nails. You don't spook easily. But you did last night. What happened?"

Debating telling the truth, she peeked up at him, at the face she'd known more than half her life. A man she'd known forever, yet at the same time, was just getting to know. Her heart squeezed. How could she not tell him the truth? "I saw a man on the news that I hadn't seen in years. From . . . before. From my life before Anna and Henry. It launched me back in time."

She could be truthful with Parker, but he didn't need to know everything.

"Not a good trip down memory lane, I take it?"

"No."

He was silent for a moment, but it felt like he wanted to say something. Instead, he just held her hand, tracing the edges of her bandage with his thumb.

"What is it?" She shifted her head from his shoulder to the chaise so she could look at him.

He shrugged, his focus on the outdoor fireplace in front of them. "I don't know much, if anything really, about you before you came to live with Aunt Anna and Uncle Henry."

"It's okay. Not many people do."

A grin quirked his lips and she knew it was from her non-answer.

"I take it Aunt Anna and Uncle Henry know about you, about your life before?"

She nodded yes, then no. "Not all of it."

"Raven?"

She couldn't help the smile at the thought of her best friend. Her fierce, loyal friend. "She probably knows the most."

"You two met in foster care, right?"

She nodded. Her smile fell as memories of her childhood came back in a rush.

"Stop shaking, Kate," Raven whispered.

She tried. She really did. But she couldn't.

Tears welled in her eyes and her chin trembled. "I can't." A single tear slid down her cheek, quickly followed by more.

Raven faced her and slapped her hands down on Kate's shoulders. Hard. "You. Have. To."

She bit her lip and willed her tears to stop, but they kept falling.

"Cry all you want later. But they're coming back," Raven glanced over her shoulder toward the darkened hallway, toward the angry voices that were getting louder. "Pull your shit together," Raven hissed as she squeezed hard on Kate's shoulders.

Kate nodded and swiped at her tears. She took a shaky breath in and held it.

"You can't show any weakness or those fuckers will have you for breakfast. Got it?"

She nodded again and let out her breath, fear drying up her tears. "Got it."

Raven moved to stand next to her, shoulder to shoulder, and squeezed her hand one final time. "The dad's an asshole and likes to hit," she murmured. "He's a creeper, but the one you really need to keep your eye on is the son. He's a sneaky fucker and doesn't take no for an answer."

Ice skated down Kate's spine as her new foster family stepped through the doorway. Her stomach rolled at the gleam she saw in their eyes.

She thought she'd gotten away from evil. She was wrong.

Kate blinked away the memories, her eyes refocusing on Parker. "Foster care was . . ." Horrible, traumatizing, a crapshoot . . . so many indescribable things. "The first family I was placed with was only for a few days. They seemed nice, but they'd wanted a younger kid. The next family was where I met Raven. She'd been with them for a couple months by the time I got there, and that family was awful. Luckily, I wasn't there that long. But Raven . . ." She shook her head, as if that little movement could erase those horrible memories. "If it wasn't for Raven, and then Anna and Henry, I don't know what would have happened to me."

"You don't call Aunt Anna & Uncle Henry 'Mom' and 'Dad,' do you?"

She shook her head. "It's not because I don't see them that way. I do."

"But you don't call them by those titles?"

A familiar rock settled in her belly, like it did every time she thought of her real parents. No, not her *real* parents. That honor went to Anna and Henry. *Those* people were her *birth* parents. "Obviously, I had a mother and father before . . . but . . . they were the antithesis of what parents should be. Of what Anna and Henry are." She wrinkled her nose. How to phrase this? "I guess the actual words 'mother,' 'father,' 'mom,' and 'dad' feel cheap to me. Even when I was younger, on some level, I knew that I never wanted to associate Anna and Henry with those words." They were a million times better than those words. "I was open to them about why, about my reasons in our family therapy sessions, and they never pushed."

"You were, what, thirteen when you moved in with them?"

"I had just turned twelve when they first took me in as foster parents. I was thirteen when they adopted me."

"Huh." He frowned. "Where the hell was I?"

"College," she chuckled, releasing his hand to elbow him in the ribs. "You're old, remember."

"Ha-ha," he replied, the two syllables deadpan. "You know, even though I was a completely self-absorbed, newly minted adult—"

"You were a teenager."

"I wasn't just any ole teenager, Kate. I was an eighteen-year-old at college, so that made me a god. I was invincible and knew everything." He shot her a wink. "In my own mind, of course."

Her eyes rolled, but she smiled at the memories. "Yeah, both you and Blake were so full of yourselves."

They *had* been like gods to her. Two carefree, outgoing teenagers—boys on the cusp of manhood—who she'd run into at various family get-togethers. Anna and Henry had been fiercely protective of her those first couple of years. They'd known better than she that she wasn't ready for the onslaught of their large, extended family. Kate would forever be grateful for their protection. Still, both boys had fascinated her from afar. Neither had been shy in regaling the adults, or anyone who'd listen, with their college antics. They'd been fearless and confident, secure in who they were, secure in their families.

The complete opposite of her.

"But," Parker continued, "despite all that, I do remember you."

"Wow." Her eyes rolled again. "I'm flattered."

He chuckled and nudged her with his shoulder. "Don't be. I was an idiot."

"You were a teenager. All teenagers are idiots."

"True, but I do remember when Aunt Anna and Uncle Henry initially told the family they'd be taking you in. They'd always wanted kids, but it just didn't happen for them." His voice grew soft. "The family was nervous for them. I remember everyone being worried they'd get their hopes up, that they'd get burned. Then we all met you." A soft, faraway smile graced his lips. "You were ridiculously shy, didn't make a lot of eye contact, didn't talk much. But you were a really sweet kid."

She snorted; she couldn't help it. "If I didn't make eye contact or speak, how could you possibly know I was sweet? I could have been a serial killer."

"Truck, smartass."

Her brow arched. What? "Because of a truck?"

"No," he chuckled. "Truck. Uncle Henry's dog."

Kate gasped as memories of a wrinkled, graying, overweight, geriatric English Bulldog filled her brain. His stinky doggy breath that no amount of mint-laced dog biscuits could hide haunted her senses. She sighed deeply, with so much fondness. Truck. How could she have forgotten about that darling pup? Granted, he'd died of old age only a few months after she'd arrived, but still . . .

Parker's chuckle turned into a full-on laugh, his face lighting. "Only you would make that face, that sigh, over Truck."

She shook her head, pointing her finger at him. "Watch it, buster. Truck was the best."

"Truck was the grumpiest and meanest bastard out there. He hated everyone. *Including* Uncle Henry, but especially me and Blake. He'd piss on our shoes every chance he got."

"Well, you guys probably deserved it," she mumbled into her malbec.

"But with you? He was the nicest damn dog. Followed you around like he was your shadow."

"That makes *Truck* sweet. Not me."

"Nope. Dogs know things. We all knew—adults included —that you had to be the sweetest girl if that grumpy bastard was so nice to you. We were really happy Aunt Anna and Uncle Henry finally got the kid they'd wanted."

Her heart squeezed and tears prickled her eyes. She blinked rapidly to hold them at bay. "I'm the lucky one, really. But that's kind of you to say, Park."

He opened his mouth. And then snapped it shut, placing his empty wineglass on the side table.

Her head tilted in question.

Silence ticked by. It wasn't uncomfortable. But it wasn't comfortable.

"Did your birth parents die?" Parker finally asked, his quiet voice loud in the stillness of the backyard.

"No." The sour rock was back in her gut at the mention of her birth parents.

She had no idea if they were still alive. Nor did she particularly care. She wanted the door to that part of her life bolted and barricaded shut.

"Did CPS remove you from them?" She shook her head, her hands toying with the stem of her wineglass. "Then what happened? How'd you end up in foster care? Damn it," he muttered, raking a hand through his hair, a pained expression on his face. "I'm sorry. If I'm overstepping, just say so. The last thing I want to do is make you uncomfortable. We've known each other forever, but I just . . . I want to know more about you."

She reached over and squeezed his forearm. "It's fine, really."

Shifting to sit cross-legged, she placed her wineglass on the table and pulled the blanket over her lap, her focus on the blanket's scalloped edge.

What happened?

She happened. She spoke up. That's what.

"They didn't want me anymore," she murmured. Meeting his gaze, her shoulders lifted, then dropped. An ancient hurt that was still too familiar and too fresh bubbled in her heart. "So, they gave me up."

CHAPTER FIFTEEN

S ilence.

The only sounds were the soft hum of the gas fireplace, the quiet breeze rustling the trees, and the croaks of distant frogs.

Kate fought to tamp down the old sorrow, the old disappointment, the old heartbreak. It had been ages since she'd revisited her childhood. Thinking of her past—the turmoil, the anger, the fear—made her feel like shit. Structure, organization, lists; she utilized every therapy tool she knew to stay in the present.

For some reason, though, talking about it with Parker made it all a little less sucky. She took solace in the confusion, anger, disgust, and flat-out disbelief that washed over his face.

"Jesus, Kate," he finally said. "What the hell was wrong with them?"

Her lips quirked. Sweet, sweet man. "I caused a lot of problems for them."

"You're going to defend them?"

She shook her head. "I'm not defending them." She wasn't.

But their conversation was moving into tricky territory. "It's a bit . . . complicated."

What was she doing, spilling this part of her past to Parker? He'd said he wanted to know more about her. She was pretty freaking sure this wasn't what he'd meant.

Favorite food? Favorite color? Did she have a pet growing up? *That's* what he'd meant. She needed to get this conversation on lighter ground. Fast.

She opened her mouth to say so but fell silent as he shifted on the chaise to face her. He gently took her hands in his, lacing their fingers together, and held her gaze. "It's complicated?" She nodded and tried to look away from the intensity of his dark green eyes. But couldn't. "Then uncomplicate it for me."

She bit back a sigh. What was it about this man that made her want to tell him everything?

"I made some questionable choices that went against what my parents believed. So, they disowned me."

"Wait." His brow furrowed. "How old were you?"

She cringed. Hindsight made all of it so much worse, so vile. "Eleven. Almost twelve."

His body tensed, his lips pressing into a thin line. "You were eleven."

It wasn't a question.

"Right," she replied on an exhale.

He brought both of her hands to his lips, placing a kiss on each before he rose and paced in front of the fireplace. It was obvious he was choosing his next words carefully.

"What the hell kind of *choice* could you have possibly made that would warrant your parents disowning you?" He paused as if a thought had just occurred to him. "I'm not a lawyer or anything, but I'm pretty damn sure you can't just disown your kid when they're *eleven*."

Kate begged to differ.

She took a moment to find the right words. "It didn't happen overnight. They didn't just drop me off at a foster home and say, 'See ya, kid!'" Though she was pretty sure if they could have, they would have. "It was a process."

A process that had started the moment she spoke out and revealed the ugly truth. A process that had taken her years and years of therapy to get over.

Her heart stilled.

No. *Get over* wasn't quite right. It was more accurate to say she'd shoved it in a dark closet while telling the therapists she acknowledged what had happened, had come to terms with it, and would work to move past it all.

"My parents claimed to the state's powers that be that I was an 'at-risk youth.' That I had a habit of running away for weeks at a time. Then when I was home, I was destructive and a danger to my siblings, my parents, and my neighbors."

That I was evil. That I was a whore.

Parker stopped pacing, disbelief etched on his face. "I can't imagine you were any of those things."

"I wasn't."

"Then how could any social worker or judge believe it?"

Now it got tricky.

She cleared her throat. "You know that thing in the news about the eastern Washington guy who just got arrested for tax fraud?"

"The cult leader?"

"Yeah." She took a deep breath in, her heart picking up its pace. "I grew up in that cult."

Shocked silence met her. The look on Parker's face could only be described as What The Fuck? It would have been comical. Had it not been *her* life.

"It didn't look like the cults you've seen on television with the bunkers and fortified boundaries. It looked like any small, single-stop-sign farming community. Kids roamed free. The neighborhood cats were fed by everyone. The neighborhood dogs claimed their favorite humans, and that's where they hunkered down for the night. The town's center was the church and everyone was a member. Everyone knew each other and was free to come and go as they pleased." Though no one ever left. Because they all followed the word of one man. Master Sebastian. "But the 'church,'" she air-quoted with her fingers, "was a cult. So, when my parents claimed that I was a danger to the community, there were more than enough people willing to corroborate their story."

It was what Master Sebastian had wanted. No one went against him. Not even her.

"No one listened to you?" The anger in his voice had her eyes shooting to his.

She'd wanted to speak the truth. Scream to everyone what had happened. But she'd known it was impossible. Even then. Even at eleven.

She'd only told two people the truth of what had happened, the two people who were supposed to protect her the most. But the second the words had left her mouth, the process of "purifying the community" of *her* began. If her own parents hadn't believed her, who would?

"I didn't speak up. I went along with what they wanted. I had to." The truth, *her* truth, hadn't mattered. The entire community had been against her. She would never have won. Even at that tender age, Kate had known that she would never, ever win.

So she'd said nothing. Even though there had been proof. Undeniable proof.

Fear and shame had kept her silent.

"Motherfuckers," Parker said in a harsh whoosh.

He'd resumed pacing, his shoulders tense, his hands swinging in fists at his side.

She wanted to reassure him somehow. "But it all worked

out, Parker. I met Raven, and then I ended up with Anna and Henry. It wasn't all bad."

<hr>

Kate killed him. She really did. This beautiful woman, who'd had such a shitty family, was trying to reassure *him*. How she'd survived her fucked-up childhood, he hadn't a clue. A cult, for fuck's sake! But Parker was beyond grateful she had.

He'd always known there was a quiet strength to Kate. Now he knew why.

"How did you meet Aunt Anna and Uncle Henry?" To his knowledge, she had been the only child they'd ever fostered.

She stayed silent for a while, her eyes unfocused, as if memories assailed her. He didn't think she was going to answer.

"Raven." Her voice was soft. And heartbreakingly sad.

He looked at her in question.

She shivered and pulled the light blanket tight around her.

His stomach knotted. It wasn't cold. Whatever Kate was going to say wasn't going to be pleasant.

"Raven and I met by chance when I was placed into the same foster home as her. She was ten, and I was eleven. The foster home was awful, and I grew up in a cult, so that says a lot. Raven . . ." A faraway shadow crossed her face. "Even though she was younger than me, she knew so much more about that world than I did."

Ice inched up his spine. "That world?"

"Violence. Sex. Men. She was ten when I met her, and looking back, it's horrific and appalling how many people had already failed her, had hurt her."

Parker's mouth opened, but no sound came out. He was at

a complete loss for words. Vomit threatened. He laced his hands behind his neck and braced himself.

"Our foster home was horrible. The family put up a good face when CPS came around, so they didn't have any issues with the state, but they were just in it for the money. The father, if you can call him that, was a drunk who was always copping feels on whichever kids were in the house—girls, boys, it didn't matter—so long as they were a kid. But he wasn't the one we had to worry about." Kate's face drained of color, her lips forming a thin, angry line. "The son," she said, so much disgust in those two words, "he was the scary one."

Parker's stomach lurched at what was coming next.

"The son was seventeen and . . . pure evil." Her breath left her in a shaky exhale. She brushed away a tear, anger making her movement jerky. "He'd do 'Eeny, Meeny, Miny, Moe' with me and Raven. To choose which one he'd fuck."

Parker's blood iced over. Holy. Fucking. Christ.

"But Raven," she paused, her face softening, fresh tears welling in her eyes. "Even if I was *it*, Raven would always take my place. To protect me." Kate met his gaze, disbelief and awe—the very worst kind of awe—crossing her face. "Can you believe that?"

He shook his head.

No. He sure as hell couldn't.

He exhaled, grinding his teeth together. What he would give to get his hands on that motherfucker . . .

"The son didn't care who it was under him." Kate stilled. "Until one day he did. She tried to step in for me, tried to protect me again, and he beat her up so bad . . ." More tears fell, and she swiped them away, lost in her memories. "The neighbors called the cops, and when they showed up, they arrested everyone in that god-awful family. They took us both to the hospital. My injuries weren't as bad as hers, but they were worried abou—" Her mouth slammed shut and her eyes went wide, as if she'd surprised herself. Kate cleared her throat. "Raven was hurt far worse than me."

Raven's beautiful face flashed in his mind. Goddamn. His throat tingled, and he blinked back tears. It broke his heart to know his friend had been hurt, that she'd gone through all that. Raven amazed him. From everything Kate had said—and didn't say—Raven had every reason to be a basket case. But she wasn't. She'd quickly become one of his closest friends, one he'd considered family even before she'd agreed to become his cousin's wife. His admiration for the woman grew a thousandfold.

"When I say that I don't know what would have happened to me if it weren't for Raven, I mean it," Kate murmured, tears falling in earnest.

Parker went to her then. Settling next to her on the chaise, he opened his arms.

His heart clenched when she burrowed against his chest, her tears dampening his shirt. He knew there was darkness in the world, that there were inhumane people out there. Knowing that darkness had touched Kate and Raven made him want to howl at the universe.

After a few moments, Kate's tears waned, but she kept her head on his chest, her arms around his waist as she snuggled deeper into his embrace. "When we were in the ER, they kept me and Raven separated." A shiver wracked her body, and he tightened his hold. "There were all these strangers, and I was all alone . . . it was an absolute nightmare."

He closed his eyes and his breath left him. The ER. Like puzzle pieces clicking into place, the terror he'd seen in Kate's eyes when she'd thought he was leaving her alone in the emergency room the night before now made sense.

"After what seemed like forever, the hospital's social worker came to see me."

A smile lifted his lips for the first time since their conversation began. "Aunt Anna."

"Yeah. Anna." She yawned against his chest. "Meeting her changed everything for me."

Parker remained silent for a moment, overwhelmed by what Kate had revealed, yet grateful that she took comfort in his arms. Thankful that she'd trusted him enough to share this story, this horrific, god-awful story that was such a crucial turning point in her life.

"It breaks my damn heart to say it, Kate, but I'm happy you had Raven."

"Me too." She sniffed, her arms tightening around him. "It makes me feel like a horrible person, but I'm so thankful she was there."

"You're not a horrible person." His lips found the top of her head. "Thank you, Kate."

She peeked up at him, her eyes red-rimmed. "For what?"

"For trusting me. For sharing this part of your past with me."

She stayed silent, her tired eyes searching his. "There's something about you, Park. I don't know exactly what it is, but I treasure it. I treasure you."

His heart pinged. God, he loved this woman. He truly did.

"I treasure you too."

The sadness eased from her eyes, and she dropped her forehead to his chest, yawning again.

"Come on." He rubbed small circles over her back before leaning away. "Let's get you to bed. It's been a long day."

He stood and extended his hand to her.

She took his hand but didn't get up, her gaze uncertain. "Will you stay with me again tonight? Please?"

This woman killed him. She really did.

Parker knelt in front of her and framed her face in his hands. He took a moment to tuck a stray lock of hair behind her ear, then brought his lips to hers. "Of course."

CHAPTER SIXTEEN

For the second morning in a row, Kate was cocooned in Parker's arms. When she'd first awoken, instead of panicking, she'd curled deeper into his embrace, warmth enveloping her as his strong arms tightened around her.

She should have been out of bed a full hour earlier, but the thought of moving out of Parker's sleepy embrace left her cold. Her spaghetti-strapped night dress had ridden up overnight, and she savored the contact of their spooned bodies, only two thin layers of underwear separating them. So she'd stayed put, memorizing the feel of his solid chest against her back, his hard length nestled to her backside, the warmth of his arms, the soothing effect of his even breathing.

Kate couldn't believe she'd told him so much last night. So much, and yet, not all of it. She wasn't sure she could ever share it all. Not with anyone.

She was raw. Her emotions had been splayed out everywhere, like poor little Jonesy. What surprised her was that revealing that part of her life, a part she'd kept bolted away, hadn't been as bad as she'd anticipated. She'd for sure thought she would be drowning in embarrassment, mortified by the exposed crappiness of her childhood. But she wasn't. If anything, it had been therapeutic.

It made no sense.

No, that was a lie. It did make sense.

Because it was Parker.

He'd been there for her for as long as she could remember. Well, not just for her, but for everyone. Parker had always been a rock. Steady and sure and so dang reliable.

Her lips pursed. That sounded bad. He wasn't a Honda.

She turned into Parker's arms, snuggling her cheek against his warm chest. Her free hand slid slowly over his stomach and side until her arm draped over his waist. No. The man was definitely not a Honda.

Kate had never intended to tell anyone about her past. Ever. But last night, ripping open that scabbed-over wound until it gaped and bled had been easier with Parker at her side.

She trusted him completely. It was as simple as that.

Stilling, her mouth dipped to a frown. Just because she trusted him didn't mean she could, or *should*, tell him everything. That would be stupid. He'd leave.

She inwardly winced. No. Parker wouldn't leave. He *couldn't*. Their families were too intertwined. Parker would still be a part of her life, but if she were dumb enough to tell him everything . . .

Her eyes closed, and she pressed her forehead to his chest. *Don't borrow trouble, Kate! You don't need to tell him everything. There's no way he could ever find out.* She prayed that the steady beating of Parker's heart would calm her, that his familiar woodsy scent would soothe her.

With an exhale, she slowly rolled onto her back. She tried to push away the thoughts of their relationship, or whatever it was she and Parker now had, exploding in her face.

A glance at her bedside clock told her it was seven-thirty. She bit back a groan. It wasn't that she didn't welcome the distraction from her self-wallowing, because she did. What she didn't welcome was the fact she couldn't lie in her warm bed with Parker forever. If she didn't hustle, she would be late.

Careful not to disturb him, she untangled herself from his arms. He stirred, but she managed to slip out without waking him. Sitting at the edge of her bed, she took a moment to steady herself.

She was overthinking things. Again.

If she kept this up, she'd drive herself crazy. She needed to focus on the present. Like the fact that there was a smoking hot guy in her bed. A smoking hot guy who seemed to really like her. She needed to focus on *that* and not jinx herself with the what-ifs.

She startled when Parker's arm snaked around her waist, the heat from his body warming her back.

"Morning." His voice was rough, and he dropped a kiss to her spaghetti-strapped shoulder.

Heat flooded her body. *This*. She needed to focus on this.

Another kiss landed on her shoulder, closer to her neck. "Want me to fix you some breakfast?"

"No, it's all right. You should get some more sleep." She tilted her head ever so slightly to give him better access. "You have to work late tonight."

He chuckled, his warm breath tickling her neck. "So do you."

"True." Parker hadn't been wrong the night before. She was exhausted. "Then at least one of us should get some sleep."

"You're so pretty first thing in the morning," he murmured. "Have I mentioned that before?" His lips found her neck, the wet heat of his tongue against her sensitive skin sending goosebumps racing over her. It was a good thing she was already seated because her legs would have liquefied.

In some far corner of her mind, she heard her phone ding. "I have to go, Park." With a groan, she turned and kissed his lips quickly, unwrapping herself from his arms.

"You should have dinner at the pub tonight," Parker said, settling back against the pillows, one arm behind his head. "I'm trying out a couple new recipes and need a guinea pig. You game?"

She stepped toward the walk-in closet. "Sure, it's a date."

"No," he chuckled. "It's recipe testing. But let me take you out on Sunday?"

Her hand froze on the closet doorknob. "Like a *date* date?" Oh my God. Did that sound as dumb out loud as it did in her head?

She peeked over her shoulder and saw a smile spread slowly over his lips.

"Yeah. Our lunch date yesterday was derailed by ole Jonesy, so how about a *date* date? Catch a movie. Go out to dinner. Come home and make out on the couch. What do you say?"

She leaned against the closet door and took in the man sprawled on her bed. Well, technically it was *his* bed, but still, the man made quite a picture. Parker's shaggy chestnut brown hair was all rumpled, his bottle-green eyes sleepy. With his chest bare, his six-pack was on full display, the delicious V of his lower abs highlighted by the sheet slung low over his hips. Her mouth watered. She wanted to lick every single inch of him. Every. Single. Inch.

A flush stole over her face.

Dating Parker? Yes, please.

Before she could second-guess herself, Kate launched herself onto the bed. Quickly crawling to the middle where he lay, she pressed her lips to his, darting her tongue out to lick at the seam of his lips. "I'd love that," she murmured. The element of surprise was on her side as she reversed direction and was off the bed before he could react.

He moved, as if he were going to come after her, but Kate held up her hand in a stop motion as she walked backward toward the closet.

He stilled.

"I have a meeting, and you have to stay there."

Mischief played across his face. "Or else?"

"Or else you're going to distract me."

"And?"

"And I've already missed enough work. So stay put. Got it?" Part of her wanted him to ignore her, but the other part really had to get moving. Adulting sucked sometimes.

He chuckled, leaned back against the pillows, and saluted her. "Yes, ma'am."

Kate sat in the conference room of Alvarez Technologies and stared blankly at the computer screen in front of her. Her concentration was crap. Instead of daydreaming about Parker or figuring out which way was up with Jake's shit-tastic books—because the sorry state of his bookkeeping deserved the whole curse word—she was mulling over her earlier client meeting. Or rather, her earlier *former*-client meeting.

The results of her morning meeting hadn't come as a surprise to her. In the three years she'd worked with that marketing company, they'd added sixteen full-time employees to their payroll. They'd grown, were making more money, and had decided to take their bookkeeping in-house. It was totally understandable. If it were her company, she'd have done the same. She would have actually done it a year sooner, so she got it. She harbored zero hard feelings and would be assisting them with their transition over the next two months.

Still. Losing a client, especially a longtime client, sucked. She should have stayed in bed with Parker.

It looked like there were more pub shifts in her future. Who needed sleep anyway?

Her forehead throbbed, and she took another sip of her coffee. At this rate, her blood would be pure caffeine by dinnertime. She focused back on the laptop with Jake's company's "correct" set of books. He'd "fixed" them and wanted her to double-check his work.

Her headache mounted to epic proportions when Jake burst into the conference room, apologies for being late flying from his lips. With a heavy sigh, he took the seat directly across the table from her. She stilled when she met his gaze over the top of the laptop.

Jake's big brown eyes begged. Like a puppy.

The man was up to something.

With one final rub of her temple, she leaned back in her chair, her arms crossed over her chest. "What do you want?"

"Please, Kate. I really need your help."

She motioned toward the computer. "I am helping you."

"Yes, thank you for helping with the books, but I'm talking about the party."

Her eyes narrowed. "What party?"

"The launch party we're throwing for the giant update on our Square Peg game app." His puppy dog eyes morphed into kicked-puppy dog eyes.

She held his gaze, brow arching in question. There was more. There was *always* more when Jake flashed the kicked-puppy dog eyes.

"In two weeks," he muttered.

Oh heck no. She shook her head. "I'm a bookkeeper. Not a party planner." Or a miracle worker, for that matter.

"You've done event planning before. You're Clean Water Campaign's bookkeeper *and* you've planned at least three of their galas."

"Yes, however, for each gala, CWC asked me at least a *year* in advance."

"This will be nothing. It's *tiny* in comparison. It's just a party. No auction, no gala, no nothing. *Just* a party."

True. Kate thought about her current workload. How she needed to pick up more shifts at the pub and put out feelers for new bookkeeping clients. She really didn't have the time to take on anything else. Or the desire to work with Jake beyond his books. Working his books was pushing it as it was.

"Please. I'll pay you double your rate."

That got her attention. Her monthly income would dip once the marketing company's transition was complete. She also needed to replenish her savings account. Not to mention buy a new car and save up for a new apartment or house. "Double my rate?"

"Absolutely. That way, you can cut back on your shifts at the pub."

Huh. That would be nice.

Her brow furrowed. "Wait. What about your new assistant? Why don't you just have her do it?"

He cringed. "Yeah . . . she didn't work out."

"Already?" Not that Kate was surprised. "What did you do?"

He flinched as if she'd slapped him. "Excuse me, but why is it *my* fault?"

"It's *always* your fault." He opened his mouth, but she kept on talking. "Let me ask you a question, Jake. Your company makes a ton of money. Why haven't you hired a CFO or—I don't know—an accounting department?"

"We're not that kind of company." His face scrunched in

distaste. "We're not all corporate."

God help her. "Your company brings in millions of dollars a year. *Millions.* You employ three coders and four graphic designers. Your overhead is ridiculously low, so you're making money hand over fist. Why don't you have someone internal managing your books?"

He shrugged. "I guess I don't trust anyone with the company's financials. *And* I also employ an assistant."

"You actually don't," she mocked. Kate usually wasn't this blunt, but her brain was hurting. "You haven't been able to keep an assistant for more than three weeks at a time. Ever. Jake, you need to find someone to manage the financial end of this place or it's going to be your company's downfall." She held up her hand when he opened his mouth. "Correct me if I'm wrong, but you run the day-to-day of this place, right?" She waved her hand, indicating Alvarez Technologies.

He nodded.

"You're also a co-owner of The Spotted Dog, right?"

He shifted in his seat. "Yeah, but it's not like I do anything. Parker handles all the food, Blake handles all the staffing, Raven's got the bar, and you handle the books. I don't actually do anything."

Idiot. She loved the guy, but holy crap was he an idiot. "Who handles the marketing? The advertising? The social media?"

He glared in silence.

Kate glared back. "Who, Jake?"

"Me," he grumbled.

"Oh, but you're right. That doesn't take a lot of time. Like when you had the Food Network people come out last year? That was super easy to coordinate, right? Or when you had the pub spotlighted in *The Seattle Times* two months ago? And the feature in *Bon Appétit* that comes out next month? Easy peasy, right?"

He let out a breath, annoyance on his face. "Your point, Kate?"

"My point, *Jake*, is that you have so much going on. The last thing you need to be worrying about is your company's books. That's something you need to hire out because you can't do your books half-assed, especially with the amount of money this place makes."

"I don't know if I'd call it half-assed," he complained.

"I would," she scoffed. Sometimes tough love was the answer. "Trust me, this is what I do for a living. Do you know who else would call it half-assed?" She didn't give him a chance to answer. "The freaking IRS!"

It was his turn to scoff. "That's a little dramatic, don't you think? I can handle the money end just fine."

"No." Her chuckle was more exasperation than humor. She waved a hand at the laptop. "You clearly can't. Your payroll is showing up as an *asset* account! This is payroll software, Jake, so *you* had to go in and manually change that setting. You claim you're paying payroll taxes, but I haven't found anything digitally or in your hard copy files to suggest you actually are. The amount of money your company makes and the corresponding amount you're mis-paying in taxes is a huge red flag. I'm shocked you haven't been audited."

A flush crawled over his face. "I have good accountants."

"Well, they must be freaking magical, because they're pulling numbers out of their asses."

He bit back a smile. "I have bank statements. Those are legit numbers."

He was killing her. Ab. So. Lutely. Killing her. "Jake. This is a multimillion-dollar company. You can't just use your monthly bank statements."

"But I do."

"And because you do, you're missing out on thousands upon thousands of dollars in tax deductions and reallocations. Haven't your accountants told you that?" She had her answer when he frowned and pouted. Like a six-year-old. "Hire one of your accountants."

The pout deepened, and she almost laughed. Almost.

"They don't want to work for me," he muttered.

Of course they didn't. She supposed she should feel sorry for him. She didn't. "Do you know why that is?"

He slouched down in his seat, his head dropping back against the top of the chair, a look of resignation crossing his face. "I'm assuming you're going to tell me?"

"Because you're a jerk."

He shot up in his seat. "What?"

"I love you, Jake, but I only love Friend Jake. Business Jake?" She motioned at him with her hand. "Total jerk. It's also why you can't keep an assistant."

His mouth opened and closed. "Well, if I'm such a jerk, why are my coders and designers still here?"

"Because you not only pay them a buttload of money, but you know they code and design better than you. You can't and don't micromanage them because they know more than you do. But with all the other stuff?" She waved her hand, indicating the rest of the office. "You always know best. *Always.*" She shrugged. "Not gonna lie, that's why I'm not going to help you with this party thing. I adore you and I don't want to have to kill you."

He was silent for a moment, studying her. "I'll triple your rate."

Her mouth dropped. Wow. He was serious. But no. She shook her head. No way.

"Triple, Kate."

Her fingers tapped on the desk as she mulled it over. Good God, that money would go a long way. The party was in two weeks. She couldn't possibly kill him in two weeks. Right?

Decision made, she squared her shoulders and met his gaze. "You have to promise to stay out of my way, Jake. Completely. Out. Of. My. Way."

She laughed at his offended look.

"I am *not* a micromanager, Kate."

She laughed harder. "Uh, that's called denial, buddy. It's technically the first sign of a problem. Ever heard of it?" After a few more moments of laughter—solely on her part—she cleared her throat and tried to pull herself together. Even still, she couldn't quite wipe the smile from her face. "Triple my rate, you stay out of my way, consider the idea of hiring an accounting department, *and* I have final say on all—and I mean *all*—of the party details. Those are my terms, Mr. Alvarez."

He frowned. "What about me?"

"You're the checkbook, my friend." She stuck out her hand. "Deal?"

"Fine," he muttered, taking her hand and shaking. "God, you're a ball-buster."

Pride bloomed in her chest. A ball-buster. No one had ever called her that before. She'd take it!

CHAPTER SEVENTEEN

"For the millionth time, Raven, it's not your fault," Kate groaned, resting her elbows on the bar top. It had been a couple hours since her meeting with Jake, and her headache had yet to subside. She pushed the papers in front of her aside and reached for her glass. The wine was helping. Because good wine helped everything.

As much as she wanted to down the entire bottle, her shift at the pub was starting soon. "Stop feeling guilty, Rave. Last time I checked, *I* was the one who dropped a tray full of glasses and then tried to scoop it all up with my bare hands. Did *you* shove pieces of glass into my hand?"

Raven rolled her eyes as she rearranged a bouquet of bright orange flowers in a glass vase. "I still feel bad."

"Well, don't. I'll live. I promise." She nodded to the vase. "Pretty flowers. From Blake?"

Raven placed an orange tiger lily between two bright orange roses. "I don't know. The note didn't have any to or from info." She gestured to the small envelope on the bar top.

Kate pulled the little card out and frowned.

Don't Speak

"That's a weird note. What does it mean?"

Seemingly satisfied with the arrangement, Raven moved the flowers to the center of the back-bar display and shrugged. "It could be a Gwen Stefani song reference or some asshole telling us to shut our mouths and just look pretty. Who knows and who cares? Either way, we can't have pretty flowers going to waste, can we?"

"True," Kate chuckled. Orange wasn't her favorite color, but the flowers were stunning.

"Nice flowers," a voice interrupted.

Kate turned to her left and smiled. "Hi, Dave. How are you?" she asked as Phone Boy's friend settled onto the barstool next to her.

"I'm good." He nodded to her hand with a grimace. "Looks like I'm doing better than you. Get-well-soon flowers?"

"More like possible-creeper flowers," Raven muttered. "At least they're pretty and match the Irish decor."

"At least there's that." Dave smiled. His gaze dropped to Kate's hand on the bar top. "Your hand all right?"

She waved her bandaged hand in the air. "It looks a lot worse than it is." It was still sore, but she wasn't lying. It was feeling better. Though it probably didn't hurt that she was popping Tylenol like Altoids. Plus, she'd added extra gauze over the stitches for more padding. She wouldn't be able to carry as much on her trays tonight, but that was probably a good thing.

"Please tell me your narcissistic, dumbass, phone-obsessed buddy isn't with you," Raven said with a smirk, placing a coaster in front of Dave.

"Raven!" Kate's jaw dropped.

"What?" Raven winked at Dave. "Were any of the adjectives I used inaccurate?"

"No. Not at all." Dave laughed. "In fact, they're all pretty spot-on."

"See, Kate," Raven snickered. "No need to get your panties in a twist." She turned her attention back to Dave. "What can I get you?"

"Nothing actually," Dave replied. "I'm just waiting to pick up Mel—"

"Hey!" Melody interrupted, leaning against the bar on the other side of Dave. "Give me two minutes and I'll be ready to go." She hesitated and frowned, then met Kate's gaze. "Are you sure you're okay to work tonight? If you don't feel up to it, Dave and I can reschedule our dinner to another—"

"I'm fine," Kate said, her eyes ping-ponging between the two. She bit back a smile as Melody's face lit up. "It'll be fine tonight. Go have fun."

As Melody strode off toward the back office, Dave watched her go. Melody and Dave, huh? They looked good together. Melody was downright stunning with her long blonde hair and overall gorgeousness. Kate had never really noticed it before, but Dave was a good-looking guy. He was probably a few inches shorter than Parker, with dirty blond hair and hazel eyes. There was something familiar about him, but he kind of had that every-man look to him. Not in a bad way, he just had that look.

"Where are you guys going to dinner?"

"Wild Ginger." A sheepish grin graced his face. "I want to make a good impression and figure I can't go wrong there."

Awww, what a sweet guy. "No, you can't."

Dave rose when Melody returned. After helping her into her jacket, he turned. "Kate? I'm sorry that Scott was such a dick."

"Thanks," she replied. Not that she was upset about Scott, but it was the polite thing to say. Frankly, she'd dodged a bullet with that prick.

"Honestly, you're better off without him." Dave nodded to both her and Raven. "Have a good night, ladies."

Once the couple was out of earshot, Raven turned to her, concern back on her face. "Are you really okay, sweetie?"

Kate rolled her eyes. "Yes. I promise. Stop worrying."

Raven placed two drinks on the rail. "I still feel like an asshole."

"Well, stop." She knew the words were pointless. If the tables were turned, she'd be just as worried and mother hen-ish as Raven.

"And then, as if almost amputating your entire left hand wasn't enough—"

"Oh my God, drama queen, it wasn't *that* bad," Kate interjected to no avail.

"To top it all off, there was a dead dog in Parker's backyard! What the hell?"

"Cat," she corrected with a shudder. However, if it hadn't been for the glass-in-hand debacle or Jonesy, who knew where she and Parker would be. Not waking up together two mornings in a row, that's for sure. Another shiver raced through her body. This time it had nothing to do with glass fragments or cats. "It's been an interesting forty-eight hours, Rave, that's for sure."

Kate turned her attention back to the papers in front of her. She could feel Raven's eyes boring into her head, but she didn't dare look up. Raven could read her like a book.

After a few silent moments, she peeked up and tried not to squirm under her friend's gaze. The way Raven's eyes were focused on her with such laser precision was a bit unsettling. Kate made a display of straightening the stack of papers, party supply brochures, and fabric swatches in front of her, making a point to tap them on the bar counter before meeting her friend's eyes. "Yes?"

"There's something different about you."

It took everything Kate had not to cringe. Her shoulders lifted and fell. "I have a new cardigan on."

The noise Raven made could only be described as a gag. "You have a cardigan in every goddamn color, so that's not it." Raven continued to stare, pursing her fire-engine red lips. "You're still uptight, so you obviously haven't gotten laid."

No kidding. Her and Parker's timing sucked. "Analyze me all you want, Rave. Just know that you're being ridiculous. Aside from this cardigan, there's nothing different." She sipped her wine and turned her attention toward stuffing the papers into her tote and placing the bag on the hook beneath the counter.

Moments later, the aromas of garlic, peppers, and something spicy hit her. She glanced up just as Parker sidled up beside her, placing two small plates on the bar in front of her.

"Try these," he said, the heat from his body warming her. "Colcannon cakes with bacon and chorizo, topped with our Guinness onion gravy. One has a sweet potato base, and the other has Golds. Let me know which you like best."

Her mouth watered. Partly from the delicious dishes in front of her and partly from the delicious man next to her. "That won't be a problem, Parker."

She bit into the sweet potato colcannon cake. The spicy chorizo, salty bacon, and sweet, buttery potatoes danced in her mouth. She licked the sauce off her lips and couldn't hold back a moan of satisfaction. Parker's gaze went straight to her mouth and his eyes heated. She bit back a chuckle.

His eyes darted away, and he cleared his throat. "Good?"

She took a bite of the Yukon Gold cake and her eyes closed in appreciation. "You have no idea." She met his gaze and pointed to both dishes with her fork. "You should serve them together. Or at least have both as options because they're both freaking delicious."

His brow furrowed, and he nodded. "That could work."

As she took another bite, his gaze returned to her mouth. It was Kate's turn to clear her throat as she arched a brow at him.

He straightened with a jerk, as if just realizing that not only was he staring, but that they had an audience. "Sorry," he chuckled under his breath, casting Raven a wary glance.

Man, he was cute.

"Holy moly, have you tasted these yet?" she asked Raven, hoping to take her friend's attention off Parker.

"No," Raven replied. Her mission failed as Raven's focus never wavered from the man. The smile her friend flashed him was overly sweet and all teeth. "Parker didn't offer *me* any."

"Well, grab a fork," Kate said at the same time Parker mumbled, "Yeah, sorry about that, Raven."

Holding Raven's inquisitive gaze, Parker stuffed both hands in his jeans pockets and rocked back on his heels. Kate wasn't quite sure, but it looked as if he were biting back a grin.

"Are you still working tonight?" he asked, bringing his attention back to her.

She nodded.

"Jake stopped by earlier and said you're helping him with the launch party." A look of disbelief spread over his face. "How the hell did he manage that?"

She grimaced and gestured to her overflowing tote bag hanging under the bar. "Clearly, I'm not the smartest person on the planet."

His nose wrinkled. "Joking or not, don't sell yourself short, baby. How'd he do it?"

She shrugged. "What can I say? I'm a sucker for good old-fashioned bribery."

Parker's smile had his eyes twinkling. "He doubled your rate?"

"Double? Please." She huffed in mock indignation. "Triple."

"Nice." His laugh warmed her belly. "If you're not feeling up to it, you don't need to work tonight. Blake's coming in later and can cover for you. You should do the party stuff tonight instead of working the pub, especially if you're billing Jake by the hour. Or have another glass of wine and then go home and rest. Your choice though, sweets."

With a wink, he turned and made his way back to the kitchen.

She took a moment to watch him walk away—because how could she not? Turning back to the plates in front of her, she took another bite and sighed. Bacon, chorizo, butter, and potatoes. It was pure, delicious goodness. She didn't even care that there was kale, cabbage, and other nonsense in it. The guy sure knew how to cook.

A flush slowly crept over her face. It wasn't one of embarrassment. No. It was because of Parker. The food he made was divine, but she'd rather take a bite out of him. Then lick it all better. But she'd settle for his food. For now, anyway.

Raven let out a low whistle. "Hooolyyy shit. That's it."

Kate turned her attention back to her friend and took another bite of the sweet potato colcannon cake. Her eyes half closed again. So stinking good. "What's it?"

"You."

"Me what?" She placed her fork down and pushed the plates toward Raven. "You seriously have to try this."

Raven took a bite, her eyes widening with surprise. "Damn. No wonder you're going all orgasmic over there."

Kate's eyes rolled, but she didn't deny it.

"I think I figured it out."

Kate sipped her wine. "I'm not following."

"You. You're different. And I think I know why."

Good God, she really needed to work on her poker face. "Yeah, new cardigan."

Raven ignored her. "You have this different kind of . . . energy . . . around you. Not quite the I-finally-got-laid vibe, but definitely a charged type of energy." Her friend's violet eyes sparked. "Parker finally nutted up and made a move, didn't he?"

The corners of Kate's lips tipped up. A different energy? A charged energy? She liked that. Almost as much as she liked being called a ball-buster. Almost.

She shook her head. "Nope. Parker didn't make a move."

Raven's brow arched in disbelief. "Bullshit."

"It's true, I swear. He didn't." She couldn't help the grin that bloomed on her face. "I did."

After a split second of silence, Raven grinned back at her.

"Part of me wants to ask where the hell my timid, sloth-paced Kate went. But I'm not gonna. Because this Kate?" Raven waved her hand in her direction. "I like this Kate. What's even better is I think *you* like this Kate."

"I do." Pride at—she didn't quite know what—spread through her. "But I'm still me."

"Yeah, but for whatever reason, you're finally allowing yourself to *be* you."

Maybe that was it. Raven hadn't been off the mark when she'd called her pace sloth-like. Kate never made the first move. Ever. Heck, she barely made the second or third moves. But with Parker?

The man made her want. To take and to claim him as hers. Whatever the female version of caveman mentality was, that's how he made her feel.

Raven leaned as close as she could with the bar between them and dropped her voice. "Did you jump him or what?"

Kate's mouth opened, then shut as her face flushed. Her brow furrowed. Had she really jumped him? *Her?*

She couldn't hold back the laugh that escaped. Dang right, she had. "Yeah, basically."

"I take it he was game?"

Heat stole over her entire body as her memory flashed to straddling Parker's lap. His mouth devouring hers, her breasts pressed against his solid chest, his hard cock rocking against her. "Uh, yeah. You could say that." Her grin was starting to hurt. In the best kind of way.

Raven's eyes danced as she clinked her water glass against Kate's wineglass. "Well, it's about damn time, my friend."

It was. It really, really was.

"Do we really have to go to this barbeque?" Parker asked from the kitchen table, peeking over the Sunday paper.

At the island, Kate poured vanilla creamer into her fifth—no, sixth—cup of coffee. It wasn't even ten, and she'd already met with three separate vendors. One week until the big party, and it was officially all caffeine, all the time. "Are you kidding? It's Blake and Raven."

"Yeah, but it's not like we don't see them all the time. You look great, by the way."

She glanced down at her outfit. White tank top with spaghetti straps, a basic white cardigan, and a teal, A-line, flared skirt printed with pineapples, palm trees, and pink surfboards that hit just above her knees. Fall had officially started a couple weeks earlier, but it was a freakishly warm and sunny Seattle weekend, and she was taking full advantage. She was hoping her bright outfit and matching shimmery pink lipstick would give her an added boost of energy. Frankly, she needed every bit of help she could get. "Thanks. But don't change the subject."

"I'm not. You look especially gorgeous, and that ensemble would be wasted at a barbeque with just Blake and Raven."

She rolled her eyes. Charm wasn't going to get him out of going to the party. "They invited other friends too. Blake mentioned that some of your college buddies are in town. Besides, Raven will kill us if we don't show."

"How about we leave early?"

Parker was impossible. Cute, but impossible. "You still want to go see a movie?"

"Sure. See a movie. Make out here. Whatever." He winked, and that sexy grin lit his face.

Kate's body heated. Tempting. So, so tempting.

She'd barely spent any time with Parker this week. The pub had been extra busy, so he hadn't come home until she was asleep. Granted, he crawled into bed with her each night —seeing as she was now sleeping in his bed—so that was a plus. She woke every morning wrapped in his arms, the warmth of his body cocooned around her. But then, before Kate knew what was what, she was up and out of bed before he was awake.

Between her regular bookkeeping clients and the party planning, she was drained. Thank God she'd fleeced Jake into tripling her hourly rate; the mere thought of having to work pub shifts on top of what she was already doing had her whimpering. When she'd remembered to eat, she'd swung into The Spotted Dog for food, but Parker was usually slammed, and she couldn't exactly jump the guy in the middle of the crowded pub. Oh, she'd thought about it. Numerous times.

Thankfully, they had managed to run into each other, alone and during daylight hours, twice that week. Both those times had turned into hot and heavy make-out sessions. Unfortunately, both times had been cut short before actual sex could occur. She'd loved every last second of touching him, tasting him, but their timing truly sucked. Each interruption left her frustrated, borderline desperate, and wanting more. And she knew he felt the same way.

Ditching the barbeque to stay home and make out with Parker was way beyond tempting. But Raven would slaughter her if she didn't show up. Her friend would never admit it, but Kate knew she was nervous about hosting this get-together. Raven had never met this group of Blake's college friends. As delicious as Parker looked in his faded jeans, flip flops, and light green polo that brought out the gold flecks in his eyes, they were going to the dang barbeque. They'd find a way to sneak out early. And then she'd jump him.

"Aside from Raven maiming us if we're a no-show, we also have to go because I kinda sorta said you'd bring a side dish. Or two." She flashed him a giant hope-that's-okay smile.

"Did you now?" He rose from the table, newspaper forgotten, and stepped toward her. "You know, I can always have some pizzas or buckets of fried chicken delivered. Blake wouldn't care."

"Ha-ha." Her dry reply contradicted her racing pulse.

"I'd much rather spend the day with just you." He took the coffee cup from her hand and placed it on the island behind her, stepping close. Her breath caught. "I've missed you this week."

The corners of her mouth ticked up, and her stomach fluttered with excitement, nerves, and a whole lot of want. "Are you making a move on me, Parker Cunningham?"

His eyes twinkled, and he stepped even closer. One arm snaked around her waist and pulled her tight against him, the other traced her jawline with his finger. "Yes, ma'am. How am I doing?"

"Good," she whispered. She leaned into him, her hands

resting on his solid chest. The quickening thump of his heartbeat sent excitement and a blast of heat through her. "You're doing good. Really, really good."

His lips met hers, and time stood still.

Her arms wrapped around him, and her body hummed as their mouths explored. When his lips found her neck, she couldn't help but sigh. She'd missed him too. She'd missed this. Them.

She pressed her body more fully against his, but she couldn't get close enough. All the sexual frustration from the week boiled over. She wanted—no, needed—more. She needed *him*.

On another sigh, she pushed against his shoulders. He pulled away, question and desire swirling in his gaze. Taking his hand, she laced her fingers with his and led him out of the kitchen.

"Come on," she murmured, need humming through her, making those two words tremble.

Parker followed her silently into the living room. She stopped in front of the leather couch and pointed. "Sit." His brow arched in question, the edges of his lips curving up. Heat washed over her face, but her chin lifted. "Please."

He kissed her hand before releasing it and sat, leaning back against the oversized cushion. "As you wish."

Before her nerves could take over, before she could overthink and second-guess herself, before she could chicken out, she did what she wanted.

She took.

She stepped closer to Parker, between his splayed knees, and his eyes darkened to deep emerald green, his jaw tensing. Another fiery bolt of excitement coursed through her. "Take your shirt off," she commanded.

His breath hitched, and then a slow, sexy smile spread over his face. "Yes, ma'am."

Reaching one hand behind his neck, Parker yanked off his polo shirt and tossed it off to the side. It was her turn to suck in a breath.

The man was gorgeous. Broad shoulders and a solid, muscled chest tapered down to ripped abs that she wanted to trace with her fingers. And tongue. Just like she wanted to follow the dusting of chest hair all the way down to where it disappeared into his jeans. Jeans that were barely containing his obvious erection.

Kate let out a breath at the sight. For the life of her, she couldn't tear her gaze away. Didn't *want* to tear her gaze away. Her mouth watered for this man.

"Are you just gonna stare, sweetheart?" Parker's voice was like gravel. The hands that were resting on his thighs fisted.

"No." Her heart threatened to race out of her chest. "You're mine."

His eyes flared, and that sexy smile turned predatory, but he remained still, letting her take the lead. She'd never been a take-charge woman with sex and intimacy, but the fact that he was ceding control thrilled her, emboldened her.

Every sexy and filthy fantasy she'd had about him flashed in her mind. And she wanted to make every single one a reality. Because she knew, down to the depths of her soul, that she was safe with him. She trusted this man. Completely.

With that realization, she leaned closer and placed her hands on his shoulders. The muscles in his neck tensed. His hands settled onto her hips. Not pulling, not pushing. Just holding. She kept her eyes locked with his and, as if in slow motion, she straddled him, pressing her body flush against his and sliding down until her core pressed against his hard length. She rocked her hips against his and felt each hard inch of his straining cock. "Parker," she whispered. Her head fell back and she couldn't hold in the moan of pure satisfaction. "You feel so good."

It was as if those whispered words set Parker on fire. His hands twisted in her hair and his lips fused to hers, their tongues tangling and dancing. Then his hands were everywhere. Touching. Squeezing. Pinching. Caressing.

"More," she breathed out. She raised her arms as he made quick work of her cardigan, tank top, and bra.

"You're so damn beautiful, Kate," Parker said, his voice reverent, his hungry gaze and hands exploring the newly exposed skin.

Tingles raced through her body as his tongue joined his hands in teasing her breasts. A moan escaped her lips as his fingers pinched her nipples and his mouth soothed and suckled.

He slipped his hands under her skirt, cupping and squeezing her backside, pressing her even closer to him. She rocked harder against him, but it wasn't enough.

She needed him closer. She wanted all of him, wanted to feel every hard inch of his length inside her. Her breath came in pants as she pulled slightly away and reached for the button on his jeans. His hand stilled hers.

"Kate." He was equally out of breath, but he waited until she met his gaze. "Are you sure?"

"Yes." She held his gaze, her hands cupping and stroking him over his jeans. She didn't quite recognize who this new, bold woman was, but when Parker's breath hissed out and his cock twitched under her hands, a smile crept over her lips. *She* was this new, bold woman. And she loved it. "I need you so much. I want to feel you inside me."

With a growl, he framed her face in his hands and kissed her. Deep and demanding, yet still soft and gentle. He pulled away and motioned to the stairs with his head. "Condoms are upstairs."

She shook her head. "I'm on the pill and I just had a checkup. I'm good. You?" Another low growl. He nodded, the muscles in his neck tensing anew. "I don't want anything between us, Parker." Her hands moved back to his jeans, undoing the single button and gently sliding the zipper down. As an adult, even with the pill, she'd never had sex without a condom. Ever. But with Parker, she wanted to feel him inside her without barriers. She wasn't quite sure why, but she needed this. Needed him. Bare. Now. "I want to feel all of you."

His eyes darkened. Under her hand, his straining cock hardened further, and she gave him a gentle squeeze. "Kate, sweetheart, you may actually kill me."

She smiled and rose slightly off his lap. She patted his hips, and he lifted up. In one move, she tugged his jeans and boxer briefs down.

"Oh, but what a way to die, right?" She grinned, her gaze never leaving his. Her hand encircled his cock, and she began to stroke, loving how he was both rock-hard and smooth, how his breath left him in a hiss with every caress.

"You have no idea." His hands snaked into her hair and he pulled her close, his kisses urgent and hot, borderline desperate. "Your skin tastes so good," he growled against her neck, her shoulder, the tops of her breasts. "I want to taste every inch of you, lick every fucking inch of you, baby. Let me taste your sweet pussy; let me eat you until you're screaming."

A shiver rocked her body at his words. Heat and arousal flooded between her thighs at the mere thought of his mouth on her. "God, yes," she moaned, panting. "But later." Bracing a hand on his shoulder, she rose to her knees. Gently grasping him with her other hand, she rubbed the head of his cock against her wet folds.

"Holy shit," he groaned, his eyes half closing. "You're so wet, baby." His hands clamped down on her waist and he rocked his hips toward her. "Take what you need."

She understood his desperation; she felt the exact same way. Guiding him to her entrance, she leaned slightly away, wanting to see his face as she lowered herself onto him.

Passion. Reverence. And outright lust.

She trembled as he filled her, stretched her. And her heart tumbled.

"Holy shit, Kate," he moaned, and his mouth found hers again in a kiss that curled her toes. "Ride me, baby."

He caressed her body, and his mouth brought unending pleasure as she rode him hard. He filled her so completely it took her breath away. Each rock of her body against his, each filthy word he growled in her ear, brought her closer to the edge.

Parker gripped her hips and held her tight against him, thrusting deep. Over and over, he slammed into her until she cried out, rocketing over the edge. Her body was still trembling when he came within her, his cry of release filling the room until their ragged breaths and racing hearts were the only sounds.

She was mush. A tingling mass of mushy mush. She sat astride Parker with her head tucked against his shoulder and his semi-hard cock still buried deep within her. His fingers traced softly up and down the notches of her spine, leaving goosebumps in their wake.

Holy. Moly.

She'd just had sex with Parker. Magnificent sex. The best sex of her freaking life.

She knew she should probably be thinking of something deeper, something more profound. Maybe about the future or what this step meant for them. But all she could think of was how she wanted to do it again. And in what positions.

The memory of Parker's words—of him practically begging to lick every inch of her; of the gruff, crazy sexy declarations he'd made about what he wanted to do to her—

had her tingling anew. No one had ever spoken to her that way, had ever wanted her in that way.

The man had just blown her mind. He'd awakened something in her, a boldness she'd never known she had, and she wanted more.

A chuckle escaped her as she considered what a sight they must be. Their arms were wrapped around each other, and her skirt was bunched around her waist. She was topless, straddling this gorgeous man with his pants shoved down to his knees. He was still inside her, the evidence of their orgasms wet between them, and she felt freaking marvelous.

Granted, it was equal parts satisfying and terrifying, but she was determined to focus on the satisfying part. Because she'd never felt this free. This at ease. Ever.

"Something funny?" Parker asked, the deep rumble of his voice soothing.

She lifted her head off his shoulder and grinned when he met her gaze. "When you make a move, you really make a move, don't you?"

He chuckled and kissed her. A long, slow, mind-numbing kiss. He hardened, pressing against her insides, and she rocked against him. God, this man was amazing.

"I'd say the move-making went both ways." He dropped another kiss on the tip of her nose. "Who knew you'd be so bossy?"

She winced, and her hips stilled, her face flushing, embarrassed that the new, bold woman she'd become may have been a bit too much. "I'm sorry. I don't know what got into me."

"Kate, look at me." Her gaze flew to his at the serious tone. "You don't ever need to apologize to me. You want to be bossy, I'm game. You want me to take charge, I'm game. I don't ever want you to be embarrassed about anything we do. I don't ever want you to be embarrassed about asking me

—or telling me—to do anything. Trust me when I say that I . . ." He dropped a kiss to her lips as his hands went to her hips, holding her tight and thrusting up. "Am." Another kiss, another thrust. "Game. For anything. For everything." His lips found the side of her neck, and he guided her hips with his hands, rocking her harder and faster. "And for the record, Bossy Kate is so fucking sexy. Don't get shy on me now, baby."

Oh, this man.

Kate moaned, sensation after sensation coursing through her. He trailed kisses down to her breasts, and she clutched his head to her as he suckled, her hips canting hungrily against his once more.

"Damn it," he murmured, his hands stilling her movements. "Hang on, baby."

"What?"

The doorbell chimed.

She frowned, her breath coming in pants. "Did I miss the first ring?"

He chuckled. "I think we both missed the first one. This is like the third or fourth ring, I think."

Still sitting atop him, she spotted her tank top on the couch and pulled it on, her movements slow and dazed. "You realize we have the worst timing, right?"

"I don't know about that." He ran a hand up her leg to her bottom and squeezed. "Our timing today wasn't too shabby."

She framed his face in her hands, and it was her turn to drop a kiss to his lips. His hand found the back of her head, holding her close.

The doorbell rang again.

"You stay," she said. She slowly rose off his lap and groaned. As he pulled out of her, each delectable inch of him set her nerves on fire. What she wouldn't give to ignore the door, take him for another ride, and finish round two. She nodded to his cock, hard and standing at attention, and grinned. "It's probably a good idea that I get the door so you can put that away."

Heart still racing, she used her cardigan to quickly clean herself, then balled it up and tossed it to Parker so he could do the same. She readjusted her tank top and skirt. She'd lost her bra and panties somewhere along the line. Unfortunately, her tank top did nothing to hide her appreciation of Parker. She did a quick finger comb of her hair and repositioned the strands to cover her very happy nipples. It would have to do.

Prepared to send the persistent solicitor on their way, she pulled open the front door. It took her a split second to recognize the not-a-solicitor on the porch. Shock had her eyes going wide and her mind going blank.

"Oh, oh my God. Carmen," she stuttered. "Hi! How are you?"

The other woman's jet-black hair fell nearly to her waist, and though it had been a few years since Kate had last seen her in person, her tan skin was still flawless. Dang those Filipino genes.

"Hey, Kate!" Carmen's dark brown eyes reflected her surprise. "What are you doing here?"

Kate stepped out onto the porch and hugged her old friend. "How are you? What are *you* doing here?" She shook her head, laughing. Holy crap. Of all the people to be standing on Parker's porch. "Sorry. What am I saying? Come in, please. Your brother's inside."

And hopefully fully clothed by now.

She inwardly winced. Dang. They really did have the worst timing.

CHAPTER NINETEEN

Parker nearly died. When he heard his sister's voice, he came close to breaking his neck scrambling off the damn couch. He yanked up his pants and tossed on his shirt in record time, then came close to death again when he tripped diving for Kate's bra hanging off the back of the recliner.

After tucking the bra and Kate's balled-up sweater behind a couch cushion, he flew into the entryway toward his sister as Kate closed the front door behind them. "Holy shit, Carm! What the hell are you doing here?" He didn't wait for Carmen to roll her suitcase into the living room before sweeping her into a hug.

When her feet hit the floor, he turned her so that her back was to the living room. The very disheveled, pillows-scattered, obviously-life-altering-sex-just-occurred-here living room.

Carmen grinned up at him. "What? Can't I visit my little brother?"

A quick scan showed that Kate had disappeared but had found and taken her castaway clothes with her. He focused back on his sister and steered her toward the kitchen, willing his heartbeat to return to normal. "Little brother?" He patted her on the head. "Looks like you've been skipping those vitamins. You still claiming five-two, shorty?"

She lifted her foot, showing off gravity-defying heels. "Shorty? These bad boys have me up to five-seven."

"Yeah, but you're still barely five-two," he chuckled. "You should meet Raven. The two of you would get along on footwear alone. Seriously though, what are you doing here?"

She ran her hand over the quartz countertop and studied the kitchen. "This place looks great. The pictures you sent don't do it justice."

He crossed his arms over his chest. Deflection. He may not see his sister as much as he'd like, but they spoke often. And he knew her. Something was up. "Carmen?"

She continued her perusal of his kitchen. "Where'd Kate go?"

Her voice was pitched too high, her tone too casual. Something was definitely up. "Carmen?"

She turned to him, leaning against the island, her smile in place, her face the picture of innocence. "What? I was in the neighborhood."

"Uh, we talked on the phone yesterday, and you didn't mention you'd be in town." He pulled out the stool next to her at the island and sat, his eyes narrowing as he recalled their earlier conversation. "In fact, you lied to me and said you had to go because 'the natives were getting restless' and that it was 'so hot you were sure they'd start a riot.'"

"I didn't lie." A smug smile grew on her face. "When I was talking to you, I was in LA. I happened to be in line for coffee, and yes, the natives were getting restless because it was my turn to order. It's also a fact that it was fucking hotter than bejesus and everyone was grumpy. So again, I didn't lie. Have I taught you nothing about semantics?"

He slung an arm around her slim shoulders and hugged her again. Damn, he'd missed his sister. They spoke often, but it had been about nine months since they'd last seen each other face to face, and that was only because he'd flown to San Francisco to meet up with her. As for the last time she had been in Seattle? Years.

After he'd finalized his divorce from Courtney almost three years ago, he'd bought the house, and Carmen had stayed with him for a few months as she'd been going through her own marriage separation and subsequent divorce.

He and Carmen were a crazy pair for sure. With their parents coming up on their forty-fifth wedding anniversary, it must kill them to know that their kids sucked at marriage. He was closing in on forty and had one divorce under his belt, while Carmen, just eleven months his senior, had three. Three! If someone checked the dictionary for "sucks at marriage," there'd be a picture of the Cunningham kids.

He eyed his sister, suspicion worming in his mind. She was up to something. "You were in LA yesterday, and now just happen to be in the neighborhood?" He didn't buy it. No way. Carmen wasn't the type to drop in unannounced. Ever. She always had a plan. Always.

She shrugged. "I do consider anywhere on the continental US to be 'in the neighborhood.'"

He nodded, conceding her point.

Around the time of her last divorce, Carmen had been promoted to President of Development and Operations at Clean Water Campaign, their family's non-profit. While his sister could have managed the position and overseen CWC's multiple international locations from Seattle, she'd chosen to do the exact opposite.

Before the ink dried on her divorce paperwork, Carmen had hightailed it out of there. She went from desk jockey to full-on boots on the ground. As a result, she was never in one location for more than a few months. She moved around so much that she didn't even have a home base. His house was as close as she came to a permanent US address. There was nothing new about his sister jet-setting all over the world, but in the years she'd been gone, not once had she come back to Seattle. So yeah, something felt . . . off.

"Seriously. What's up?"

The laughter in his sister's dark brown eyes dimmed. He would have missed it if he didn't know her so well. "Everything's fine, worrywart. I was in LA and met up with Mom and Dad."

He frowned. "Wait. Mom and Dad are in LA? I'm supposed to have dinner with them tomorrow night."

She nodded. "They fly back to Seattle tomorrow morning, then head down to Rio next week."

Apparently, he was the boring non-globetrotter of the family.

"Anyway, I met up with them yesterday," Carmen continued. "The International Clean Water Symposium is down in Vegas next month and I'm officially the keynote."

"Wow, congratulations! That's impressive." And not at all surprising. His sister had always excelled at everything. Well . . . there were those three marriages. So *almost* everything.

"Thanks. I figured I'd bum around here until the conference. God knows I don't want to be in LA for that long." She shuddered. "Or Vegas, for that matter."

"Bum around? You?" Right. The woman was a bona fide workaholic. She was even worse than Jake, and that said a lot. At least Jake came up for air every few days. Not Carmen.

"Okay, fine. I've scheduled some meetings here with investors and a couple board members. I also have some potential fundraising meetings and other things lined up."

"Now that's more like the Carmen I know. Detailed and vague, all at the same time." He winked.

"Hey," Kate said, entering the kitchen and stopping at the opposite side of the island. "It's so good to see you again. It's been a long time."

"It's good seeing you too, Kate." Carmen's eyes darted between him and Kate, then settled on Kate. "I was wondering where you ran off to."

Parker couldn't help but smile as a flush stole across Kate's face. Damn, his girl was stunning. Yeah. That's right. *His* girl. Was that a bit Neanderthal and high school? Sure. Did he give two shits? Nope.

"Oh, I just had to fix my makeup and stuff." Kate cleared her throat. "Do you have plans right now? We were about to head over to Blake's for a barbeque. I'm sure everyone would love to see you."

"That sounds great," Carmen replied, tilting her head to the side as she studied Kate.

Kate's flush deepened, her brow knitting in confusion. "What?"

"Oh, nothing." Carmen flashed another innocent smile and turned her attention to Parker. "It's okay that I stay here, right? My old room?"

"Uh . . . no, actually. Kate's in that room." Technically, Kate's *things* were in that room, seeing as they'd been mostly sleeping together in his room. Heat rushed over his face, and he cleared his throat. "You can take the room at the end of the hall." Damn it. Of course he had to go and blush in front of his sister. She was going to bust his balls forever for this.

Her brows rose in surprise, her eyes twinkling. "Oh, I didn't realize Kate was living here."

"She is," he said at the same time Kate said, "I can move."

"Really, Carmen," Kate rushed on, her eyes darting

between him and his sister. "You can totally have that room if you want."

Carmen straightened, elbowing Parker on her way toward Kate. "Don't be ridiculous. The end of the hall is fine." She linked arms with her. "That's a great color lipstick. Not really long-wearing though, huh?"

Kate's eyes narrowed in wary confusion. "Um, I guess." She nodded her head toward the living room. "You know what? I'll go take your bag upstairs while you and Park catch up."

Carmen shook her head. "Oh no. Don't worry about it. Parker can get it later."

But Kate had already untwined her arm from Carmen's and was halfway out of the kitchen. "It's not a problem at all," she called over her shoulder.

Parker crossed his arms and pinned his sister with a glare. "What are you doing?"

"So." She grinned, wagging her brows. "You and Kate, huh?"

He wasn't going to confirm or deny. "Zip it, Carm."

She walked back to him and hopped onto the stool next to him. "I'm guessing this is a relatively new thing with the two of you?"

His lips stayed sealed. Never give your sibling ammunition. Ever.

She studied him for a moment, and years of not squirming under her scrutiny came into play. "Stop already, brat," he grumbled.

Her eyes widened. "Oh, so this is like a super-duper new thing."

It wasn't a question. His eyes rolled, and it took all his power to bite back a smile. It was like they were teenagers again. "Seriously, Carm. Stop."

"Fine. It's a new thing. I get it. But aren't you even a tiny bit curious how I figured it out?"

He shook his head. "I haven't said a thing."

She continued as if he hadn't spoken. What did it say about him that all the women in his life disregarded what he said whenever it suited them? "It's because I'm at the end of the hall."

He glared at her. "What?"

"If this wasn't new, Kate would already be moved into your room, and I could have my usual room. But I can't because she's there. Or at least her stuff is. Ergo, this is a brand spanking new thing. For the record, I'm more than happy to be at the end of the hall." She shuddered. "I don't even want to chance hearing something that would trauma-tize me for life."

"Oh my God," he groaned. Parker snagged her around the neck and noogied her head. "Stop already. And ease up on Kate."

She laughed and pinched his stomach, twisting like only an older sister could, until he yelped and released her. "I've missed you, Park."

They both stood and made their way to the stairs. His phone dinged, and he fished it out of his pocket. He cringed when he pulled up a text from Blake asking where the hell he was and what he was bringing.

"Damn," he muttered. "We were supposed to bring a side dish to Blake's, but we, uh . . . got sidetracked." He glanced at his sister and smiled. "We'll just bring you instead. I suppose you'll do."

Carmen's brows rose and fell in another exaggerated wiggle. "You and Kate got sidetracked, eh? Is that what you crazy kids are calling it these days?"

He groaned. "Christ, you've been here less than thirty

minutes and I already have to tell you to butt out? That's like a new record for you."

She chuckled. "I didn't say anything."

"Right." He playfully shoved her toward the stairs. "Get ready. We're leaving in ten minutes."

She paused on the stairs, turning back to him, that oh-so-innocent smile back on her lips. "By the way, you still have lipstick on your neck, little brother."

He shooed her away. When she disappeared up the stairs, he peeked at his reflection in the hallway mirror. Sure enough, remnants of Kate's sparkly pink lipstick trailed up the side of his neck. He grinned. Fuck yeah. And didn't bother wiping the lipstick off.

CHAPTER TWENTY

Kate stepped out onto Blake and Raven's massive patio and snagged the glass of white wine Jake held out for her. A wide grin broke across his face as he moved toward Parker and Carmen behind her. "I assume this gorgeous woman is why you two yahoos are late?"

Carmen let out a low whistle and made a production of eyeing Jake up and down. "Well, holy shit. Look at you, Jake Alvarez."

"Darlin'," Jake drawled, holding his arms open for a hug, "I didn't think it was possible to improve on perfection. But there you are."

"Still the handsome charmer, I see." Carmen laughed and stepped into his arms as both Kate and Parker groaned.

"Well, hot daaamn!" Blake whooped as he sprang from his seat and crossed the patio. He swooped Carmen up in his arms and swung her in a circle. "You don't call? You don't write? What the fuck? I thought you loved me best?!"

Carmen laughed as Blake set her back down. "Still a smartass." She slapped him playfully on the cheek. "Good to see some things don't change, cutie."

"Who the fuck is that?" Raven hissed in Kate's ear.

Kate choked on her drink. She looked at Raven, who was shooting daggers at Blake and Carmen. In all their years as friends, she couldn't remember a single time her best friend had been jealous of anyone. Ever.

"Wow," Kate chuckled. "Claws back in, my friend. That's Carmen."

"Who the fuck is *Carmen*?"

Kate put her arm around Raven and squeezed. Oh, her sweet, sweet jealous friend. "Carmen. As in Parker's sister, Carmen."

"Uh, no. That's not Parker's sister. He's white and that chick's Asian."

"Yup, and she has been since birth." Kate laughed. "You didn't know what Carmen looks like? That she was adopted?"

"No." Raven frowned. "Whenever anyone talks about Carmen, it's just 'Carmen.' Not 'adopted sister' or 'adopted Asian sister.'" Raven's frown grew, and she let out a sigh that could only be described as grouchy. The fight was leaving her friend. "Apparently, it's because you guys aren't a bunch of dicks. Apparently, *I'm* the dick because I missed the connection. I'm sure I must have seen a picture of her at some point but just figured she was a girlfriend or something." Raven leaned closer. "But if you're bullshitting me and she's like Blake's long-lost lover or something, then—"

"Babe," Blake called out. "Come and meet my favorite cousin."

Kate arched a brow. "Told ya." She elbowed her friend. "Go. She's really nice. I promise."

As Raven made her way to Blake and Carmen, Kate bit back a chuckle. Raven had her bartender smile plastered on her face but was muttering impressive curse word combinations under her breath.

"What was that about?" Parker snagged her hand and pulled her toward a small couch. It didn't escape her notice that this particular couch was at the far end of the patio, away from everyone else.

She settled onto the couch next to him, her crossed legs leaning against his thigh. They sat close, but it was casual enough that if anyone was looking at them, they wouldn't think anything of it. After all, it *was* a small couch.

"Oh, Raven's just having a little bout of insecurity."

His jaw dropped. "Raven?"

"I know, right?" she replied with a chuckle of disbelief.

"Because of Carmen?"

She nodded, then her chuckle turned into a laugh at the bewildered confusion on Parker's handsome face. "Raven is confident. We both know that. But Carmen? She can intimidate the best of them."

The disbelief intensified. "My sister?"

Yet another nod. "Raven didn't know that Carmen's Filipino, so she wasn't exactly prepared for Blake to fawn over another woman. Besides, not only is Carmen brilliant, but she's probably the nicest person I've ever met."

"Uh, no," he snorted, and clinked his bottle of beer to her glass of wine. "If you asked any of her business associates to describe her, trust me when I say 'nice' isn't the word they'd use in conjunction with Carmen Cunningham. Besides, the 'nicest person' honor definitely goes to you, sweetheart."

She rolled her eyes but savored the warmth his compliment brought. "To top it all off, your sister is freaking flawless. The woman looks exactly the same as she did in college. Better, even."

He shrugged. "What can I say? I got the amazing immune system, and she got the amazing genetics."

"I don't know." Her face flushed as memories of their earlier activities flashed in her mind. She nudged him with her shoulder and turned her attention to their group of friends. "You're not too hard on the eyes yourself, Cunningham."

After a moment, she realized Parker hadn't replied. She glanced over at him and her heart stopped at the intensity and fire in his gaze.

"What I would give to be alone with you right now," he murmured.

Her stomach flipped. If they were alone, she would jump him. Totally throw herself at him, rip off her clothes, and beg him to have his way with her. Another wave of heat crept over her body and settled between her thighs. What this man did to her . . .

She let out an unsteady breath and fanned herself. She couldn't help it. "You are too much, Parker Cunningham."

He chuckled and took a pull of his beer, his gaze never leaving hers. "Right back at you, baby."

Good lord. At this rate, they'd be having sex in front of everyone in no time. She cleared her throat. "So, I don't think we'll be able to sneak out of here early with your sister and all."

His head dipped in agreement. "Yeah. We're here for the long haul." His free hand settled on her knee, his fingers tracing little circles that turned her insides molten. "I know this probably isn't the time or place for this conversation, but whatever it is that's going on with us, Kate. This?" He gestured between the two of them with his beer bottle. "I like this. I like us."

Her chest squeezed, and she couldn't help the smile that grew. "Me too." She nodded in the direction of their friends. "What about them?"

"Them?" He shrugged. "I love them all, some more than others. But this has nothing to do with them. They're just noise. It's me and you. That's all that matters."

There were stomach flutters. And then there was this. "Me and you."

The corner of his lips tilted up. "I want to see where this goes. Because I like you, Kate. A lot."

Oh, this man. "I like you too, Park. A lot."

His hand found hers, and he brought her fingers to his lips before resting his hand back on her knee, their fingers still intertwined. "We can take this as fast or as slow as you want." He nodded to their friends. "As far as they're concerned, if you want to keep this between us, I'm cool with that." He flashed her that lopsided grin she loved so much. "But if you want me to lay one on you right now, I'd be cool with that too. Whatever you're comfortable with."

She laughed. He really was something. "Thanks, Park. That means a lot."

"Hey, chef," Jake called. "You're needed at the grill!"

"Yeah, yeah," he called back, and took another swig of his beer. "I believe there's ribeyes, T-bones, and porterhouses. Any preference?"

Her lips pursed. "Aren't T-bones porterhouses?"

"Ah, my little carnivore," he replied, his green eyes sparkling. "Porterhouses are T-bones, but a T-bone isn't a porterhouse. Want to know why?"

"No, not really. But this foodie-geeking-out thing you're doing right now is adorable." She chuckled and squeezed his hand when his face scrunched. "And kinda hot. Surprise me on the steak. As long as it's not chicken with a side salad and no dressing, I'm good."

He looked at her in question.

"A story for a different day." She laughed. "It all sounds good. Surprise me."

CHAPTER TWENTY-ONE

"So, you and Kate, huh?"

Parker grunted in response, his body tensing at the impact of his fists against the punching mitts his cousin held. Blake circled, repositioned himself, lifted his chin, and Parker let another combo fly. Again and again they went, circling left, circling right, until his arms were jelly.

Kate. He should still be in bed snuggled up with her instead of at the boxing gym with his damn cousin. Morning sex with Kate was his new favorite thing. He'd been hoping it would lead to shower sex, which he was certain would become his second new favorite thing, but his freaking cousin and his freaking unending text messages.

Blake: *Where are you?*

Blake: *Let's go!*

Blake: *Any day now, buttercup.*

Blake: *If you're not here in five minutes, I'm sending Raven after your ass.*

It was his cousin's last text—and Kate's solemn yet snickering, "You know Raven will actually show up here, right?"—that finally got him out of bed.

So, there he was. Twenty minutes late to their standing Monday morning sparring session at the gym. He was surrounded by shirtless dudes. Sweat and bleach permeated the air. Yeah. He'd rather be with Kate, but that didn't mean his cousin had to know that.

"I don't know what you're talking about," Parker replied, using his teeth to unfasten the Velcro closure on his right glove. "Done?"

Blake nodded and wiped the sweat from his brow with his forearm. "Bullshit. You know exactly what I'm talking about. The two of you were cuddled up like two little high school kids at the barbeque yesterday."

Removing his other glove, Parker grabbed his towel and mopped the sweat from his face and chest. "That makes zero sense."

Blake's brow arched as he put the mitts in his gym bag. "High school kids, dumbass, think they're being sneaky, but they're not."

"Dude," Parker cleared his throat, not knowing how to proceed. Blake was his cousin and best friend. But Kate was his . . . Kate. "I'm not admitting anything to you. This is all in Kate's court. What she wants other people to know about us is up to her."

"Ahhh, so the two of you are an 'us' now?" Blake wagged his eyebrows.

Parker gave up and shook his head, a grin spreading over his face. "You know we are."

Blake golf clapped, and a smirk stretched across his face. "About. Fucking. Time."

"Fuck off," he chuckled, the grin still on his face. "It's new, so don't fucking say anything, okay? For real. It's up to her on what she wants other people to know." He glared at his cousin, his early humor seeping away, and hints of trepidation rumbled low in his gut. "I mean, hell, this could all go sideways. You know I'm not the best bet."

Blake crossed his arms over his chest, his eyes narrowing. "Not the best bet? What the fuck are you talking ab—"

"Parky!" a shrill voice interrupted.

"Damn," Parker muttered at the same time Blake groaned, "Kill me fucking now."

Courtney wedged herself between the two men. Dressed like a walking Lululemon ad, she completely ignored Blake and threw her arms around Parker's waist.

Parker froze, didn't move a muscle, didn't hug her back. Nothing. But that didn't deter Courtney from squeezing him tighter. "It's so funny that I ran into you here! What a coincidence!"

"Yeah," Blake muttered behind her. "Such a fucking coincidence since we're here every Monday at the same damn time and have been for nearly a fucking year."

Blake wasn't lying. While Parker and Jake had been regular members of the boxing gym for the past five-plus years, his cousin had finally joined about a year ago. Raven had gotten sucked into some crazy shit last fall, and though it had all eventually gotten resolved, Blake had needed an outlet for all the anger and helpless frustration that remained. Over the past year, they'd only missed a handful of Monday sparring sessions—including their hungover Monday a couple weeks prior. So yeah, it was no secret to anyone how he and Blake spent their Monday mornings. And it was most definitely not a coincidence.

Courtney's cloyingly sweet perfume was making him nauseous. He'd spent the last hour around sweaty guys and their body odor, so that said a lot. "Let go of me," Parker said, not bothering to hide his annoyance.

"Oh," she giggled. She slowly unwrapped her arms, running her hand over his bare stomach in the process.

"Sorry, Parky. It's just so good to see you." Her eyes crawled over his chest and he barely suppressed a shudder. *Blake was right. Kill me now.* "Your form is looking great. We should get together sometime and . . . spar."

Blake gagged. Audibly gagged. And that's all it took for Parker to lose his shit.

He laughed. Full-on belly laughed. He couldn't help it; the entire situation was ridiculous. He wasn't sure what Courtney was up to, but he wanted no part of it. He could hold on to the annoyance, but as awful as it sounded, he hadn't cared enough when they were married, so why the hell would he care now?

Courtney looked at him, confusion evident on her face. Her arms crossed over her chest, and she shifted on her feet. And Blake still looked like he was going to puke, which set off another round of laughter.

When Parker finally got his amusement under control, he cleared his throat, trying to pull himself together. "Look, Courtney. This," he waved a hand between them, "is not happening. I don't know what your angle is, but it's not happening. I'm seeing someone and—"

"And it's not fucking you," Blake interjected as she shot a scowl his way.

"We have to get going." Parker gathered up his gym bag and towel, stepping away from his ex-wife. "Good luck finding a, uh, sparring partner."

He and Blake hustled away from her. Neither looked back, but Parker was certain she was shooting daggers his way.

"Seriously, man, I almost puked in there," Blake exclaimed once the gym door closed behind them. Parker laughed when another shudder ran through his cousin. "What the fuck was that?"

"No clue," Parker chuckled, turning toward his car and

speaking over his shoulder, "but if that woman doesn't get the hint soon, I'm going to borrow your fiancée and have her set Courtney straight."

"You do that. I'm sure Raven would be more than happy to assist. I'll see you later at the pub. And Parker?" He turned back at the concern in his cousin's voice. "That shit you said earlier about not being the best bet? Don't think I forgot about that. Don't let what happened with that evil woman fuck with your head. You're a dumbass, sure. But you're a damn good bet."

Parker nodded and sent a salute to his cousin. Courtney's shrill voice echoed in his ears. Maybe Blake was right.

But maybe not.

Parker looked out at The Spotted Dog staff gathered for their not-quite-mandatory-but-show-up-if-you-want-a-say-in-your-schedule monthly-ish meeting. "Hey, gang," he called out. "Can I have your attention, please?"

The soft murmur of conversations quieted. Scheduling, staffing, and other business issues were discussed over brunch every fourth Monday.

Parker wasn't an idiot. Getting people to come in for a team meeting—though paid, it *was* on everyone's day off—sucked. However, free food and free Bloody Marys, Irish coffees, and mimosas were a good incentive and almost always brought the troops in.

"Now, you guys may or may not recognize this degenerate," Parker teased as he nodded to Jake, who rose to stand next to him. "But he has an announcement that I think you'll all find of interest."

"Morning, everyone," Jake said. "I know I've been a little silent on the silent partner front, but as most of you all know since my crew upstairs is down here a lot—"

"Drinking away their sorrows," Blake cut in.

Jake paused, then shrugged. "Basically. We've been working ourselves to death because we're set to release the newest and biggest world update for our Square Peg app next week. We just overtook both Minecraft and Roblox in subscribers, so this is a pretty big deal for our little operation."

The group broke out into hoots and applause. Parker laughed and slapped his buddy on the back when Jake's grin turned aw-shucks-ish.

"Thanks, guys," Jake continued. "Our new world features an Old West-style saloon."

"As one does," Blake cut in again.

Jake turned to Blake. "You running this or me?"

Blake grinned. "By all means," he said, and motioned for Jake to continue.

"As you all know, users can customize their pegs however they want. In this new world, the main hangout and where you can buy new skins and accessories is a saloon called, naturally, The Spotted Dog."

Parker had to chuckle. Jake's damn eyes were twinkling with excitement.

"Ahhh, that's why Ty and Dana have been down here sketching the place," Ali said, referring to two of Jake's graphic designers.

Jake nodded. "The Spotted Dog in Square Peg is going to basically look exactly like this place. But, of course, pixelated and more Wild West-ish than Irish. The game will also have fixed characters inside the saloon, and with all your permissions, we'd like to base these characters on all of you."

A murmur of excitement zinged through the group.

Parker slapped Jake on the back again and gave him an I-told-you-so look. Jake had been so nervous about asking the staff to be characters in the game and hadn't believed Parker when he'd said he was sure the staff would go for it.

"However," Parker said over the din, "if you don't want to be a part of it, it's not a problem. It's just something Jake thought would be fun." He turned to Jake. "I get to be in it too, right?"

"Fuck yeah, brother," Jake laughed, returning the back slap. "What's the point in owning a mobile game company if you can't feature all your friends in the most popular games?" Jake turned back to the gang. "Ty and Dana have sketches of everyone already, and they'll be here in about half an hour to meet with everyone to get your formal approvals. I'd prefer the faces to look like you—well, if you were pixilated—but it's completely your choice. You can also pick what type of character you want to be. They'll show you what new skins and accessories we have. Like I said, it's all very Wild West."

"I'm totally going to be a saloon girl," Melody said with a laugh. "Raven, you should totally be the saloon madam, but with a kickass bullet bandolier!"

Parker raised his hand to quiet the troops. "Because Jake can't keep an assistant for more than a week, he somehow convinced Kate to help plan the launch party." He glared at Jake. "You know, with all that free time Kate has between working here and all her other business clients."

Jake's hands rose in innocence as he sent a wink Kate's way. "Hey, she agreed. I only had to bribe her a little."

Parker's heart stuttered when Kate rose and joined him and Jake in front of the group. As her arm brushed his, he had to remind himself to not take her hand, to play it cool. When the scent of her fruity shampoo wafted over him, it took all his willpower to not bury his face in her hair. Like he had this morning when he'd returned from the gym and found her in the kitchen. She'd been wearing his T-shirt and nothing else. It had taken him less than five seconds to boost her onto the kitchen counter and get them both naked. He'd been so deep inside her, and she was so tight and—

Holy fucking shit, STOP!

He had to shut down this line of thinking fast. Immediately. Because springing a boner in front of the entire staff would be awkward, to say the least. His mind whirled with baseball stats, menus, Emeril freaking Lagasse—*anything* except the woman next to him.

"Jake needed a venue for the release party, and I figured that it would be fitting to have the party here," Kate announced. "I also thought it would be fun if everyone dressed up like your characters in the game."

Parker laughed as the staff whooped in excitement. Yup, focusing on the staff was a good way of cooling his errant thoughts. He really needed to pull himself together. "The party is going to be this Saturday night. We're closing the pub for the party, and we'll need all hands on deck. It'll be a time crunch, but Kate's in charge of getting everyone costumed for the party. Like Jake said, Ty and Dana will be here in about half an hour. Once they show you the skins and accessories, make your decision ASAP so they can coordinate your costume with Kate."

He scanned the grinning faces before him. "That's it for now, folks," he said, and gestured toward the kitchen. "Everything's on the stove, so grab some food and drinks and then we'll talk schedules and goals."

Two hours later, all the staff had gone, but the buzz of excitement still lingered in the pub. Blake and Raven pushed paper at the bar while Kate and Jake finalized the costumes and party details in the back office.

As Parker wiped down tables, he couldn't help but smile.

Kate really was amazing. How she handled everything, he hadn't a clue. Between her regular bookkeeping clients and the pub, though she'd had to cut back on her shifts this past week, how she was able to work for Jake too and stay sane was a miracle. Jake was one of his best friends for sure, but even Parker knew there was a difference between working *with* the guy and *for* the guy. He'd take *with* every damn time.

The sound of the front door opening had him turning. Instead of seeing one of his coworkers, a woman in her late twenties or early thirties walked in. "Sorry, miss," he said as she approached. "We're closed."

"Oh, I know. I'm sorry to impose." She paused, her eyes darting around the room. "I'm just looking for someone and was hoping you could point me in the right direction."

The woman was rail-thin and twitchy. Too twitchy. The back of his neck tingled. He crossed his arms over his chest. There was something off with the woman. The faster she left, the better.

The woman's breathing quickened. "I'm looking for Katie Rose Westerly."

"Sorry. There's no one here by that name." He nodded toward the door. "I'm going to have to ask you to leave."

"Please! I was told I could find Katie Rose here. That she—"

"Who the fuck are you?"

Parker whipped his gaze to Raven as she stalked toward them, a startled Blake on her heels. Whoa. His mouth hung open at her furious demeanor. Smartass and spunky? Yeah, that was Raven. But raging and belligerent? Not at all.

As his eyes ping-ponged between the two women, he had to give the twitchy woman some credit. While her gaze wavered, it never left Raven. "I'm Meredith Macey. I need to speak with Katie Rose Westerly as soon as possible. I need to talk to her about her daughter."

A glass shattered.

Ice shot down his spine as he spotted Kate, water and broken glass lying at her feet. She stood unnaturally still. Her skin had gone ghostly pale, her eyes wide with shock, her face filled with a grief he'd never seen before.

The hairs on the back of his neck stood at attention.

Holy. Shit.

CHAPTER TWENTY-TWO

Katie Rose Westerly.

The last time she'd been addressed by that name had been by her birth mother. The woman's exact words were: "Katie Rose Westerly, you're nothing but a dirty whore. You are dead to us, you evil temptress!"

She'd been a month away from turning twelve. And pregnant.

She'd told her mother who the baby's father was, and while she'd expected her mother's anger, she hadn't expected the absolute disgust and blame. She hadn't expected to be banished. But she should have.

A daughter. The woman, this stranger, had just said she had a daughter. A shiver tore through her body.

Oh my God.

Kate's vision wavered, and her breath stuck in her throat. Her mind raced, but she couldn't find any words. Rooted to the floor, all she could do was stare. She had given birth to a child when she had only been a child herself. She hadn't been told if she'd had a boy or girl, only that the baby was healthy.

She hadn't wanted to know. Ever. And Anna and Henry

had respected her wishes. But not knowing hadn't stopped her from wondering, from hoping the child was happy. That they were safe. In a way, not knowing if the baby had been a boy or girl had helped her move on; it kept a safe distance between herself and the child she'd birthed.

Giving the baby up for adoption hadn't been a question. A twelve-year-old wasn't capable of being a mother. Though it had taken years and years of therapy to work through the guilt, she understood that. But hearing she'd had a *daughter* . . .

Something deep in her chest broke. Knowing that one little fact was . . . something else, something she couldn't describe. Happiness, amazement, joy, shock, horror, shame. So many things.

"Who are you?" Her voice sounded far away to her own ears.

The skinny woman met her gaze and gasped. "Katie Rose!"

Her stomach turned at those two words. Then an anger she'd never before felt surged through her body. Before she knew what she was doing, Kate advanced on the woman. The stranger's eyes widened in fear.

Someone grabbed her by the waist and held her away. "Who are you?!" Kate screamed, her heart threatening to beat out of her chest.

"I'm Meredith Macey. I grew up in Rockberg," the woman explained in a rush of words. "I lived down the street from you in the house with the purple mailbox."

Kate stilled at the woman's words, a memory of that house flashing in her mind. She leaned against the body holding her. The sour ball in her gut twisted. Holy crap. "Mary?"

The slight woman nodded. "I go by Meredith now."

Kate understood completely. She took two deep breaths

in, her attention never wavering from the woman in front of her. Sandalwood and spice filled her senses. Parker. He was the one holding her up. Taking one last breath, her shoulders squared. "I go by Kate now. What do you want?"

Meredith looked around the room, her gaze darting from Raven to Blake to Parker and back to Kate. "Can we talk privately?"

"No." Kate wanted this over and done with.

Meredith seemed to be debating what to say. "Master Sebastian was arrested for tax fraud."

Her stomach twisted at the mere mention of the man's name. "And?"

"And he'll go free," Meredith replied. "He has enough money to buy his way out of a stupid tax charge. But if you help me, we can put him away for life. Your daughter—"

"No," Kate spat. "I want nothing to do with you. Leave."

Meredith's mouth dropped. "But you can't—"

"Make her leave," Kate said to Raven.

Before Meredith could utter another word, Raven grabbed a handful of the woman's hair and yanked her toward the door.

"Please, Katie—er, Kate!" she begged as she was halfway out the door. "You have to help us. You owe it to us! You owe *me*, damn it! You owe me!"

Kate trembled as the front door slammed shut, the adrenaline and anger fleeing. She turned and buried her face in Parker's chest, his arms wrapping tightly around her.

"I got you, sweetheart," he murmured against the top of her head.

Her eyes prickled and her throat grew thick. "A daughter, Parker," she whispered as the first tear fell. The pressure in her chest built. She wrapped her arms around his waist and held on. "I didn't know I had a little girl."

· · ·

Twenty minutes later, in Raven and Blake's apartment, Kate was curled on the couch with her back against Parker's chest and his arms around her. A shot of tequila warmed her belly. Her mind was in a haze, but it had nothing to do with the tequila. Rather, it was the confirmation she'd received from Anna over the phone that she had, indeed, had a healthy little baby girl two decades earlier.

"Are you okay, sweetie?" Raven asked from the opposite couch, concern shimmering in her violet eyes. "Do you need another shot of tequila? Or whiskey? Or ice cream?"

Kate couldn't help but smile at her friend. "I'm good for now, Rave. I'm shocked and . . . a little numb, I think. But thanks."

"Well, if you change your mind, I have Phish Food and Häagen Dazs's Dulce de Leche. I've obviously had a little bit of both, but of course I'll share with you."

"Wait," Blake said, sitting next to his fiancée. "You won't even share your ice cream with me."

Raven shot Blake her classic are-you-a-freaking-moron look. "Yeah. That's right. You have a penis."

Kate chuckled. God, she loved Raven. "Well, in that case, I'll take the Dulce de Leche."

"That's probably for the best," Raven said as she rose. "Phish Food and all that chocolaty goodness is more for guy troubles." She wagged her eyebrows as she headed to the kitchen. "And you two seem to be doing all right."

Ignoring her friend's last remark, Kate called out, "Big spoon, please."

Moments later, she'd untangled herself from Parker's arms and the creamy, sweet caramel ice cream was melting in her mouth. "You were right, Rave," she sighed, leaning back on the couch, her feet tucked underneath her. "This makes everything a little better."

"Doesn't it, though?" Raven replied, scooping a bite of Phish Food into her own mouth.

"Babe, you just said that pint was for guy troubles." Blake's expression could only be described as wary. "What guy troubles could you possibly have?"

Raven glared at him. "Keep talking and you'll find out soon enough, Sullivan."

Man, Kate loved those two.

"Can I have a bite?" Parker asked from beside her.

Kate shook her head. "Sorry."

He looked at her in question.

She took another bite. Her gaze dropped down his body and then back up again.

"I don't get it." His face mimicked Blake's wariness.

"Penis," Kate clarified around a mouthful of ice cream. "We don't share our pints with those who have penises. It's like a rule."

"It's more like a law," Raven interjected. She held out her pint. "Switch?"

Kate scooped one more bite, then leaned over the coffee table to switch. "Yeah. Sorry, Park."

"But getting back on topic," Raven said. "How did that Meredith chick find out you had a baby?"

"I have no idea," Kate replied. "I mean, I guess it would all be part of public records, right?"

"You know, you never specifically said who, but I always kinda assumed. I didn't want to pry. Salt in old wounds and all that."

The love Kate had for the woman across from her squeezed her heart. "And I appreciate that, Rave. More than you'll know."

Seconds ticked by as they ate their ice cream. Then Raven frowned. "Would it all still be part of public records if you were a minor?"

"I don't know." Kate tapped her spoon against her lips. "The adoption stuff would have been sealed, but the birth record is still a birth record, regardless of me being twelve."

"Holy shit," Parker breathed out.

Kate closed her eyes and winced. Crap. She hadn't told him about that part. "Sorry, Park."

"Look at me, baby." She did. His gaze was fierce. "You have *nothing* to apologize for. You just caught me by surprise."

"Still. I'm sorry. This isn't how I wanted you to find out." Her voice dropped to a whisper. "I didn't want you to find out at all. I'm sorry."

His hand came up and cupped her face. "Again, baby, there's nothing for you to apologize for." He was quiet for a moment, his intense stare holding hers. "This was that 'choice' you'd mentioned. The one that went against your parents."

She nodded.

"The cult guy?"

She nodded again. "They didn't believe me when I said it was his." Their enraged voices echoed in her mind, twisting her stomach. "They said I was purposely accusing him to hide my own 'true depravity.'"

Parker's eyes darkened with anger, and he looked away. After a deep breath, he pulled her so she sat across his lap. His arms wrapped tightly around her, and her nervous heart calmed.

"I just need to hold you for a little bit," he murmured, laying his lips on the top of her head.

Raven rose and held out her hand to Kate. "Blake and I will go pick up some food. Give you guys some time alone."

Kate handed over the pint and spoon and mouthed a silent "thank you" to her friend.

· · ·

They sat in silence, Kate resting her cheek on Parker's chest, his arms wrapped snugly around her. The only sound was the steady beat of his heart.

"What are you thinking?"

"I keep hearing Mary, I mean Meredith, screaming, 'You owe me.'" The more it echoed in her mind, the more grief and abject desperation she heard. "I have no idea what she means. I barely remember her from Rockberg."

"She was probably just running her mouth."

Her lips pursed. "Maybe."

"You don't think so?"

"I don't know what to think." She sat up and met his worried gaze. "Do you think I should meet with her?"

The frown between his eyes deepened. "No."

Something nagged at her. She didn't know what it was, but it turned her stomach. "But how did she know about me? Parker, *I* didn't even know if I had a boy or girl. How the hell did *she* know?"

His lips pressed into a straight line. "I have no idea. But you don't know her, Kate. You don't know if you can trust her."

True. "But she knew about the baby girl. Anna confirmed it."

"Then you need to talk to Aunt Anna and Uncle Henry." He tucked a lock of hair behind her ear. "You know them, and you trust them. Maybe they can shed some light on how Meredith could have found out."

The other woman's anguished plea reverberated in her head. *"You owe me!"* A shiver ran through Kate. You couldn't fake that kind of desperation. "What if—"

Parker's phone rang. He fished his phone from his pocket, and she saw Carmen's name on the display.

"Answer," she said. "Go ahead."

With obvious reluctance, he tapped the answer button.

"What's up, Carmen? You're on speaker, by the way. Kate's here."

"You guys need to come home. There's a butchered cat on the front porch." The way his sister's voice trembled had the hairs on the back of Kate's neck rising. Her next words were muffled, as if she held her phone away from herself. "Jake's with me, and he already called Matt."

Parker's body tensed. "We're at Blake's. We'll be home in five."

Kate's breath caught in her chest.

Another dead cat? And if Jake had called his twin brother, Matt, a detective with the Seattle PD, it didn't bode well. At all.

What was going on?

CHAPTER TWENTY-THREE

They pulled into Parker's driveway at the same time Matt's unmarked police car parked in front of the house. As she and Parker got out of the car, Jake and Carmen headed down the front steps toward them. Trepidation crept through Kate as she caught sight of Carmen. The woman's usually tan complexion was ashen.

Parker pulled his sister into a hug, and Jake slung an arm over Kate's shoulder.

"Don't go up there." Jake's voice shook, and he cleared his throat.

The uneasiness running through her grew. Nothing shook Jake.

"Let Matt take a look first." Jake nodded to his brother, who headed directly to the front porch with a brisk wave and grim face. A second detective, holding a camera, followed close behind Matt. "I don't think you should see what happened to that cat."

"Was it mauled like the other cat?" She asked after a few moments of silence, wariness coating every word.

"No, Kate," Matt said, joining their group in the driveway.

"It most definitely was not mauled. We need to reassess the situation with the first cat." Matt shifted his focus to Parker and Carmen and lifted his chin at the woman. "Hey, Carm. It's good to see you again."

"I wish it were under better circumstances." She pressed a hand to her stomach with a shudder. Jake stepped away from Kate and toward Carmen, wrapping his muscular arm over the woman's slim shoulders.

Matt gestured toward the porch, concern clouding his dark brown eyes. "That was pretty grisly. You going to be okay?"

Carmen nodded, taking two deep breaths. She nudged Jake with her shoulder. "Good thing we didn't stop for food first."

Addressing Carmen and Jake, Matt motioned to his partner taking photos on the porch. "Detective Tran will take your statements separately." He turned to Kate. "I hate to say this, but I need you to look at what's up there."

"This is *my* house, Matt," Parker said. His arm wound protectively over her shoulder, pulling her to his side. "I'll look. She doesn't need to be involved."

"You're welcome to look." Matt hesitated a moment too long, and Kate's heart tripped. "But this involves Kate."

Ice shot down her spine in surprise. Parker's body tensed. The hand on her shoulder squeezed, the pressure oddly reassuring her. She wasn't alone. "It's okay, Park," she said, swallowing hard. "We'll both look."

What was only a few feet to the front porch felt like miles. She gripped Parker's hand and hung on as if it were a lifeline. Climbing the four short steps to the porch, her eyes widened at the horror before her.

She gasped and staggered backward. Both her hands flew to her mouth. Parker caught her by the waist and pulled her close, his strong arm encircling her. It was like a scene out of a movie. A really, really effed-up movie.

They'd chalked up the injuries of the first cat to being mauled. It only took one look at this cat—another orange tabby—to see that it hadn't died naturally.

It had been tortured.

The poor thing's limbs had been butchered into chunks, and sharp bits of bone protruded through its blood-matted fur. Pieces of its broken and mutilated body were placed at odd angles on a bed of crushed, blood-stained flowers. The only part of the cat that hadn't been mutilated was its face, its decapitated head sat off to the side on its own pile of flowers.

Her vision swayed as the blood drained from her face. Vomit threatened. Holy shit. Who would do something like this?

"I'm sorry, Kate, but I need you to look at the negative space."

Matt stood next to her, but his voice seemed far away. She shook her head. "I don't understand what you mean."

"Don't look at the animal pieces. Look at the flowers and how they're laid out."

She pushed away the nausea and tried not to focus on the bloody bits of fur and bone. Instead, she focused on the multitude of orange flowers. Something tickled at her memory, but in a flash, it was gone. She frowned.

Concentrating on the blood-stained flowers, she began to make out letters. It took a few seconds for her brain to catch up to what her eyes were seeing. When it finally did, her heart stopped. Bile rose in her throat, and she raced toward the edge of the porch, emptying her stomach with a violent heave.

Breathless and trembling, she folded her arms on the railing, resting her forehead on top. She tried to banish the image in her head, but it remained. Like a sick horror movie scene replaying on a loop. That, combined with the sour, acidic taste in her mouth, had her stomach turning and emptying again.

Parker rubbed circles over her back, but it did nothing to calm the tremors running through her. The pieces of the cat's body created an outline of letters, and the flowers spelled out a single word.

Katie.

———

Parker had never felt so helpless in his life. He suppressed a shudder.

Cat pieces. Holy shit. What kind of sick fuck would do that?

While additional personnel from the Seattle PD and Animal Control took care of the gruesome scene on Parker's front porch, Carmen and Jake went inside the house to give their statements to Detective Tran. Kate remained outside, and answered the expected questions from Matt, like whether she could think of anyone who could be responsible or if she had any jilted ex-boyfriends, former clients, that sort of thing. Parker remained silent, waiting for her to mention what had happened earlier at the pub with Meredith.

She didn't.

So he did.

He had to hand it to Matt; their friend didn't blink an eye. Not with the revelation about Kate having had a baby at twelve, nor about who had fathered the child. Matt was the consummate professional. He took notes and then simply asked Kate to confirm everything in her own words.

With each question Kate answered, she pulled further and

further away from him. And not just emotionally. When he sat beside her, she not-so-discreetly moved to another seat.

After another half hour of Kate's monosyllabic replies, Matt and his partner left. Parker felt like absolute shit. Kate had thrown up a wall—not to mention she'd actually thrown up—and it just about killed him. If you didn't know her, she was the picture of calm, her body completely still.

But he knew her. Kate's hands were clasped daintily on her lap, but her nails dug little crescents deep into her skin.

"I know you're mad at me for telling Matt about what happened with Meredith, but he needed to know. It can't be a coincidence that she showed up and then this happened, that the name spelled out was Katie and not Kate."

"Of course." She didn't meet his eyes.

Of course? His teeth ground together as frustration built. "Then why didn't you mention it yourself?"

The rise and fall of her shoulders were barely perceptible. "I don't know," she replied, her voice just slightly above a whisper. A split second later, she surged to her feet. "I can't be here. I'm going for a walk," she announced, her voice firm, though slightly shaky. Finally acknowledging his presence, she swung a challenging gaze his way. "Alone."

CHAPTER TWENTY-FOUR

Kate clenched her shaking hands and hustled down the sidewalk, her eyes darting around for any signs of . . . she didn't know what. She couldn't believe Parker had told Matt about her past and her pregnancy all those years ago. Her chest tightened at the memory, her angry steps eating up the sidewalk. The sane part of her understood that the upset she was feeling was an overreaction. Because yes, the cats and Rockberg *had* to be connected in some way. And yes, Matt needed to know all the information to do his job, to figure out what was going on.

But it still felt like a betrayal. It still hurt.

It hadn't been Parker's place to say anything, dang it.

Her steps faltered, and nausea swirled anew.

It had been *her* place, *her* responsibility. But no matter how hard she'd tried, she couldn't form the words. She'd wanted to tell Matt everything, but a giant weight had slammed down on her chest every time she'd opened her mouth. She couldn't think. She could barely breathe. Only one-word answers had been able to pass her lips.

Self-disgust crawled over her like thousands of tiny spiders. For what had happened in her past; for how she'd reacted in the present. Anger and hurt and terror all fought within her. All of it turning the bile in her stomach.

The well-counseled part of her knew she was being completely irrational, that she needed to give herself a break, that the last few hours would have been too much for anyone, but she couldn't help it. She couldn't stop the self-loathing and the beginnings of panic. She'd worked so hard at being normal. At putting her messed-up childhood firmly behind her. At being competent and efficient and at freaking blending in.

Now, everyone would know.

She doubted anyone would blame her, but they'd all *know*. And they'd look at her differently. With pity.

When the walls had started closing in on her, she'd bolted from Parker's house. As much as she wanted to lean on him for support, she couldn't. Because even though he'd tried to hide it, she could see it in his eyes. The pity.

Tears tingled her nose, and she scrubbed her hands over her face, her palms pressing hard into her eye sockets. Everything was falling apart.

No! She blew out a breath and straightened her spine. "No," she repeated to the silent sidewalk.

What would Raven do, dang it?

She'd keep going, that's what.

Willing her tears away, she continued walking with Raven's classic words of encouragement—*"Pull your shit together!"*—echoing in her head.

Kate had made it a few blocks from Parker's house when a familiar Mercedes stopped at the opposite end of the street. Her heart stopped.

A woman hopped out of the passenger side and slammed

the door shut, not acknowledging the vehicle as it drove off. All thoughts Kate had of pulling her shit together fell away.

Tears flooded her eyes and stung her nose. Trying to swallow a sob, her steps quickened until she was jogging. Within a few strides, she was wrapped in familiar arms, the comforting scent of Chanel No. 5 surrounding her.

"Oh my sweet, sweet girl," Anna murmured, smoothing a hand over Kate's head. "What a day it's been for you."

The sob tore free, and Kate clung to the woman she loved above all others. The mother of her heart. She couldn't stop the tears even if she wanted to. Because at that moment, everything inside her hurt. Everything.

The fear of some unknown crazy who'd tortured a helpless animal as some sort of sick message to her. Despair that she'd messed things up with Parker. Then there was the pain and emptiness tearing at her soul. She'd worked so hard to overcome her past, yet countless years of therapy had been undone by a single bombshell.

Somewhere in this world, she had a daughter that she'd never know.

Kate would never be to her child what Anna was to her. That simple fact hurt on a gut-wrenching level. But by God, she hoped beyond anything and everything that the child she'd given birth to had found her own Anna. Because the opposite was unthinkable. The possibility that Kate had given her up only to have her suffer a childhood of horror was terrifying and heart-shattering all in one. That thought was too much.

Sitting on a bench at Kerry Park, Kate accepted yet another tissue from Anna. With a loud sniff, she told her story of the mutilated cat while keeping her gaze on the Seattle skyline.

As she was talking about the questions Matt had asked, she stopped mid-sentence and faced Anna. "Wait. How did you find me?"

"Parker."

Kate waited for more, but nothing came. "Did he call you?"

A small smile played at the edges of Anna's lips. "He was worried about you, sweetie. He said that you were upset at him, that he'd messed up, and that you ran off. He wondered if I knew where you'd go."

"And you just happened to be in the neighborhood?" Kate couldn't keep the skepticism out of her voice.

Anna chuckled. "I actually was, if you can believe that. And I know that when you stew, you like quiet places." She nudged Kate with her shoulder. "Preferably with a view. I figured you'd either come here or head over to Marshall Park."

"Thank you," Kate said, her eyes watering anew. "I didn't know how badly I needed you until I saw you."

Gently touching Kate's cheek, Anna pressed a soft kiss to her forehead. "I love you, sweet girl." She drew Kate's head down onto her shoulder. "Don't ever forget that."

"I love you too." Kate sniffed.

They sat in comfortable silence. Closing her eyes, Kate let out a weary sigh, banishing all thoughts of the unknown stranger mutilating cats and the pitying looks from Parker. She simply took comfort from Anna being there, from her steady and unconditional love.

As the sun set and the sky turned a mix of purples, pinks, and reds, she broke the silence and asked the question that had been plaguing her all day. "How do you think Meredith found out about me and the baby girl?" Her breath caught on the last word.

"I don't know," Anna replied, confusion echoing in her voice. "I've been thinking about that since we spoke earlier. Have you given thought to meeting with this Meredith woman?"

Kate sat up, not bothering to hide her shock. "Don't you think that's dangerous?"

Anna rolled her eyes. How the woman could make an eye roll look classy had always mystified Kate. "Sweet girl, you've been watching too much bad television. I'm not suggesting you meet this woman in a deserted alley down by the docks in the middle of the night."

A flush rose to Kate's cheeks. Well, when she put it that way . . .

"You want to know how this woman got your information," Anna continued. "The most direct way to figure out what's going on is to ask her. During the day. In a public place. Preferably with someone you trust nearby."

"I don't know how to find her." The flush spreading over her face deepened. "I kinda threw her out of the pub before I got her contact info."

Anna's brow arched. "Threw out?"

"Well, technically, Raven was the one who threw her out."

The brow arched higher.

Kate squirmed in her seat. "By grabbing a fistful of her hair and dragging her out of the pub."

"Raven is loyal, I'll give her that." Anna looked to be fighting a smile, but then laughed. "Raven did mention the hair incident when I spoke to her earlier today. I believe her exact words were, 'I was more than happy to toss the bitch out by her hair! How dare that fucker hurt Kate like that!'"

Kate smiled for the first time in hours. God, she loved Raven. "I don't know what I'd do without her."

"Hopefully, you'll never find out. But," Anna paused,

"don't bring Raven with you when you meet up with that woman."

"*If* I meet with Meredith."

Anna shook her head. "You'll meet up. She'll find you. But don't bring Raven. She's too hot-tempered. The mere sight of her would scare off Meredith. Bring Parker."

Kate sighed. Parker. She probably shouldn't have run out on him, but the pity in his eyes had been more than she could take. She shook her head. "He just feels sorry for me."

"Don't insult the man, Kate. It's beneath you." Kate's eyes widened at the snap in Anna's words. "Of course he feels awful for what happened to you all those years ago, sweet girl. He would be a horrible human if he didn't."

"I don't want his pity." Because that's how he would look at her now. That's how *everyone* would look at her.

"Do you feel bad for what happened to Raven when you were in foster care with her?"

A few moments of silence ticked by.

"Of course I do," she finally grumbled, knowing where the conversation was going.

"So, you pity her then?" Anna's words were sharp. "Should Raven be ashamed of her past?"

Kate's frown grew. "Of course not," she mumbled.

"Then why should you? Your past, your childhood? It wasn't pretty at all. Instead of looking at it as something you need to suppress and deny, reclaim it, sweet girl. As ugly as it was, it's part of what made you such a strong woman today."

She shook her head, and a tear spilled over. "No," she whispered, not bothering to wipe away the next tear that followed. "It wasn't me. That was you and Henry."

"No, sweetie." Anna kissed her forehead, and Kate welcomed the tiny bit of warmth blooming in her chest. "It was *you* who did all the work. Henry and I were just lucky and honored you allowed us to help prop you up. Are you proud of Raven and how far she's come?"

She nodded. "You know I am."

"Then be proud of how far *you've* come."

"But Anna, it's not the same thing." She crossed her arms over her chest, slouching farther down onto the bench. "I don't want Parker to look at me and se—"

"Kate." If she weren't feeling so awful, she'd be impressed by how much exacerbation Anna put into that one word. "If you think that pity is *all* Parker feels for you, then you're a fool. Don't go insulting him because of your pride. He doesn't pity you. He cares *so much* about you. You're just looking for an excuse to pull away."

"I'm not. I'm—"

Anna leveled her with a fierce mom look, and Kate's mouth snapped shut. Fine. She *was* looking for an excuse, any excuse, to pull away.

"As much as you want to, don't revert to your old ways of trying to handle everything on your own."

Her mind flashed to Parker and how his steady presence —in so many freaking instances this past month—had calmed her, had made her feel less alone. "I'm trying, Anna. Really. I'm a lot better now."

"I'm glad to hear that because it would make me crazy when you were younger. Whenever things got difficult, it was," Anna snapped her fingers, "immediate silence. You shut down and don't speak to anyone. Then—"

"Wait." Kate sat upright, the tiny hairs on her arms rising. "What did you just say?"

"That you gave everyone the silent treatment?" Anna's brow furrowed. "Are you okay, sweetie?"

Kate shook her head, the blood draining from her face.

Don't Speak

The note from the flowers. The *orange* flowers. It had to be connected.

Kate sprang up from the bench, unsure if she should puke or be thrilled she'd found a connection. "We have to go," she said, tugging on Anna's hand. With her free hand, she fished her phone from her pocket and dialed Parker. "Meet me and Anna at the pub," she said in a rush. "I'll explain when we get there."

CHAPTER TWENTY-FIVE

When Kate entered The Spotted Dog, her gaze landed on the bright orange flowers that had been delivered a little over a week ago. The bouquet was still going strong and sat on the back bar in a pretty glass vase. There were multiple flower varieties, but they were all a bright and vibrant orange, the exact color and varieties as the flowers they'd found under the poor cat.

Her heart stuttered and bile rose in her throat.

Holy crap. Orange had been his favorite color.

Her vision went hazy as Master Sebastian's voice whispered in her mind.

"Orange represents new life and glory, Katie. Its brightness is in the sunrise, celebrating each new day. It's in the sun's rays that remind you that Master gives you life. It's in the sunset, so you do not forget to give glory to Master for all the blessings of your day. It's in the stars, so you always know Master is watching over you. Master will always be with you, Katie. Always."

A shiver wracked her body.

Damn. How had she not made the connection earlier?

Kate tried to shove the memories away, but if the tiny

note card trembling in her fingers was any indication, she wasn't doing a good job. Anna rubbed gentle circles over her back, and Parker stood silently a few feet away. Her hands still shook. Repressed memories were a powerful thing.

Don't Speak

Turning the card over, she looked for some sort of clue. Anything. But aside from those two little words, the note card was blank. She ran her thumb absently over the ridged corner of the card, and when she realized what she was feeling, her heart kicked. The corner of the card wasn't ridged. It was an embossed logo. The florist's logo.

"What is it?" Parker asked.

She pointed to the card's small embossed logo and waved at the flowers, her mind whirling with the possibilities. "The flowers under the cat were the same as these."

And the cats . . . there was something there too . . . something that tugged at the back of her mind. It was as if the answers were right in front of her, but she couldn't figure out where to look.

Focus, Kate! Her lips pursed as eyed the flowers. "How many all-orange arrangements could this store have sold?"

"It is October," Anna began, "but that bouquet has some high-end, rare blooms in it. Either way, the person most likely would have paid in cash."

"True," Kate nodded, every crime show episode she'd ever seen replaying in her mind. "I know this florist. They're a small family business, but they're expensive. They're sure to have an electronic point of sale system, so they'd have some sort of record, even if the person paid in cash, which would have been done in person."

"And who pays with cash these days?" Anna added. "The florist may recall what the person looked like."

Following Anna's lead, Kate continued, "Maybe they even

have a security camera and could match the security feed with the time of purchase."

Before she could finish her sentence, Parker had his phone to his ear. "Matt, it's Parker. Kate may have found a connection to the flowers."

After relaying their theory to Matt and agreeing to meet with him first thing in the morning, Kate walked Anna to the door. "Thank you," she said quietly. "I'm so glad you found me. I didn't know I needed to see you so badly."

Anna wrapped her in a hug, and Kate held on. "Remember that you're not alone, sweet girl," she murmured. She gave Kate one final squeeze, then straightened, her hands firm on Kate's shoulders, and kept her voice low. "You may want to strangle that man right now," Anna paused, her head nodding in Parker's direction, "but he meant well. Lean, sweet girl. There's a whole slew of us for you to lean on. But no one more willing than that man over there."

With a slight nod, Kate kissed Anna on the cheek. "Thank you again."

Locking the pub's door behind Anna, nerves filled Kate. She turned back toward the bar. Toward Parker.

He stood across the room, arms crossed over his chest, leaning back against the bar with an unreadable look on his face. A part of her wanted to run to him. To do as Anna had said, to lean into his strength. But the other part wanted to run away. Some sort of trouble was after her—the psychotic and terrifying sort that mutilated cats—and the last thing she wanted was to put Parker in danger.

Instead of running to or from him, she took a fortifying breath, slowly letting it out. She straightened her shoulders and calmly headed his way. Each slow step toward him high-lighted how tense and confused, how absolutely the opposite of calm, she felt. She wanted what they'd had just this morning: the easiness, the affection, the little touches. Not a regression to this awkward feeling of not knowing how to act around him. She didn't know how to get back to what they'd had.

She stopped when she was a few feet away, and before she could figure out what to say to ease the tension, he uncrossed his arms and moved in front of her in two strides. He reached out to her but changed his mind last minute, shoving his hands into his jeans pockets instead.

"I know you're mad at me, Kate. I'm sorry."

Mad? Sure. Shocked? Hurt? Betrayed? Absolutely. "I can't believe you did that. How could you tell Matt about my past? About the baby?"

He stared at her a moment, disbelief crossing his face. "How could you not?"

"I would have told him."

"Really?" He paced away, then abruptly turned to face her. "When?"

Prickles of anger mixed with the hurt. She embraced the anger. "When I was ready!" Her stomach rolled. "Did you forget about that god-awful butchering on your porch?"

"It's because of that butchering that I told Matt!" He scrubbed his hands over his face and resumed pacing. The sound coming from him could only be described as a growl. "Don't you see? There's a fucking crazy-ass nutjob out there butchering cats for you. There's no time for you to 'be ready.' The police need to know everything *now*." He raked his hands through his hair and cupped the back of his neck. "I'm sorry I hurt you. I swear to God that wasn't my intention. But I'm fine with you being mad at me. If the alternative is that this fucking whack job gets anywhere near you, then I'll take you being mad at me every damn time." He waved his hands toward the flowers. "It's all connected. I don't know how, but it is."

Parker was usually the epitome of calm and steady. His

jerky movements and frantic tone, the way his eyes darted around the room, had her temper fizzling. He was scared for her. Truly scared for her.

Like a tiny pinprick in a balloon, the anger eased from her body. "I know. You're right. This is all somehow connected to the cult, but I'm not sure how. Or who. Orange was Master Sebastian's favorite color. It had a deep and symbolic meaning to him. He often lectured that it represented new life and glory, that it was basically a representation of him, and that we—that *I*—should be grateful for him."

Kate took in the man before her. His hands were clasped behind his neck again, his biceps flexing under his fitted long-sleeve shirt. A worry line ran between his brows, his green eyes cloudy with frustration and concern. Though it still felt like a betrayal, she knew Parker's intent hadn't been malicious. Her heart pinched. "I understand why you felt you had to tell Matt about my past, I really do. But it wasn't up to you to take over and tell him everything. Not without talking to me about it first."

"I'm sorry, Ka—"

"No, Parker. I don't think you understand." Because she'd never explained. That was on her. So, she'd explain now. And hope he'd grasp the enormity of it all, of her hurt. "Aside from Raven, Anna, Henry, and my therapist, I have *never* spoken out loud about the baby I had. *Ever*. It wasn't your place to say anything."

"I'm sorry, Kate. Truly." His hands dropped to his sides. He stared at her for a few moments, as if debating what to say, before speaking again. "I like to think that you and I are a team. We're good together, right?"

He looked at her so earnestly she couldn't help the corner of her mouth from ticking up. "Usually."

"Baby, I desperately want to protect you," he said, his deep green eyes blazing with emotion. "But you're right. I spoke out of turn. Instead of blurting out everything about your past, I should have spoken to you alone and asked you—no, *begged* you—to tell Matt yourself. Or at least asked if it was okay for me to say something. It was a dick move and I'm sorry. So, so damn sorry." His arms opened a fraction. "Please forgive me?"

It wasn't a question—she'd always forgive him. How could she not? She stepped into his embrace and sighed, wrapping her arms around his waist. Feeling a slight tremble run through him, she buried her face in his chest. His racing heartbeat calmed hers, his soft, woodsy scent comforting her. "You're forgiven, Park. Just promise me you won't do it again."

"I promise," he murmured. "I'm so sorry I hurt you."

With her arms still around his waist, she pulled slightly back to look up into his face. "If Meredith reaches out to me again, will you come with me to meet her? Not to take over, but just to be with me, support me?"

If she hadn't been waiting for it, she would have missed how his body momentarily tensed. She sighed in relief when his arms tightened around her and his lips pressed to the top of her head. "Of course."

"Will you be with me now?"

His head tilted slightly, confusion swirling in his gaze. "I'm right here, sweetheart."

"No, Parker." Her heartbeat thumped loudly in her chest as she called upon that new, bold woman. "Will you *be* with me? Make love to me? End this horrific day on a positive note, like the way we started it? Together?"

"You honor me, Kate." His eyes blazed with an emotion she couldn't decipher. He held her gaze until his forehead rested against hers. "Yes, I promise to worship you tonight. And always." His lips caressed hers in a gentle kiss that stung her eyes with the sweetest tears. "Let's go home."

· · ·

Kate's nerves and insecurities returned with a vengeance on the short car ride home. Was she really going to drag Parker into the chaos of her life? They turned onto his street, and the shame and horror of her past crept through her until it was lodged in her throat, choking her.

Parker pulled into the garage and cut the engine. She didn't move. So many things were swirling in her mind like a drunken, chaotic mess. The worry of not knowing what had happened to her child twisted with the terror of the unknown person threatening her and possibly those she loved.

Her breath came in shallow pants. She heard Parker's car door open but still didn't move.

Paralyzed. Simply paralyzed.

When her door opened, the first tear fell.

"Baby," he whispered.

The care emanating from that one word had more tears falling. Before she could take her next breath, her seat belt was unbuckled and his arms were around her. When he lifted her, she nuzzled into him. Closing her eyes, she inhaled his calming scent as he silently walked her through the house.

Moments later, he lowered her onto his bed. He began to pull away, and she jolted in panic. "No," she said, her arms locking around his neck. "Don't go."

He laid his forehead to hers, then kissed the tip of her nose. "I'll be right back, baby. I need to lock up."

With a reluctant exhale, she let him go, then curled into a tight ball.

As promised, a few minutes later, the bed sank under his weight as he sat next to her. "Talk to me, sweetheart." He smoothed a hand over her hip and leg. "Tell me what's going on in that beautiful head of yours."

She remained silent as he removed her shoes and climbed

into bed, curling his body around hers, tucking her snug against his front. Wrapping her in his arms, he kissed the top of her head. "Talk to me, Kate."

"I'm scared," she said, the two words shaky.

"There's nothing wrong with that, sweetheart. But remember, you're not alone. We're a team."

She nodded, though her eyes welled anew. "Sometimes I feel like we can face this, but then . . ."

He shifted so she was on her back, looking up at him. "Then?"

"Then I feel like I don't deserve to be on your team." A tear escaped the corner of her eye and slid into her hairline. "It's too much, Parker. *I'm* too much."

He caressed the side of her face, his thumb tracing the track of her tear, and she leaned into his palm.

"You're not too much, baby. You are everything."

Her heart warmed as she remembered to breathe. He kissed her, and it was unlike anything before. His lips were gentle and soft as always, but there was something more this time. Something that soothed the tight ball of shame and terror that had been lodged in her gut.

His mouth explored her neck and his teeth gently nipped at her earlobe, then he soothed the slight sting with his tongue. "Let me show you how much you matter, Kate," he murmured.

His lips were back on hers, and she tangled her fingers in his hair. When his hands cupped her breasts, his fingers teasing her aching nipples, she moaned against his lips. "Too many clothes," she muttered, tugging at his shirt. She needed to feel his skin on hers. Now.

With a growl, he sat up. A second later, his shirt was gone. Another second later, so were the rest of his clothes. Her breath caught—it always did when she saw him naked—but before she could fully appreciate his form, her clothes joined his in a heap on the floor.

He hovered over her, his hard body resting between her thighs. His bottle-green gaze locked on hers, an intense emotion she couldn't put into words on his face. "You are everything to me, Kate." Her stomach fluttered and heat settled low in her belly. And deep in her soul. This man . . .

"Everything about you is precious," he murmured, trailing kisses first down her neck, then her chest. His tongue swirled over her nipple before he pulled it deep into his mouth. Electricity zinged through her body and her back arched, seeking more. "You're so damn perfect, baby."

He moved lower, his hands molding her breasts as he kissed her stomach. Her breath caught as he traced an ancient stretch mark on her lower abdomen with his tongue. "Perfect, Kate," he said, holding her gaze as he pressed a kiss to it.

Her heart clutched hard, butterflies and . . . love . . . erupting within.

Never before had she felt this cherished.

He moved lower still, and his hands spread her legs wide. Settling between her thighs, his eyes locked with hers, and he inhaled deeply. She would have been embarrassed, would have tried to close her legs, but the heat and lust rioting in his eyes had her lifting her hips, her center, to his mouth. She groaned when his tongue slicked over her, and she couldn't hold back a moan when he sank his fingers deep within. She shouted his name and soared as his fingers pumped deep into her and his lips locked onto her clit. He licked her through her orgasm, setting off tiny spasms of pleasure.

Never before had she felt this desired.

Another shiver wracked her body, and she tugged on his hair. "I need you inside me," she said, her voice hoarse.

With another kiss to the stretch marks on her stomach, he shot her that lopsided grin she loved so much. Covering her body with his, he wrapped her right leg around his hips and caught her left leg in his elbow, opening her wide. He filled her with a single stroke, sending tingles racing over her body. His movements easy and deep and torturously slow.

"Faster," she begged.

"No," he growled. Then his lips crashed against hers, the desperation of his kiss at odds with his slow and steady thrusts. "We have all night, sweetheart. I promised to make love to you and worship you." She gasped as he pumped deep into her and held. "And I'm just getting started, baby."

Another rock of his hips and another gasp. Throughout the night, he worshiped her, every inch of her body, every inch of her soul.

Never before had she felt this loved.

CHAPTER TWENTY-SIX

Kate didn't have to wait long for Meredith to contact her. The next morning, a simple note with Meredith's name and phone number was slipped under the front door of The Spotted Dog.

A few hours later, Kate sat at a scarred wooden table at a small café in Seattle's International District. Parker sat next to her with Meredith across from them.

After the care Parker had lavished on her last night—making her truly believe she was precious to him—she'd come to this meeting with renewed determination. Not exhausted and full of nerves, the wreck she knew she'd have been if not for this wonderful and patient man.

Meredith shifted in her seat, her eyes darting around the café, her hands with their chipped, hot pink polish fiddling with the coffee cup's sleeve. "Thank you for meeting me."

Kate gave her a curt nod. She wasn't here for small talk. She wanted—no, *needed*—answers. "How did you know I had a child?"

After a moment's pause, Meredith drew in a deep breath.

"Master Sebastian said we had to pray for you because you had lost your child, that it was your punishment for being a woman of evil morals." She met Kate's gaze. "That we had to cleanse the community of your influence on the rest of us."

Kate held up her hand, her brow knitting. There was so much to unpack there, but she focused on the most pressing. "That I lost my child?"

Meredith nodded.

What this woman was saying made no sense.

She glanced at Parker. His gaze was steady on hers, but he didn't say anything. Under the table, he took her hand, laced his fingers with hers, and simply held on. Kate turned her attention back to Meredith. "Again, how did you know I had a child?"

"Because it recently came out that your father betrayed Master Sebastian. Your father betrayed Rockberg."

Concern bloomed in Kate's chest as Meredith's breath quickened, the other woman's anxiety apparent. "I don't understand. What are you not telling me?"

The anguish on Meredith's face had the fine hairs on the back of Kate's neck rising. Without taking her eyes off the woman, she squeezed Parker's hand. Hard.

"When you were banished, I replaced you. I became Master Sebastian's Chosen One."

Kate's breath caught. It had never occurred to her that the monster would have another young girl take her place. It should have—he was an evil predator. But she'd done everything she could to banish all thoughts of him. Her stomach rolled and vomit threatened. "I'm so sorry," she whispered.

Meredith nodded, quickly swiping away a single tear. "When I was fourteen, I became pregnant."

"His?"

She nodded. "He was the only one I'd ever been with, the only one I was allowed to be with. But he told my parents that someone else was the father. When I told them it was him, that I'd never been with anyone but Master Sebastian, my family didn't believe me."

"Oh my God, Meredith," Kate breathed out. Disgust soured Kate's gut. Their stories were the same. "I'm so sorry." She truly was. But she still didn't understand how it all connected.

"After I revealed my pregnancy, I was deemed impure. Master Sebastian went to the Council and ordered my Purification." Fury dripped from Meredith's every word.

Kate startled. "What?"

"Purification," she spat, so much fury and disgust in that one word. "Where the members of the fucking Council beat you within an inch of your life, making sure you miscarry. Then the Council votes whether to keep you in the community or banish you."

Kate's jaw dropped. The other woman's eyes were glassy and far away, lost in her horrific memories. Letting go of Parker, she reached across the small table and took Meredith's cold, trembling hands in her own.

After a few silent moments, Meredith's hands stilled, and she leaned back, crossing her arms over her chest. "After his recent arrest," she began, her voice holding a slight tremor, "Master Sebastian's personal journals were found. Your case changed the Purification process."

Kate shook her head. "I'm not following."

"After *you* became pregnant, your father was supposed to carry out the Purification process. At that time, it was the responsibility of the family. Your father said he had completed the Purification and had approved of your banishment."

Kate's mouth opened and closed. She had no words. The blood drained from her face and left her lightheaded.

"After you'd been banished, the journals said that your

father admitted his lie to Master Sebastian. After that, the Purification process moved from the family to the Council."

Ice slithered down her spine. Her father was supposed to have beaten her into miscarrying? And he'd lied about doing so?

It was all too much to take in. She leaned back in her seat and bumped into Parker's arm. Seconds later, his hand rubbed soft circles between her shoulder blades. Leaning into his touch, she found her voice. "What happened to my father?"

"The journals just said that he was 'punished accordingly.'" Meredith shrugged, sadness marring her face. "After you were banished, I don't recall ever seeing him. I saw your mother, but never him. Then again, I was just a kid."

Holy crap. "Who knows about this?"

"My dad was the one who found the journals and told me. I ran away from Rockberg when I was seventeen, but he and I secretly kept in contact."

"Surely there's something in the journals that will incriminate Master Sebastian. Does your dad still have access to the journals? Can't he help you?"

"He's dead."

Kate gasped. "I'm so sorry."

"He fell off a ladder and broke his neck. At least that's how the story went." Meredith chuckled, the sound bitter and humorless. "The reality was that my dad had been in a wheelchair for the last decade. No way he was up on a ladder. But what Master Sebastian says goes, right?"

Kate's eyes widened, but she stayed silent. Was Meredith implying Master Sebastian was responsible for her father's death? Was he responsible for Kate's own father's disappearance?

Did she actually care?

If someone had asked her yesterday, the answer would

have been a definite no. But knowing her father was supposed to have carried out this god-awful 'Purification' but hadn't? That he'd banished her instead of keeping her in Rockberg with Master Sebastian?

Her mind flashed to a long-suppressed memory. Of her father silently walking her into a drab, nondescript CPS office that smelled of coffee and stale cigarettes. And leaving her there. Her heart clutched painfully as she recalled staring at his retreating form, the words begging him to stop locked in her throat. He'd never once looked back.

Kate didn't know what to think. She surely didn't know what to feel. There was too much to process. "What do I have to do with this?"

"Don't you see?" Meredith asked, an edge of desperation in those three words. "You were *never* supposed to have had his child. The journals list at least twelve Purification cere-monies. Twelve! And that's just from a handful of journals!" Meredith glanced around the café, seemingly surprised by her raised voice. Dropping her voice, she leaned in and continued, "The daughter you had is the only proof of what a monster Master Sebastian really is."

Kate stilled. Something kept nagging at her. "How did you know I had a daughter?"

Meredith flushed. "I pretended to be you and did a birth parent request for the original birth certificate with the state."

Kate's breath caught and disgust turned her stomach. There were so many things wrong with that sentence.

It couldn't be that simple, could it? The horrific image of the cat flashed in her mind and her heart tripped. If the woman before her could find that information so easily, what could the monster who'd mutilated the poor cat find out?

"If you can find your daughter and have her submit a DNA sample, we can—"

"No. It was a closed adoption. It's sealed." She leaned back in her chair, her arms crossing over her chest. "I'm surprised you didn't keep pretending to be me and unseal the records yourself."

Meredith cleared her throat. The flush on her face deepened. "There's a lot more official paperwork involved to access a sealed adoption file. Forms that involve photo ID and notarization. But as the actual birth mother, you could file the paperwork and a judge—"

"No," Kate repeated. "She'd be twenty years old." Her heart squeezed and stole her breath. She knew that this girl, this young woman, wasn't her daughter. Not really. Being a parent was more than just birthing someone. "I'm not going to do that. What if she doesn't know she was adopted? Why would I—a complete stranger, mind you—ask her for a DNA sample? Why would I want her to know that she was the product of a pedophile and a twelve-year-old? You realize you're asking me to blow up an innocent person's life, right?"

"He has to pay, Kate. I have three other women from Rockberg who are willing to testify against him, that he raped us when we were children. If we have you testify *and* DNA proof, then—" Meredith broke off as her phone rang.

"Unknown Caller" flashed on the woman's phone screen.

Snatching her phone up from the table, Meredith barked out an impatient, "Hello?"

Kate's growing unease intensified as Meredith paled, her gaze darting around the café again. Mumbling something incoherent, she disconnected the call. She rose with a jerk, her chair loudly scraping on the floor. "I have to go," she whispered, slinging her purse strap across her body. "Please think about it, Kate. It's important. Your testimony is crucial.

This whole thing is bigger than me and you. Bigger than your daughter. I'll call you soon."

Kate watched the café door close behind Meredith, then turned to Parker. "What just happened?"

CHAPTER TWENTY-SEVEN

Parker's arm pinned Kate snug against him. Her warm, naked body curled along his side, her head tucked in the corner of his shoulder and chest. His mind scrambled to take in everything from the last forty-eight hours.

Meredith showing up and dropping her bombshell, the tortured cat, his fuck-up telling Matt about Kate, meeting with Meredith yesterday, and then the crazy and hectic shift at work last night with both the flat top and one of the refrigerators dying.

The work stuff was an inconvenience. What worried him was everything he'd heard from Meredith. Purification process? Kate's birth father going missing? Meredith's father dying from a mysterious fall?

He knew to take what the other woman said with a grain of salt. But. Holy. Fuck. This was bigger and way more dangerous than he'd imagined. If Meredith was telling the truth—even remotely—then Kate was in serious danger.

They'd shared everything they'd learned with Matt. Parker had learned his lesson, so he'd thoroughly hashed it all out with Kate before making the call to Jake's twin. But still. To say the entire situation was unsettling was a gross understatement.

He pulled Kate closer, and she snuggled in deeper, her leg draped over his. Calm crawled through him. It didn't fully settle him, but having her in his arms rounded out the edges of his worry, putting him a little more at ease.

"Things are so crazy," she murmured. Her hand absently stroked over his chest, her nails softly dragging through his chest hair. His body stirred. He couldn't help it. Any time Kate was this close, he wanted her. Throw in her hands running over his body and he was a goner. "Do you think Meredith was telling the truth?"

He tensed and scolded his body. This wasn't the time. As much as he wanted it to be, Kate didn't need the distraction or comfort of sex. She needed to get her thoughts out there. After their meeting with Meredith yesterday and their talk with Matt, they'd barely had time to process what they'd learned. They'd each been pulled in different directions with the other chaotic details of their everyday lives. "What does your gut say? You know her better than me."

"But I don't," Kate replied. "I barely knew her when I was in Rockberg. It's not like we were friends then, and I've obviously had zero contact with her since I left."

"I don't know, Kate." He ran his hand over her hip. "From what you've told me about it, it seems like what she said—or claimed, anyway—would have been in line with the cult's actions."

"True. All her accusations were horrifying, but sadly, they weren't surprising. Still . . ."

"It's a lot to take in."

"Yeah," she agreed. "Especially without any proof, so to speak." She was silent a moment, her hand still tracing circles over his chest. "You know, the first cat and flowers happened before Meredith showed up. They were both around the time Master Sebastian was arrested. I know it's all related somehow. For the life of me, I just can't figure out how."

"But after Meredith showed up, the second cat was so much more violent. And personal. That's what worries me." He pressed his lips to the top of her head and held her there. "I think you should tell Anna and Henry, even Blake and Raven, what's going on. The more of our people who know, the more eyes we have. And the safer you'll be."

She was silent for so long, if it weren't for the soft motion of her fingers, he would have thought she'd fallen back asleep. When she finally spoke, her voice was unsteady. "Everyone has been nothing but supportive. I hate dragging them into this. We don't even know what *this* is."

"Kate, you know they all—"

"It's all so dark, Parker. So sordid. If what Meredith said was true, it's even worse than we thought. Then there's the cats." He felt her heartbeat quicken against him before she shot up into a sitting position, pulling the sheet to her chest. He eased himself up and sat next to her, soothing a hand up and down her back. "There's a psychotic, demented human out there who's capable of torturing innocent cats—on purpose—to make some sick point!"

He didn't know what to say. Everything she'd said was true. And terrifying. So, he continued to rub her back in the hopes it would provide some comfort. For both of them.

"I can't bring them into this," she whispered. Turmoil and confusion flittered over her features and gutted him.

"Baby, you can't isolate yourself from the people who care about you, who love you."

"Then there's you," she continued as if he hadn't spoken, her voice holding the beginning twinges of panic. "You've been the greatest friend and opened your home to me after the storm."

His brows rose and his stomach stirred with discomfort.

"Greatest friend"? What the hell? They were sitting in his bed. Naked. He was pretty sure he'd graduated from the friend category.

"And what do I do?" she plowed on, her question apparently rhetorical. "Bring you nothing but craziness and chaos. The timing has been all wrong."

The hairs rose on his arms. Holy shit. He took in a quick breath and forced himself to calm. She was panicking, processing. That's all. She didn't mean it like it sounded. Or so he kept telling himself. Because this conversation was taking a shitty turn toward the "we need some space" exit.

He'd know. He'd had similar conversations before. Different circumstances for sure—there were no mutilated cats, cults, or mysterious strangers from the past—but the same general reasons: timing, craziness, and/or chaos.

"Ever since I moved in with you, I've brought you nothing but trouble." She threw the bedsheet aside, but before she could hop out of bed, his arm locked around her waist and he pulled her back toward him. "Parker, I have to go. I'm not being fair to you. You need space from me. I'm a toxic dumpster fire right now. It's best if I left or—"

"Kate, ca—" He cut his words short. He was going to say "calm down"—perhaps the most horrible thing he could utter at a time like this. Thankfully, he shut his trap before those two stupid words flew out of his mouth. "We're a team, Kate. We talked about this the other day, remember?"

Her struggles ceased and her body sagged. "I'm not being fair to you."

"Look at me." He loosened his hold and drew her across his lap. He waited until she met his gaze, and his heart gave a painful tug at the worry and panic in her shimmering brown eyes. "One of the things I've always loved about you is how you care so much about everyone around you. You have the biggest heart and are always looking out for everyone else.

Raven, me, Blake, the girls at the pub, Anna and Henry . . . everyone. This isn't about what's going on or not being fair to *me*. Or you dragging everyone into the chaos and craziness that's happening right now."

"But it isn't fair," she whispered, her eyes glittering with unshed tears.

He pressed a kiss to her forehead, and when he pulled away, she burrowed into his chest. His arms tightened around her. What he wouldn't give to take her panic and worry away. "What isn't fair, baby, is that there's someone out there scaring you. Doing crazy-ass shit to get your attention."

"But none of you asked for this craziness."

"You didn't either, Kate."

She sniffed. "I don't want to drag you, or *anyone*, into this."

"All those people you're always looking out for? The ones you don't want to burden with what's going on? Asking us to step back so you can go at this alone, *that's* not fair to us. Because we all love you. And when you say that I need space from you, *that's* not being fair to me. Because I love you, Kate. We're a team. We face the craziness together. Me and you."

She stilled in his arms and he fought a grimace. Damn. Not exactly the smoothest declaration of love.

She pulled away and met his gaze. Emotions swirled across her face so fast he couldn't catch them. "Say that again?"

He took a moment to trace the features of her face. The strong dark brows, her sharp cheekbones, her jawline. He cupped her face in his hands. She was so damn beautiful it hurt. "I love you, Kate. More than you'll ever know. Craziness, chaos, and all. I'll always choose you—to be with you, to be by your side. Always."

Oh, this man. Kate's hands came up to cover his and she let out a breath. The tears she'd been trying to madly blink away won the battle and slid down her cheeks. Catching them with his thumbs, Parker brought his lips to hers for a kiss so sweet, more tears fell.

She didn't know what she'd done to deserve him. She'd woken up warm in his arms, and as she'd replayed their conversation with Meredith in her mind, the stress, uncertainty, and downright terror had begun to build. Until she couldn't breathe.

She'd panicked. She knew it. Just like she knew what Parker had said was right.

He'd unknowingly echoed Anna's words, her advice to not shut down and push everyone away. Which was exactly what she'd been in the process of doing. If Parker hadn't snagged her and kept her in his bed, she would have bolted as fast and as far away as she could get. She was terrified someone close to her—someone she loved—would get hurt. That Parker would get hurt.

But he had caught her. He had kept her in his bed. And then he'd proceeded to destroy her, in the best possible way, with the sweetest and most wonderful words she'd ever heard.

They truly were a team.

"Thank you, Park," she sighed against his lips. "Thank you for sticking with me."

He paused from trailing kisses along her jaw, his emerald green eyes solemn. "Always, Kate. Always."

"Parker," she whispered, fresh tears springing anew. "I was so scared that being with you like this would hurt our friendship. But it hasn't. You're my best friend, and I'm so in love with you." As her tears spilled, she caressed the side of his face, his scratchy morning stubble loud in the nearly silent room. He turned into her touch, kissing her palm, and her heart filled. "I'm so scared you're going to get hurt. I don't know what I'd do without you."

"All the what-ifs are out of our control. We can't let that debilitate us or hold us back. Me and you, Kate. We're a team. *That* is something we can control."

She nodded. "Me and you," she murmured, framing his face again. She ran her thumb over his lower lip, then tugged him closer, her mouth claiming his. She snaked her fingers into his hair and deepened their kiss, their tongues tangling.

Parker's growl set her on fire. She shifted on his lap so she sat astride him. They were both still naked, and she couldn't control the moan that escaped her lips when she ground herself against his erection. With each swipe of her tongue against his, with each rock of her hips, the final bits of nervous tension eased from her body. Oh, what this man did to her.

Her phone rang, and they both froze, their breathless pants and her ringtone the only noises in the room. When the ringing stopped and her phone chimed with notifications for both a voicemail and a text message, the lopsided smile she loved exploded on Parker's face. "Uh, baby, was that the Darth Vader march?"

"Yeah, sorry," she grimaced, reaching toward the nightstand. "It's Jake's ringtone."

Parker burst into laughter. "Of course it is."

A quick scan of her texts showed one cluster after another. She grimaced. What part of "*I* have full control, not you" did Jake not understand? She glanced at her phone again as a third text came in from the photographer she'd hired for the launch party. Her eyes rolled as yet another text, this time from the costume designer, lit up her phone. Apparently, Jake didn't understand any of it.

"Ugh, he is the worst micro-freaking-manager ever," she grumbled. "I'm sorry, but I have to go. For some reason, the idiot is calling my party vendors, changing things, and now they're messaging me all confused." She dropped a quick kiss on Parker's lips and crawled off him. "I'm seriously going to kill Jake."

She yelped as Parker's hand smacked her butt. Then she nearly melted when he yanked her flush against him and palmed her butt cheek, soothing his hand over it. "Oh, trust me, baby," he growled in her ear, his hardness rubbing against her backside, *"I'll* be the one killing that bastard today."

CHAPTER TWENTY-EIGHT

Kate scanned the crowded pub and let out a relieved breath that was 40 percent *thank God this is over* and 60 percent *heck yeah!* Gone was all the pub's Irish-lite decor. Tonight, The Spotted Dog was officially a Wild West-ified saloon.

The last few days had been a whirlwind. Her world had exploded on Monday. The remnants then caught fire on Tuesday when they met with Meredith. But on Wednesday, when she'd thought the tatters of her life were going to get sucked into a black hole . . . there'd been Parker. A smile tilted her lips. And she knew it was an ooey-gooey one. But she didn't care.

If it hadn't been for Parker, Kate never would have survived the last few hectic days. For one, she'd be in jail for the murder of Mr. Jake Alvarez, Founder and CEO of Alvarez Technologies. Her face scrunched at the mere thought of that man. She'd known Business Jake was a night-mare to work for, but the reality was much more horrific. The only upside was that she'd been so focused on fixing Jake's meddling and screw-ups—in the name of *helping* because, of course, he knew best—she'd had zero time to worry and stew about Meredith. Not that she'd heard anything more from the woman. And thankfully, there'd been no more hurt or dead animals left out for her.

Things on the crazy front were quiet. She didn't know if that was a good thing or bad. But her current reality dictated that she was too busy to worry about what wasn't actually happening.

Parker had been equally busy over the last few days with emergency repairs in the pub's kitchen. They'd barely seen each other during the day, but each night was theirs. They settled in together, savored each other, and relaxed in each other's arms. Then they woke up early, enjoyed each other's bodies again—who knew she'd be such a fan of shower sex? —and did their hectic day routine all over.

Kate also hadn't seen Carmen, who worked and networked more than all of them combined. She was convinced the woman didn't actually sleep. Either Carmen had indeed won the genetic lottery, had an amazing concealer and foundation regime, or had a fabulous Botox doc on standby. Or all of the above.

But they'd made it to Saturday. All of them. Tonight was the long-awaited Square Peg launch party.

Parker's kitchen was fully functional, and he had Adam and Vince running the show. She'd already yelled at Jake twice for interfering and had stuck Carmen on Jake duty to keep him away from everyone who wasn't a guest. Three vendors came up and thanked her. She shook her head. Freaking Business Jake.

Scanning the busy pub again, Kate's breath caught, and she stopped dead in her tracks.

Hooolyyy S-balls.

For the life of her, she couldn't take her eyes off him. She feared there was actual drool coming out of her mouth. But really, she didn't care. All she could do was stare. There was good-looking. There was hot. And then there was Parker freaking Cunningham.

Snug jeans hugged his tight butt, and a red and black plaid shirt molded to his wide shoulders. Scuffed-up cowboy boots—did Parker actually own cowboy boots?—and the sexiest black cowboy hat she'd ever seen completed his swoon-worthy look. She fanned herself with her hand. She couldn't help it. The man took sexy-hot to a whole new level.

Dragging her gaze up from his chest, she paused as she caught the hard glint in his eyes. Parker was usually the definition of laid back, but right now, he looked anything but. Granted, he still looked good enough to eat, but tension radiated off him. His rigid shoulders, the harshly set jaw, the flinty glint of his bottle-green eyes.

Kate's brows rose as a woman with long brown hair and a tiny, skin-tight, electric blue dress approached him. The dress was so short, one shrug of the woman's shoulders would have her flashing her pert backside to the entire pub. And she wasn't just any woman.

Courtney.

Even from across the room, she could see Parker's wide shoulders tense further. After a moment, he leaned down toward his ex-wife, speaking close to her ear. When Courtney placed her hand on Parker's chest, Kate's teeth ground together.

Shrug her hand off, shrug her hand off, shrug her hand off . . .

Her breath hitched when Parker's hand covered Courtney's. Moving it from his chest, he continued to hold her hand tight against his side. After a quick glance around the room, he led her toward the back office.

Kate's heart stuttered. What did she just witness? The rational part of her brain said that Parker had taken his ex-wife somewhere private to talk. The other part of her brain

—the insecure part that she tried to shut up—balked. Talk. Right. Because when she wanted to talk to someone, particularly an ex, she always held their hand.

She let out a frustrated grumble. What was she doing?

She was being an insecure idiot, that's what. She loved Parker. *Loved* him. And she knew he loved her back. If she could slap herself upside the head, she would. Instead, she was determined to ignore the tiny sparks of anxiety roiling in her gut. Because not only did she love the man, she trusted him. Completely.

However, she sure as heck didn't trust Courtney.

To top it off, Kate's life was currently as dramatic as a bad soap opera, and there was a good amount of guilt on her end for dumping it all on Parker. Like the man really needed a telenovela dropping into his perfectly calm and ordered life.

"Holy Christ, that bitch refuses to go away."

Kate glanced over at Carmen and grinned. Looked like she wasn't the only one who didn't trust Courtney.

"You know, Carm, I don't know what her deal is. Park says he's been clear with her that they aren't getting back together."

"And yet the bitch is still here," Carmen said with a roll of her eyes.

"They've been divorced for years. He doesn't know why she's still around, either."

"Of course he doesn't, Kate, because guys are idiots."

She bit her bottom lip to hold back a chuckle and waited. Carmen was many things—brilliant, driven, beautiful—but one of her best qualities? She was fiercely protective of her brother.

"Courtney's a gold-digging, status-seeking bitch. Always has been. They're almost at their three-year post-divorce mark. Do you know what that probably means?"

Kate shook her head.

"Either the court-ordered alimony payments are winding down, or she's already spent the money she got in the divorce."

Her jaw dropped. *That* had never occurred to her. Not once.

"Trust me, Kate. I know all about paying alimony to gold-digging assholes."

True. With three divorces, Carmen would definitely know. She wasn't a hundred percent sure, but she was almost certain the woman's trust fund was equal to Parker's.

Carmen glanced around and her eyes narrowed. She nodded toward a trio of women in tiny dresses and sky-high heels. "Speaking of gold diggers, I need to go and save our party host."

Kate chuckled. "Jake duty calls."

Carmen took a step away, then paused. "And Kate? Don't worry about Courtney. She'll get what's coming to her."

Kate couldn't help but smile at the muttered curses coming from Carmen as she strode away on her sky-high stilettos.

Not worrying about Courtney was easier said than done. But she trusted Parker. She had to remember that. He'd handle his ex. Somehow.

Those perfect words he'd said to her reverberated in her mind. *"I love you, Kate. More than you'll ever know. Craziness, chaos, and all. I'll always choose you—to be with you, to be by your side. Always."*

Those were the words she needed to remember. *They* were what mattered.

With one last glance at the now-empty hallway leading to the back office, Kate squared her shoulders and put her faith in Parker. He needed to work out whatever drama he had with that woman. If he needed her, then Kate had his back.

They were a team. Courtney had no part in it, and the sooner that woman got it through her head, the better.

<hr>

Parker's gaze roamed over the pub. Everywhere he looked was filled with happy faces. Kate had pulled off another miracle. With all the crazy in her life, she'd still managed to coordinate this party, from the custom cocktail napkins and shot glasses to the faux cacti and the Old West decor.

Kate was so amazing it was no wonder that he loved her. He'd happily tell her how perfect he thought she was every day for the rest of his damn life. Granted, this wasn't the time or place for those kinds of declarations of forever, but he didn't care.

He was on a mission to sneak her away for a private moment. To congratulate her on coordinating a great party. Preferably on the office couch. Or over it. Hell, even on top of the office desk would work. He wasn't too particular. Either way, he needed to find her.

Parker paused as he caught sight of a brunette striding his way. And damn it, it wasn't the brunette he was looking for. His molars ground together.

What the hell was Courtney doing here?

"Hi, Parker." He was sure the smile she gave him was supposed to be coy and seductive. It was neither.

He took a moment to rein in his irritation, then leaned toward her so he was sure she'd hear him over the crowd. "What are you doing here?" Because there was no way in hell Jake had invited her. His friend tolerated her about as much as Blake did.

"I'm here with a friend." He tensed further when she laid her hand on his chest. "Can we talk?"

Her fingers started to move, caressing his pec. He grabbed her roaming hand and held it still against his chest. "No."

"Please, Parker. Hear me out."

They were divorced, for fuck's sake. Had been for multiple years. He wanted this over. He wanted to be done with Courtney. He leaned down again and bit out a sharp, "Fine."

He removed her hand from his chest but held on, not wanting her hands roaming anywhere else. He scanned the crowded bar and frowned, then turned down the hallway and marched them into the office, flipping on the light. Slamming the door shut behind them, he released her hand and crossed his arms over his chest. "You have five minutes."

"I'd like to give us another chance."

He shook his head. Fucking. Hell. "Courtney, we've been over this numerous times. No."

"But Parker, I know I made mistakes, but so did you. I think we can make it work this time. I still love you. I still want you. And I think if you're honest with yourself, you'll see that you feel the same way about me."

Parker could only stare. She continued to talk, but he wasn't registering anything. Why wouldn't she give this up? Why was she still talking?

Marrying Courtney in the first place had been a mistake. He'd known it both the day he'd said his vows and the day he'd signed the divorce papers. Hell, Parker had known it the day he'd asked her to marry him. When she'd squealed an excited *"Yes!"* his first thought had been, *What the fuck are you doing?* But like the dumbass he was, he'd ignored his reservations and put the engagement ring on her damn finger.

When Blake had asked if he really wanted to go through with the wedding, he'd wanted to bolt. But he hadn't. Not because he'd loved her so much, but rather, he hadn't wanted to disappoint his parents by walking away on his wedding day. He hadn't wanted to put them in that embarrassing position. With the clarity of hindsight, he realized his mistake.

He'd carried a lot of guilt because he'd been an asshole to Courtney. To his wife. He should have treated her better. But he just hadn't cared enough. That was one thousand percent on him.

Courtney had cheated on him, but when it came down to it, he didn't blame her. Not fully. He'd checked out of their marriage long before she'd cheated. That was his fault.

He didn't know how to do marriage. He'd failed fantastically at his first one and had sworn off the entire institution after signing the divorce papers. He'd been done. One hundred percent done.

He'd also had a front-row seat to his sister's three divorces. Witnessed how she'd entered each marriage sure that this one would be forever. Then, as each marriage had failed, he'd watched as she'd put up a good front and thrown herself deeper into her work. A little piece of her had seemed to die with each divorce decree. He didn't want that for himself.

But then there was Kate.

Parker couldn't imagine, didn't *want* to imagine his life without her. Marriage scared the hell out of him, but Kate made him want to try again.

Because it was Kate.

The love he felt for her was beyond anything he'd experienced before. Beyond anything he'd thought possible.

He should be with Kate right now, trying to sneak her away to a dark, secluded corner. Not standing here in the pub's office with his ex-wife. He needed to be with Kate. Right now.

"You know what?" He ignored Courtney's raised eyebrows as he interrupted her, just as he'd been tuning out everything she'd been saying. Which said everything that needed to be said in and of itself. "Forget your five minutes. Hell, forget even one. We're done. We're not doing this," he waved his hand between them, "anymore. *I'm* not doing this anymore."

"But—"

"No buts, Court. We're over. We've been over. There is *zero* future with us. I don't want to be friends with you. I don't want anything to do with you." He spun away from her toward the door. He was through with this drama.

"Are you sure about that?" she asked from behind him.

He swung the door open. "Absolutely. You need to leave." He turned back to Courtney and his jaw hit the fucking floor. She stood before him. Naked. Her bright blue dress pooled at her feet.

"What the fuck?" Panic gripped his chest.

He froze as she stepped over the dress lying on the floor and sauntered toward him. "Are you sure we're done, Parker?"

"Holy shit, Courtney! Put your goddamn—"

"Holy fuck!" a deep voice interrupted. "What the fuck?"

He may have yelped. He may have squealed. He didn't know, and he didn't fucking care. He leaped away from the advancing—naked!—Courtney and barreled into his cousin. They almost tumbled to the ground in a heap, but again: He. Didn't. Care.

What mattered was Parker had managed to slam the door closed. He'd somehow gotten the damn thing shut and put a barrier between him and his fucking naked ex-wife.

He held the doorknob in a death grip as it wiggled under his hand.

"Parker!" she screamed from the other side. "Open the damn door!"

Hell no. "Put some fucking clothes on!"

"Jesus Christ, Park," Blake muttered, scrubbing his hands over his face. "I think I have to bleach my eyeballs. Holy shit."

"What the fuck are you two idiots doing?"

Relief coursed through him at Raven's voice. "You have to help. I'm begging you, Rave," he said, Courtney's muffled curses still filling the hallway. "She wanted to talk—"

"Why the fuck did you agree to that?" Blake cut in.

"Stupidity," Raven murmured, shifting the pint of beer she held to her other hand.

"Then she got naked," Parker said, shuddering as Raven's brow arched in question. "Like full-on, dropped-her-dress, wasn't-wearing-any-underwear naked—"

"Christ," Blake gagged. "Don't remind me. My poor fucking eyes."

"You know what's sad, Sullivan?" Raven asked as if there weren't a screeching woman barricaded in the pub's office. "I came looking for you so I could sneak you away and do dirty things to you."

"Oh really?" Blake's eyes brightened, and Parker couldn't help but snort. His cousin was a damn horndog for his fiancée. "That's awes—"

"But now," she interrupted, shoving the pint of beer at him to hold, "instead of doing all the filthy things I wanted to do to you—and trust me, buddy, they were *filthy*—now I have to rescue you fools from Parker's naked, psycho, stalker ex-wife."

"That is super awkward. On so many fronts," Parker cringed, then immediately smothered his chuckle when her death glare aimed his way. "But I really appreciate this. For real, Rave. More than you know."

"I love you, babe, and I swear when you're done with crazy in there," Blake said, nodding to the shut door, "you can have your filthy way with me because you're the sexiest, the hottest, the absolute best!"

"Fuck off, Sullivan." Her eyes rolled so hard Parker was worried she'd strain something. "You guys are so stupid," she muttered, though the smile on the edge of her lips softened the blow. Waving her hands, she cleared her throat. "Step aside, children."

Neither man argued. Parker let go of the doorknob and both men bolted down the hallway without looking back.

"Duuude," Blake drawled once they were out of the hallway. He shook his head and took a long drink of Raven's beer. "She just dropped her dress? Did she honestly think you'd be so turned on you'd just whip your dick out and fuck her?"

"I have no fucking clue." Parker raked a hand through his hair and grimaced. "This stays between us. You can't tell anyone. You have to promise."

Blake chuckled.

He glared at his cousin. "Seriously. You have to promise that you and Raven won't mention this to anyone. Not even Jake."

Blake's chuckle turned into a full-on belly laugh. "No way in *hell* am I promising that, cuz."

"Fucker," Parker muttered. "Kate's going to hear about this, and holy shit, how am I going to explain it?"

"The truth? That your ex makes batshit crazy look cute and cuddly?" Blake shuddered. "For real, who the hell does that shit?"

"What a freaking night, man." Parker took in the pub, still packed with Jake's party people. "I need a Kate fix. Have you seen her?"

"No can do," Blake said, finishing the last of his beer. He motioned for Parker to follow him to the bar. "Kate took off a little bit ago, prior to me needing to sanitize my eyes. Melody wasn't feeling well, so Kate and Mel's guy, Dave, were going to take her to the hospital."

"Holy shit." Parker's eyes widened with concern. "Hospital?"

"I could be wrong, though. I only heard half of what Kate said. Something about Mel being dizzy, maybe a migraine or something. Maybe not the hospital?" Blake shrugged, and a sheepish look flashed on his face. "Sorry, it was loud, and she took off in a hurry."

Damn. Hopefully Mel was okay.

With a sigh, he scanned the pub. It looked like his Kate fix was going to have to wait.

CHAPTER TWENTY-NINE

Kate circled the pub to make sure everything was going according to plan. And why wouldn't it? Now that Carmen was on Jake duty, The Spotted Dog ran like a well-oiled machine.

Madam Raven looked stunning in her rose-colored, floor-length dress, her long black hair piled high atop her head. How Raven was able to effortlessly run the bar with the dress's low-cut, corseted bodice hanging off her slim shoulders was beyond her. Kate did have a moment's worry when the cocktail shaker came out, but thankfully Raven's girls did not make an escape.

Kate snickered. She had a feeling Blake would be sneaking his fiancée away at the first opportunity.

The cowboy kitchen crew was churning out mouth-watering food and the saloon girl servers in their sassy, colorful dresses, thigh-high stockings, and gravity-defying heels were passing hors d'oeuvres and shots—with their shot glass bandoliers, of course—like the beautiful pros they were.

As for herself, she'd taken a page out of Carmen's play-book and opted for a simple, sleeveless little black dress, but with sensible heels as opposed to Carmen's standard stilettos. She'd had her eye on an emerald green saloon girl dress with a gorgeous asymmetrical hem, but figured she'd play it safe. And thank goodness she had. If she'd opted for sky-high heels and the sexy dress, she would have tripped on all the fabric and broken her ankle hours ago. Freaking Business Jake.

Scanning the large crowd, she spotted a very hot, very muscled Jake. Her lips twitched. Speaking of the devil . . .

As the head of Alvarez Technologies, Jake had embraced the event's theme and donned a cream-colored cowboy hat that perfectly matched his blue and cream embroidered Western shirt. His smile was beaming as he held court with Carmen next to him. Like *right* next to him, practically tucked under his arm.

Huh. A smile tugged at Kate's lips. There had to be a story there, because they looked way too cozy for simply being on Jake duty.

Her gaze continued to roam and paused on Melody. The woman was leaning just inside the hallway leading to the customer restrooms, her serving tray clumsily dangling from her hand. But it was the way Melody's head leaned sagged against the wall, the red feather plume in her hair smashed and askew, that had Kate's eyes narrowing.

She rushed across the room toward her friend. Reaching her, Kate placed her hand on Melody's back and felt a slight tremor under her hand. "Mel, are you okay?"

The young server let out an unsteady breath, slowly shaking her head. "I don't know what's wrong." She tried to straighten, and immediately wobbled, her serving tray clattering to the ground. Kate's arms shot out to steady her.

"Easy," she murmured, concern building as she maneuvered her friend to lean fully against the wall. "Let me get help. Are you going to be okay right here? Just for a minute?"

Melody grunted as she rested her head back against the wall, her eyes closing. "I don't know why I feel so bad, Kate," she slurred.

Hoping Melody wouldn't topple over, Kate hurried back into the pub's main room. Spotting Blake back by the shuffleboard table, she turned—and slammed into a hard body.

"Whoa!" Strong hands momentarily clamped down on her upper arms, preventing her fall. "Everything okay, Kate?"

"Oh, Dave!" Relief coursed through her as she dragged him back toward the restroom hallway. "There's something wrong with Mel."

"Holy shit," he muttered, wrapping his arms around her trembling friend. "Honey, what happened?"

"Dave," Melody sighed, her head falling onto his chest. "I don't know. I feel awful."

"What did you have to eat, sweetie?" Kate asked.

"Just dinner before the party, like everyone else," she replied, barely able to pry her eyes open, her words even more slurred. "I felt fine, and then all of a sudden . . . dizzy . . . so, so dizzy . . ."

Kate's heart stopped when Melody's eyes shut again and her legs gave out. Thankfully, Dave didn't let her fall, and he effortlessly swooped her into his arms.

"Dave," Kate breathed out. The first hints of panic began to stir. "Should we call 911? Maybe someone here is a doctor or nurse?"

"I think it'll be faster if we drive her to the hospital. My car's parked about a block down." His concerned gaze swept the room. "I don't want to cause a scene. Can we take her out back?" He motioned with his head toward the emergency exit at the end of the hallway.

"Good idea." Kate nodded. "It opens to the dumpster alley. Left goes to Galer Street and right goes to Garfield."

He moved toward the exit, Melody limp in his arms, and

called over his shoulder, "I'm parked on Garfield, just past Second, almost to Third. While I get Mel settled, can you grab her purse and stuff and meet me at my car? Silver Acura. Let Blake or Parker know too? I know she wouldn't want them to think she walked out. Especially tonight."

"Of course! I'll meet you out there as soon as I can," Kate replied, and hustled in the opposite direction.

Within a few minutes, Kate hit the back door with her and Melody's purses slung crossbody and their jackets tucked under her arm. Racing out of the alley, she turned left on Garfield and ran toward Second Avenue. Once there, she scanned the parked cars along the street for Dave's silver Acura and frowned. Nothing. Her heart raced in an unsteady rhythm. Had he already taken off to the hospital?

She crossed the street and checked the row of cars parked in the opposite direction. Scanning the vehicles, her eyes paused on a blue minivan parked the wrong way. Then, a flash of red caught her attention.

Her eyes narrowed, and a chill inched down her spine. Her heartbeat echoed loudly in her ears as she cautiously made her way toward the minivan. Through the clear windows, she could make out the back of a blonde head slumped against the passenger window, a red feather plume sticking out of her updo.

Why was Melody slumped in the passenger seat of a blue minivan? What had happened to Dave's silver Acura?

Kate had to be mistaken. She had to be seeing things.

The fine hairs on her arms rose as she approached the vehicle. Getting a better look into the minivan, her blood chilled. It was definitely Melody.

Rounding the hood, she stepped into the street to approach the passenger side. She tapped on the glass. "Melody," she called. "Melody, are you oka—"

Kate gasped at the sharp pinch on the back of her neck.

Her hand flew to her nape as she spun around. She gasped again, falling backward and slamming into the minivan's door.

Dave loomed over her, effectively pinning her between his body and the vehicle, his hazel eyes dancing with merriment. Her stomach rolled.

"How about a toast?"

"What?" Her voice was barely above a whisper. She wanted to run. She wanted to scream. But the gleam in his laughing eyes kept her rooted to the ground. "Dave, what are you doing? What's wrong with Melody?"

His arms rose to either side of her, not quite touching her, but caging her in. "There was a toast earlier to Jake and his company."

Confusion flooded her. What was he talking about? She couldn't focus. The burning in her neck intensified. Her head began to swim.

A low laugh rumbled through Dave's chest. "I think we should have our own toast tonight, shouldn't we?"

Something flickered in his gaze, but she couldn't decipher it. A wave of nausea rolled through her.

"To spiked drinks, perhaps?"

Her stomach pitched. Holy shit. Melody.

"No?" Dave chuckled, holding up an undersized needle. "Then how about to small syringes?"

Her heart stuttered. Her limbs were becoming leaden with each breath. She whimpered in pain at the fire in her neck. Oh my God. What had Dave done to her?

"You're right," he continued, dropping the syringe and crushing it under his heel. "Not that either." His hazel eyes glowed almost yellow in the streetlight. Or was that whatever he'd injected her with? "I know. I have the perfect toast for us. To new life and glory."

What? Why did that sound . . .

His face grew somber when she didn't respond. "To new life and glory," he repeated. "Say it."

Her breath hitched. "To new life and . . ." The words died in her throat. *To new life and glory.*

Master Sebastian.

Her heart stopped. It couldn't be.

Dave.

Hazy memories assailed her, but she couldn't bring them into focus. The blood drained from her face as her vision swayed. His arms closed in around her and she slumped into him.

Laughter surrounded her as her feet left the ground. "Took you long enough, Katie."

CHAPTER THIRTY

The launch party was winding down, but there were still a dozen or so stragglers remaining.

"Get your fucking hands off my sister," Parker growled, slapping Jake on the shoulder a little harder than he should.

In the last five minutes of watching them from across the room, his best friend hadn't once taken his arm from around his sister's shoulders.

"Fuck off, little brother," Carmen replied, a sweet smile on her face. "I've been tasked by Kate to keep this guy close."

Bull. Shit. "There's barely anyone here, Carm. Try again."

"Trust me," his sister said. "The second this man moves away from me, chaos ensues."

Jake shrugged, moving his arm from around Carmen's shoulders down to her waist. "It's true."

Parker's eyes narrowed when Jake's fucking hand moved even lower and squeezed Carmen's hip. His eyes pingponged between the two, landing on Jake. "Yeah, I'll buy the chaos bit. But, dude, could you be a little less . . . I don't know, man . . . handsy with her?"

Carmen rolled her eyes. "I've also been on GD duty—

which was out of the goodness of my own heart, I might add —so Jake *has* to be handsy with me."

"Also, true," Jake nodded, his damn hand squeezing his sister's hip again. "It's a genuine hardship being this touchy with your sister, but someone has to do it."

Parker groaned. What the fuck? "Do I even want to know what 'GD duty' is?"

"Gold digger duty," Jake replied, his eyes twinkling with nothing good. His head tilted toward Carmen. "Her words, not mine."

"Before this launch, they were already circling," Carmen said, nodding to the handful of women remaining while she wrapped an arm around Jake's waist. "But now? After the success of this latest launch?" Her eyes widened as she tucked herself close to Jake's side, her free hand resting low on Jake's stomach. "Look out."

"Christ, fine," Parker muttered, shaking his head. His best friend and sister? All cozied up? Even if it was supposedly for show, it was all way too much for his comfort. And seriously, if her hand drifted any lower, she'd be cupping the fucker.

Fucking. Awkward.

With a groan, he waved a hand at the two. "This . . . I, uh . . . yeah, all right . . ."

Jake laughed, moving his arm back to Carmen's shoulders. "Relax, bro. We're just fucking with you."

"Holy shit, Park," Carmen chuckled. "You make it too easy. Ease the fuck up, little brother." She turned slightly under Jake's arm and the assholes bumped fists.

"You guys suck," he muttered, which only caused them to laugh harder. The fuckers.

"However," his sister said with a grin, "I promise I wasn't lying when I said I'm on both Jake and GD duty. Trust me when I say those circling women smell fresh blood. Don't let their Louboutins and little Louis Vuittons fool you. They're looking for sugar daddies."

"I'm not quite sure what the fuck a Louboutin is, but Jake, man, you deserve to be eaten alive by one of those gold-digging sharks."

"That's probably true," Jake snickered, glancing around the pub, nodding and waving at a few people heading out.

His friend was always working, always busy, always on, but this was the most relaxed Jake had looked in a long time and Parker was glad to see it. Even if some of the humor lighting his friend had been at his own expense.

"I'd say this was a pretty successful evening," Parker said. "Barring that short time frame where you guys tried to scar me for life, of course."

"True. On all fronts." Jake smiled, his eyes still scanning the nearly empty pub. "Did you see my brother tonight, by chance? He's working but said he would try to stop by if he could."

Parker shook his head. "Sorry, no. I—" His phone dinged with an incoming text, and he pulled it from his pocket. "Speaking of the devil," he muttered.

Matt: *Recognize this guy?*

Seconds later, a photo appeared on Parker's screen. Chills ran down his spine as he glanced at the image. It was a little blurry, but he didn't need to enlarge it to recognize the subject. He did anyway. Just to be sure.

His stomach turned. He recognized the guy, all right, and his phone was immediately to his ear. The second Matt spoke, he barked, "What the fuck, Alvarez?"

Parker saw the alarm and concern on Jake and Carmen's faces, but he could only focus on Matt's voice. "It's security footage from that florist. Like Kate had hoped, we were able to match the time of purchase of those orange flowers to the store's security footage. Crappy TV procedurals for the win, brother. Who is he, Park?"

"Dave. Don't know his last name, but he's dating Melody. He's a friend of this tool Kate used to see."

"Well, tell Kate to hold tight. I left a message on her cell, but when you see her, let her know we're looking for him and we'll bring him—"

"Holy fuck," Parker whispered, panic stealing his breath. His stomach turned violently. "Kate's with him, Matt. Fuck!"

"Talk to me, Cunningham."

"Fucking hell!" His brain scrambled to remember what Blake had said. "Mel wasn't feeling good or something, so Kate and Dave were going to take her to the hospital. But that was at least two fucking hours ago!"

"We're on our way, Cunningham. Hang tight. Don't lose your shit now."

CHAPTER THIRTY-ONE

A dull throb slowly woke her. Kate's mind was hazy, except for the pounding. It was like a heartbeat. Slow, steady, but gradually getting louder.

The soft beat turned into a steady drum, a pounding that pressurized her temples and reverberated throughout her body, all the way down to the soles of her feet.

Prying her eyes open, it took a few moments for her vision to focus. She lay on her back surrounded by darkness, except for a tiny sliver of light from under a door. Turning her head to the side, she winced, a groan spilling from her lips as fire tore over her neck and shoulders. Her vision wavered but held.

Moving her arms, she bit back another moan as shards of pain raced from her fingers up to her shoulders. Her hands were bound to the table next to her hips with what looked to be a short chain of zip ties—one plastic tie was snug around each wrist, then another tie connected each wrist to the table.

A quick and shockingly painful wiggle of her body confirmed her legs were bound at her knees, a thick strap of some sort holding her down. Her shoulders were free, but even a tiny movement of her torso had nausea sweeping over her.

What was going on?

Kate's mind raced, but it was one giant, jumbled mess.

The pub. Meredith.

No. That wasn't right . . .

Costume party. *Melody.*

She closed her eyes as the images in her mind refocused and flooded over her.

Dave.

Heart racing, she didn't bother trying to free her limbs. Every movement sent tingles and a sharp pain shooting through her body. Eyes scanning the room, they slowly adjusted to the dimness and settled on the wall opposite her. Specifically, a small half window just below the ceiling. It was caked in mud and tiny, just two small sliding panes. She couldn't tell if the window led into some sort of egress. She didn't know if the window would even open, but it told her she was in a basement of some sort. Unless the window was boarded up from the outside—God, she hoped not—it was still dark out.

She hoped that meant she'd only been unconscious for a couple hours. A shudder ran through her. Unless she'd been out for over twenty-four hours. If that were the case, then she was in even bigger trouble. She could be anywhere.

Surveying her immediate surroundings, she made out a chair next to the narrow table she was strapped to. She lifted her torso slowly, her abdominal muscles screaming and shaking at the awkward angle. She held still as the room swayed. Bile rose in her throat and her mouth watered. Leaning onto her elbow as best as she could, she quickly turned her head. The room spun and her stomach heaved. Vomit dampened her shoulder and puddled on the table near her head, the sound of it splattering and dripping onto the hard floor below loud in the otherwise silent room.

Coughing, Kate eased back down and stared at the ceiling. Her chin trembled and tears slid from her eyes. She didn't know where she was or even what day it was. She was strapped to a freaking table, lying in her own vomit. Despair coursed through every pore of her being.

More tears slid down the side of her face. But she couldn't give up. If she did, she'd surely die.

Taking a deep breath in, the dank, musty odor of the basement, mixed with her puke, had Kate's stomach rolling anew. She took in the dark, bleak room and the straps and ties binding her knees and hands to the table. If she was going to die, she was going to put up a fight. She'd been through too much to go out without one.

She would *not* give up. She couldn't. She still had too much to do.

Kate was going to be Raven's maid of honor. She and Anna were going to get mother-daughter tattoos. And Parker . . .

More tears slipped out of the corners of her eyes and made their way down into her ears. There was still so much she had to do with . . . to say to . . . Parker. A whole lifetime of things.

Wiggling her body against the restraints, she bit her lip against the pain. She had to get free. She ignored the vomit tangling her hair as she worked to give herself even an extra inch of space. She ignored the fire consuming her wrists as the plastic zip ties cut into her skin. She ignored the pain shooting through her shins and thighs as the strap holding her lower half down hyperextended her knees.

As she worked her wrists against the unforgiving plastic, her eyes landed on a covered lump in the corner and, next to it, a small metal table. She wasn't sure she wanted to know what was under the stained cover. Nor did she want to know what had caused the dark stains.

Kate's body stilled and her breath shifted at the faint sound of footsteps, at the soft whistling tune. As the steps grew closer, the song tickled a long-ago memory.

Her mouth opened to scream for help, then slammed shut.

"Three Blind Mice."

The song's supposed historical ties to three Protestant loyalists who were burned at the stake for plotting against Queen Mary had made it a favorite of Master Sebastian's. Her heart kicked painfully in her chest.

The sound of metal sliding across metal was obscenely loud in the silent room. She didn't dare move, didn't dare breathe. The door silently opened, and the hallway light spilled into the barren room.

"You don't need to pretend, Katie." Dave's voice was a soft, gentle murmur as he propped the door open with a brick. "I know you're awake."

Goosebumps erupted over her chilled skin.

"There are cameras in here, and I saw the minute you woke up."

Bile rose in her throat again. His voice was so calm, so soothing . . . so deadly.

"Dave," she whispered, her voice trembling. The image of a young teenager flashed in her mind: strawberry blond hair, hazel eyes, a kind smile. He'd never stood out, never said much, but he'd always been there. Always silently shadowing Master Sebastian. Always his father's right hand.

"Katie." His voice held a humorous lilt.

Her hands shook, her whole body shuddering in panic. "Why are you doing this?"

He hovered over her as he tested the strap across her knees. She couldn't hold back the yelp of pain as he pressed down, sending fire through her legs. He continued to ignore her question as his focus shifted to the zip ties at her wrists.

"So much blood, Katie," he tsked, running a finger over her cut flesh.

She ground her teeth together against the sting. *Pull your shit together, Kate!*

Her mind focused on Parker. On Raven. On Anna. On Henry. On everyone she loved. And on everyone who loved her.

She refused to cower before this sorry excuse of a man. He could break every bone in her freaking body, but she would *not* cower, damn it. He would *not* win.

"You brought this on yourself, you know." His relaxed and conversational tone belied the maniacal look in his eyes.

Her resolve wavered at that gleam. She was sure Dave was going to treat her like that second cat. He was going to physically break every bone in her body. A shiver tore through her.

But still, Kate took a steadying breath. She would hold strong. She had to.

"Everything would have been fine, but no. You had to go and meet up with Mary."

"I didn't tell Meredith any—"

"Mary," he snapped. "Her name is, and always will be, Mary. Just like *you* will always be Katie."

"You're right," Kate replied, purposely keeping her voice calm. "I didn't tell Mary anything. I don't know any—"

"Then you believed all the filthy lies she spewed," he interrupted, pulling something from behind his back. It took a moment to register that it was a knife.

She knew nothing about knives, but the jagged ridges along the top of the blade had her insides quaking.

"I'm truly sorry it has to come to this, Katie. But really, you can blame Mary. I was more than happy to just keep an eye on you. But no. Mary had to come and find you. Then you had to agree to help her."

"I didn't, Dave. I didn't agree to anything." Her breath caught as he ran the flat part of the knife along her arm.

"But you did. You couldn't leave it alone. You know that lying will not be tolerated, Katie. You know that. *'For he that will love life, and see good days, let him refrain his tongue from evil, and his lips that they speak no guile.'*" She gasped as he flicked the point of the knife against her arm. One shallow tick mark. "Did you know I was actually happy for you?"

Her mind scrambled. She needed to find a way out. Though her heart beat an erratic rhythm, she concentrated on staying calm. Lowering her gaze from his, she strived for a meek, docile tone. "I don't understand, Dave. What are you talking about?"

"When you finally kicked Scott to the curb. By the way, that took you way longer than it should have. Do you know how tedious it was befriending that idiot? But I had to keep an eye on you somehow. Then when you booted him and ended up with Parker, I was happy for you, Katie." He shrugged and resumed running the flat of the knife along her forearm. "Hell, I was happy for myself. Parker and his crew are so much more tolerable than Scott and his band of phone-obsessed douchebags. Getting to fuck Melody was a bonus. She's such a gullible little whore. The things she let me do to her . . ." He shook his head, disappointment crossing his face. "Sweet girl, but definitely a whore."

Bile clawed its way up her throat, but she pushed it back down, along with the worry for her friend. She could only afford to focus on one thing. On Dave. "Were you just going to keep an eye on me forever?"

"Yes."

Her eyes widened in shock. She didn't know what she'd expected him to say, but a simple "yes" hadn't been it. He gripped her chin hard and forced her gaze to his. The maniacal gleam was gone. Never in a million years did she think she'd wish for it back. But she did.

The dead eyes that looked down at her sent chills running through her.

Empty. Soulless.

"You had to go and mess that up, Katie. What's worse is you made me hurt those sweet little cats."

A memory tickled her brain. Young Dave in Master Sebastian's barn, tasked with taking care of an abandoned litter of kittens. "When you were a teenager, you talked about wanting to be a vet," she whispered. Her recollection of the young man with the menagerie of animals always around him warred with the man hovering over her, the man who had done so much damage to two innocent cats. "You loved animals, Dave."

"I still love animals," he said, his voice growing tighter with every word. He leaned closer, his face inches from hers. "But you . . . YOU!"

She jerked at his shout. The zip ties dug deeper into her flesh and the point of his knife slashed into her forearm. She gasped as his hand shot out, grabbing her by the throat. The fire in his eyes dimmed and the cold, dead stare was back.

"This is all your fault, Katie."

She shivered at his monotone voice. It was as if the outburst moments earlier had come from another human.

"He promised it all to me. Rockberg was going to be mine. All the money. All the glory. All the Chosen Ones. Father promised." His grip tightened on her neck and she gasped for breath. "We didn't care that he got arrested. He'd been arrested before. He always beat their pathetic charges."

She tried to twist free from the punishing grip on her throat, but the sharp sting of his knife at her side had her stilling.

"But Mary," Dave continued, dragging the knife through the soft flesh of her stomach. "That stupid whore had to go digging. Imagine my surprise when her rantings about Father having another child were actually true."

He abruptly straightened, and Kate inhaled deeply as the hand on her throat and the knife on her stomach pulled away.

"That whore wants him in jail for rape." He paced away from her and scoffed. "How ridiculous is that." It wasn't a question. "Father is Master. The only place he's going is back to Rockberg, where he and I will rule together." He stood next to her again. "Now, Katie, where's the girl?"

Kate's heartbeat was erratic, and her body throbbed in pain, but she lay utterly still. Dave's calm, eerie voice was beyond terrifying. "I don't know," she whispered, her voice hoarse. "I met with Mary, and she wanted me to find my daughter. She wanted me to file the paperwork that would unseal the adoption records, but I didn't. I don't know anything about her."

"Hmm," he murmured, bringing the knife to her throat.

"Dave," she said, afraid to breathe. "She has nothing to do with this; she knows nothing."

"It's okay, Katie."

His wrist twitched, and a sharp sting later, a drop of blood slid down the left side of her throat. Then another twitch, and another drop. And another.

"I don't want you to worry, Katie. I'll find her. I'll keep watch over her." Dave's eyes glittered as he watched the blood trickle down to her nape. The stings burning her neck were no match for the dread pooling in her belly. "Someone has to determine if she's worthy of her great lineage. If she is, she can rule with Father and myself in Rockberg. If not, she can be one of our Chosen Ones."

Her chest clenched in revulsion.

"I'm sorry it's come to this, Katie. I didn't want it to end like this, but like I said before, you brought it upon yourself. I was content to watch over you. The first cat and the flowers were just a reminder after Father was arrested. But then Mary . . ." Yet another twitch of his wrist, and another trickle of blood, this time on the opposite side of her throat.

"Dave, you don't have to do this." Despite Kate's best efforts, panic saturated her words.

"Yes, I do. Mary has been dealt with, and I can't let you go. You know too much." He stroked the back of his hand—the one holding the knife—down the side of her face. "I know you understand. Loose ends, Katie. Loose ends."

Her heart raced. Holy shit. This was it.

Parker's face flashed in her mind. Then Raven's, then Anna's. A split-second montage of everyone she loved had tears springing to her eyes—tears of determination. *Fight!* If Dave was going to kill her, she wouldn't make it easy.

She had to fight.

With Parker's image at the forefront of her mind—because that was what she was focusing on, a future with the man she loved—she thrashed against the restraints. She no longer felt the bite of the plastic at her wrists nor the pressure pushing against her knees. She felt nothing as she whipped her torso around as much as she could. If he was going to stab her to death, she refused to be a still target.

He clamped his hand over her mouth, the fleshy part between his thumb and index finger smashing her lips painfully against her teeth. She thrashed her head and his grip eased a fraction. Kate bit down. Hard.

The taste of copper flooded her mouth as Dave cried out. The butt of his knife connected with her forehead, and he tried to pull away. Kate's vision wavered, but she clamped down even tighter. The knife butt whacked her again, this time harder and on the side of the head.

Stars filled her vision.

Her jaw slackened, and he pulled his bleeding hand free. Anger and venom colored his features. Switching the knife to his injured hand, he slammed down on her throat with his good one, squeezing until the stars turned into bright, flashing lights. Everything slowed, and Kate saw the glint of the knife's blade coming toward her.

Her chest pinched tight.

This was it. This was the end.

As her vision darkened, her cloudy mind focused on Parker. And what could have been.

A sudden crash shook the table she was strapped to, the startling clamor followed by two loud thuds. Dave was suddenly gone, and oxygen rushed into her burning lungs.

Kate's vision swam as she gasped for air. Confused and disoriented, her gaze darted around in panic. Where had he gone?

"Holy shit!" Melody appeared in front of her like an apparition. "I think that crazy fuck is out cold, but we have to hurry!"

Before Kate could process what was happening, Melody had cut the zip ties connecting her wrists to the table, leaving Kate with bloody plastic zip tie bracelets. Melody eased her up to sitting. The room swayed and Kate's entire body protested.

"You okay?" Melody asked, making quick work of the strap holding Kate's legs to the table. Kate winced at the tingles that shot down her legs as circulation returned.

"We have to hurry," Melody implored, helping her turn on the table.

Kate bit back a screech when her legs dropped to swing from the table edge, fire shooting from her knees.

"Can you stand?"

For the first time, Kate noticed Dave lying face down on

the ground, motionless, the small metal table from across the room next to him. The covered lump in the corner was now just a crumpled and stained, balled-up piece of fabric.

"Kate!" Melody snapped, softly slapping her across the cheek. "Focus! Can you stand?"

Kate concentrated on her friend and nodded. There were three Melodys, all of them blurry, so she focused on the one in the middle. She was so dizzy, and the lightning shooting through her legs was too intense for words. "Yeah, I think—"

Both women froze as a soft moan filled the room.

Melody stepped quickly away, grabbed the legs of the small table, and smashed it down on the back of Dave's head. Kate's jaw dropped.

"Crazy motherfucker," Melody spat.

"Holy crap, Mel. Remind me to never mess with you," Kate muttered as she slung her arm over her friend's shoulders.

"Well, don't fuck me under false pretenses and we won't have a problem, sweetie." Melody wrapped a surprisingly strong arm around Kate's waist. "On three, ready?"

She nodded, taking a deep breath.

"One, two . . ."

"Three," they said in unison.

Kate's breath whooshed out as she stood. The arm around her waist tightened, and she leaned harder into her friend. Her legs wobbled, and she grimaced against the feeling of nails being driven into her knees.

The room continued to sway in her blurry vision. She swiped a hand over her eyes and startled at the sticky mess.

"Your head is bleeding pretty badly," Melody murmured as they made their way into the bright hallway. "Fuck, Kate, *all* of you is bleeding pretty badly."

Kate grunted in response. She felt as if she'd been hit by a truck, and then the driver had put it in reverse and run her over again. She tried to look at her friend, but her eyes wouldn't focus. "Are you okay?"

"It feels like the worst hangover of my freaking life, but don't worry about me. One step in front of the other, okay, sweetie? We're almost to the stairs."

Kate's eyes narrowed as the hallway before her swayed like a demented video game. "I don't know, Mel," she slurred.

She flinched at a loud crash. The lights flickered—or maybe that was just her sight going—and shouts filled the hallway. It all sounded like it was coming from a faraway tunnel.

Kate was sinking. Which made no sense. She tried to focus on Melody, on what her friend was saying. Mel's lips moved, but Kate couldn't make out the words.

The edges of her vision darkened. Until everything was black.

CHAPTER THIRTY-TWO

The aroma of coffee filled his kitchen, and there was subdued chatter around him. Parker blocked it all out. His body was coiled tight, his jaw ached from grinding his teeth, and he was a heartbeat away from either puking on the floor or punching a hole in the wall.

He abruptly stood from the kitchen table, knocking his chair over. The quiet conversations stilled, all eyes swinging his way. Fuck it. He didn't care. He had to move, had to do something. *Anything.*

But damn it, there was nothing he could do. Nothing. Except wait for his fucking phone to ring. He scrubbed his hands over his face and didn't bother biting back the growl that escaped. Fuck!

Eight hours had passed since they'd discovered Kate and Melody were missing. Eight fucking hours since he'd received the call that the Seattle PD had found Meredith, beaten within an inch of her life, in the alley behind The Spotted Dog. Eight hours since they'd found Melody's jacket in the middle of the street a few blocks away from the pub.

It was almost six in the morning, the sun would rise soon,

and Parker had never felt so damn helpless in his entire life. He flopped back into the chair one of his friends must have straightened and scrubbed his hands over his face yet again.

A gentle hand settled on his shoulder and squeezed. "They'll find her, sweetie," Raven murmured, standing next to him.

"I just got her, Rave. I can't lose her." His voice was like gravel, and the lump in his throat nearly choked him. "She means everything to me. Every. Fucking. Thing." A glance at his friend revealed violet eyes brimming with tears.

"They'll find her," she repeated, steel tingeing her words despite the tears. "They have to. She has to be okay."

Taking a deep breath, he took her hand from his shoulder and squeezed, hoping to reassure them both. "You're right. Kate *will* be okay."

Raven nodded and hastily swiped at escaping tears. His cousin, seated to Parker's right, pulled her onto his lap. She buried her face into Blake's shoulder. What he wouldn't give to be able to do the exact same thing with Kate. Right freaking now.

Parker took in his quietly busy kitchen. Raven, Blake, and Jake sat with him at the breakfast table, untouched coffee in front of them. Carmen, Aunt Anna, and Uncle Henry sat at the kitchen island, quietly video chatting on his iPad with his and Carmen's parents, who were calling in from Brazil. In the living room, he knew Ali and Becca had fallen asleep on the couch while Vince and Adam had crashed in the leather recliners, the members of The Spotted Dog's crew not wanting to go home until they heard about Kate and Mel.

They'd all come together, without question, to wait for any word of what had happened.

Looking around his kitchen, there were little hints of Kate everywhere: a sweatshirt draped over a chair, the book she read while drinking her morning coffee, her stainless-steel water bottle with hair ties wrapped around the lid. But what almost killed him was that the fruity scent of her shampoo still lingered in the air, as if she'd breezed through the kitchen only moments ago.

A vise clamped down around his lungs. He couldn't lose her, damn it. He couldn't. Rubbing a hand roughly against his sternum, he let out an unsteady breath. "Where is she? Where would that fucker take her?"

"Matt will find her," Jake replied, his voice steady and clear. "He'll do everything he can to keep her safe. You know that."

Parker nodded. He trusted Matt and his capabilities one million percent. His friend had called earlier to check in and let him know they'd found a possible location for Kate and Melody. He'd said he'd be in touch. That had been over two hours ago.

If only his fucking phone would just ring.

Parker's hands fisted as his mind drifted to Dave. Harmless, nice-guy Dave.

Rage had his fists trembling. "If he fucking hurts her—"

"God help him if he does, Park," Blake said, his cousin's eyes shimmering with suppressed anger.

No one had suspected Dave was anything except a nice guy dating one of their colleagues. A friendly guy who happened to be buddies with one of Kate's exes. *That's* what ate at Parker the most . . . that the psychopath had fooled them all.

Parker's mind drifted to the jumble of information Matt had thrown at him over the course of the night. Earlier in the evening, Dave had met up with Meredith, and he'd beaten the living crap out of her. He'd left her for dead in the alley behind the pub.

The nearly invisible, ultra-high-definition security cameras they'd installed in the alley had recorded all of it.

Including how Dave had shoved the frail woman's beaten body into the space between the trash and recycling dumpsters, stood, wiped his hands on his slacks, and then headed into the pub for the launch party. Like it was fucking no big deal.

A little over an hour and a half later, the alley cameras had picked up Dave, with a barely conscious Melody cradled in his arms, leaving out the back door of the pub and heading down the alley. The care he'd appeared to show for Melody—from the concern on his face to the careful way he'd carried her—had been so fucking believable. Dave had looked like a worried and doting boyfriend. Then minutes later, the cameras had shown Kate bursting out of the same door and flying down the alley, heading in the same direction as Dave and Mel.

Matt had relayed that despite her injuries, Meredith had somehow crawled out from between the dumpsters and passed out in the middle of the alley, in the opposite direction that Dave and Kate had traveled. Meredith had been found by a homeless woman. In an absolutely dizzying blur that Parker had only vaguely heard, Matt had managed to connect the dots between Kate, Meredith, and Dave.

Now all they had to do was find Kate and Melody.

Time seemed to stand still, but then the slowly rising sun began to turn the sky outside his kitchen window a soft pinky-orange. Parker's phone rang, Matt's name flashing on the display.

Exhaustion forgotten and heart in his throat, Parker snagged the buzzing device. Hitting the answer button, he brought the phone to his ear and opened his mouth. And froze.

Holy shit, what if something awful had happened to Kate? His heart thudded painfully. Nausea turned his stomach, and his breath was trapped in his chest. For the life of him, he couldn't form the words: *Is she okay?* Instead, he croaked, "Matt?"

"We got her, Park. Both Kate and Melody. They're alive."

Relief like he'd never felt surged through him, and he couldn't catch his breath. A gasp from Raven brought him back to the present. The horror over his friends' and family's faces made him exhale, made him realize that tears were streaming down his face. "They're alive," he told the room, his voice unsteady. The terror on everyone's faces turned to tears of relief.

"Listen up, Cunningham," Matt said. "I'm at Snoqualmie Valley Hospital with both Kate and Melody and—"

"I'll meet you there," Parker interrupted, shooting to his feet. He calculated how fast he could make the thirty-plus-mile drive to Snoqualmie. It was still early, so traffic shouldn't be too bad. He could—

"No, man. Mel's about to be released, and my partner will take her back to her place in Seattle. But they're prepping Kate now for an ambulance transport to Overlake Medical Center in Bellevue. She should be ready to go in a few minutes."

A chill inched up his spine and he froze. "Wait, why?"

"Kate needs surgery. Torn meniscus in both knees and some other shit. I'll stick with her, but meet us at Overlake."

"Thanks, Matt," Parker murmured as he let out a breath.

Holy fuck. Relief, anxiety, and worry all turned in his gut. All he knew was that he wouldn't be okay until he saw her for himself. Touched her. Held her in his arms.

Within minutes, he'd barked out orders. Vince and Adam were taking Ali and Becca to Melody's apartment to await her return. He, Blake, and Raven were heading directly to the hospital, with Aunt Anna and Uncle Henry following close behind. Carmen would put a hospital bag together for Kate, then she and Jake would swing by Melody's to ensure Mel had everything she needed. Once Mel was squared away, they'd head over to the hospital.

A hand settled on Parker's shoulder and squeezed. He turned and met Blake's tear-filled blue eyes.

"Breathe, cuz," Blake said, taking the keys from his hands. "Kate's alive. That's what matters. We'll get her through the rest of it."

Parker nodded, tears spilling down his cheeks, and the vise around his chest eased slightly. "Yeah, we'll get her through." Roughly wiping away the tears with his forearm, he blew out a breath. "Let's go."

CHAPTER THIRTY-THREE

Parker lost track of how long he'd been watching over Kate's still body, tucked snugly under the plain white hospital sheet. Hell, he hadn't even bothered paying attention to that detail—time—anymore. Since the second he'd learned she'd been missing, time had been an ever-changing factor. Sometimes going too fast, at other moments, crawling by so slowly he thought he'd go insane.

Time didn't matter anymore. Parker's sole focus was the soft rise and fall of Kate's chest, her even breathing, the occasional twitch of her lax limbs. She was alive. *That's* what mattered. The doctors had assured him that she'd be waking from surgery soon.

When he'd first arrived at the hospital, bursting through the ER doors with Blake and Raven on his heels, the doctors and nurses had refused to tell him anything. Immediate family only. He'd nearly howled in frustration and anger. He was pretty sure he'd tried to grab the doctor in front of him.

It had all been a bit of a blur, but what was still clear to him was that he'd been so damn close to Kate and no one would tell him a fucking thing.

Luckily, Matt had appeared and pulled him away from the doctor. Parker had been saved from doing something incredibly stupid because, frustrated or not, clocking a doctor who was simply protecting a patient's privacy wasn't the wisest move . . . *and* it would have gotten him booted from the hospital. However, Matt's information had done nothing to calm Parker's anxiety. If anything, it had thrust it into overdrive.

Meredith had regained consciousness and confirmed that Dave was actually John-David Devine, the only son of the alleged Rockberg cult leader and tax evader, "Master" Sebastian Thaddeus Devine. Or, as the fucker's birth certificate stated: James Sebastian Jones. The reality not nearly as charismatic or heavenly in name or deeds.

Meredith had mentioned following Dave earlier in the week to a remote location, but since she'd been unfamiliar with the area and had gotten scared the farther she'd driven away from any nearby towns, she hadn't been able to provide an exact location. But Matt and his team, in conjunction with the King County Sheriff's Office and the Snoqualmie Police Department, had been able to check local property ownership records and find a couple possible locations for where Kate and Melody could have been. They'd pinged both women's phones, and with that additional information, had identified where they were being held.

In the early morning hours, they'd found the women in the basement of a secluded cabin between the towns of Snoqualmie and North Bend. Kate had been unconscious with Melody hovering over her. Dave had also been unconscious thanks to Melody's bravery and a sturdy metal table. The fucker was still unconscious, but Matt had reassured him that they had guards stationed outside his hospital room.

After hearing Matt's account, Parker had tried again to

get the doctors to give him an update on Kate—this time, in a much calmer fashion—but it was the same thing.

Nothing. Immediate family only.

Parker had been ready to beg and plead—or bribe, if need be—for any information, but again, luck had been on his side. This time, in the form of good old-fashioned string-pulling.

He'd been about to lose his shit for the second time when Uncle Henry and Aunt Anna had arrived. Not only were they immediate family, but his surgeon uncle also had admitting privileges at the Bellevue hospital and had been able to get Parker into the post-surgical recovery room so he could be there when Kate was wheeled out. She'd still been out cold when they'd moved her to a regular room, but he'd refused to leave her side.

What if she woke up earlier than expected and got scared? He knew hospitals weren't her thing. What if she came to and thought she was all alone? What if she thought he'd abandoned her?

Sure, Aunt Anna and Uncle Henry were there too, but that didn't matter. *He* had to be there on the off chance she woke early.

Looking at Kate's still body, her raw wrists, the shallow cuts along her arms and neck, the deeper cuts he knew were hidden beneath the sheets and her hospital gown, the panic and anger came in waves. Taking a deep breath to calm his now-racing heart, Parker forced down the rage.

He hadn't been there when she'd been rescued from Dave's house, but he was here now. And fuck anyone who tried to get him to leave her side.

Yes, she was safe now. The surgery had been a success. But if he thought too hard about what she'd gone through, it slayed him. Kate's injuries were severe. Dave had strapped her to the table so tightly it had hyperextended her legs, fully tearing the menisci in both knees and fracturing the tibial plateau of her right leg.

Parker let out a breath and stilled. Holy fuck. He'd almost lost her.

Kate. *His* Kate.

He was done being an idiot, damn it. Almost losing her to a madman had been fucking terrifying. If the way his heart and hands were shaking were any indication, he was *still* terrified. But he'd be damned if he lost her now to his own sheer stupidity.

If he did lose her, it would be because she walked away. And then he'd fight tooth and nail to get her back, to fix whatever he'd fucked up. Because if anything went wrong, it'd surely be his fault.

And he'd fix it.

He'd fight. Because it was Kate. He'd always, *always* fight for her. For them. Even though it scared him, the thought of being without her terrified him even more.

He thought back to the last time he'd been in the hospital with her, when she had cut her hand. On some level, he'd known he loved her then. But he'd been hesitant, content with whatever she'd wanted to give him because he needed her in his life. As a friend, as a lover, as anything.

When they'd turned to more, he'd still hesitated, still fought his feelings.

He'd feared he would fail her. As a boyfriend, a partner, a husband.

But now he'd almost lost her—in the most permanent way. That terrified him more than anything, so fuck that noise.

He *would* fail her. He was human. He was stupid. So fucking stupid. But he loved her more than anything. So he'd try again. And again. And again. He was never going to give up on them.

"I love you, baby," he whispered, bringing her hand to his lips and keeping it there. "I love you more than anything. I promise I'm never going to give up on us. You're everything, Kate. Everything."

Kate was having the best dream. She was perched on a fluffy cloud, a cool breeze soothing her, and Parker was whispering the sweetest words to her.

"I promise I won't give up on us too," she murmured.

Moments later, the cloud beneath her heated. Gone was the cool breeze, and her toes were uncomfortably warm, her legs unbearably hot. The cloud she'd been floating on disappeared and was replaced by a bed of prickles, as if tiny bugs were biting her legs over and over again.

Kate tried to move her legs out of the way and the bites turned to fire. She gasped. Her eyes flew open and quickly slammed back shut at the bright, painful light.

"Easy, Kate," a soothing voice murmured from far away. "It's okay. You're all right, baby."

Parker.

Relief calmed her racing heart. Her eyes remained closed, but she felt his strong hand stroke over her head and down the side of her face. She burrowed her cheek against his palm, seeking his touch.

Cracking an eye open, she winced against the brightness. For a second, everything was a blur, but then the face before her came into focus.

The shaggy hair, the bottle-green eyes with flecks of gold, the sharp cheekbones, the strong scruffy jaw, the perfect kissable lips. Tears sprang to her eyes and her heart squeezed.

Parker. *Her* Parker.

"Hey," she croaked, then groaned. There was getting hit by a truck, and then there was this. Everything was both sore and numb. How that was even possible, she hadn't a clue. It just was.

"Are you in pain?" Concern crossed his features. "Let me get a nurse."

"No," she murmured, her voice hoarse. Images, like a deranged horror film, flicked in her mind. The basement, the restraints, the knife. Dave. "I'm okay." Then Melody. Matt. The hospital. Parker.

Kate was better than okay. She was alive. And Parker was in front of her. She didn't bother trying to blink back the tears, and they spilled down her cheeks.

"Hey," he soothed, sitting next to her on the edge of the hospital bed. "You're okay, Kate." He caught a tear with his thumb. "No need for tears."

She shook her head, dislodging another stream. Her chest was tight and she couldn't catch her breath. "I didn't think I was going to see you again."

"Ah, baby," he whispered as he leaned close and gently wrapped his arms around her, pressing his lips against the top of her head. "I love you so much, Kate."

"I love you too, Park." She breathed him in, the familiar woodsy scent that settled her heart, soothed her soul, and set her on fire in the best way possible.

The hospital door opened, and a nurse in scrubs with cowboy hats on them walked in. "Good, you're awake," she said, her no-nonsense tone somehow comforting. Had Jake's launch party at the pub only been the night before? It felt like weeks had passed. That horrid basement, the different hospitals . . . it had all been so disorienting.

Parker stepped to the foot of her bed as the nurse checked the machines, monitors, tubes, and bandages. Kate's eyes never left him; the soft smile playing on his lips had her transfixed, kept her grounded.

"I'll be back in a few minutes with some pain meds and food," the nurse said as she moved toward the door. "Then I'm sure the doctor will want to check on you."

"Thank you," Kate said.

"Aunt Anna and Uncle Henry are down in the cafeteria. Want me to text them?" Parker asked, gesturing with his phone.

She shook her head and held out her hand to him. She needed him closer, needed to feel him. Needed him next to her. Looking at this man she loved, who, by his rumpled clothes and bloodshot eyes, she imagined had never left her side, a calm settled over her. She had so much she wanted to say, but she needed to touch him first. They had the rest of their lives for talking.

Once he was next to her, she patted the bed beside her with their joined hands. "Sit with me."

His brow arched. "I'm pretty sure we're not going to fit."

She pressed the bed button to raise herself to a somewhat sitting position, grimacing slightly when her legs protested. "Help me move to the side. I want you next to me." His brow furrowed in hesitation. "I want you to hold me, Park. Please."

The crease between his eyes disappeared, and he let out a resigned sigh. She bit back a smile. God, he was cute. "You let me know if anything hurts," he murmured as he gently moved her. Dropping the bed's side rail down, he carefully scooted next to her. It took some careful maneuvering, but once he'd settled in and wrapped his arms around her, Kate was in heaven.

They lay quietly for a moment, the beeping machines and the buzz of the compression wraps on her legs the only sounds in the room.

His heartbeat was a steady drum beneath her ear, his

arms solid and holding her safe and secure, his hand drawing soothing circles on her back. *This.* This was what she'd fought for. This was what she'd thought she was going to lose.

Kate snuggled deeper into his chest, ignoring the dull pain that lingered over her entire body. God, she loved this man.

"I'm so happy right now, Park," she murmured.

She felt the chuckle in his chest. "Even though I'm sure every part of your body hurts?"

"Yup," she nodded, swallowing past the lump building in her throat. "Even though everything's on fire. But at least it's a dull fire now." She turned her head and pressed a kiss to his shirt-covered chest, then rested her head back on him. "Want to know why?"

"Hospital-grade pain meds?"

She blinked back tears and grinned at the smile she heard in his words. "That too. But it's this. I didn't think I'd ever have this again."

His arms tightened around her and his lips came to the top of her head.

"Park, I didn't think I'd get to tell you how much you truly mean to me, or get the chance to show you how much I love you."

"We have our whole lives, Kate," he whispered, his voice rough. He shifted slightly and tipped her chin so she could meet his gaze. Her heart squeezed at the love she saw, and she knew with her entire being that it was mirrored back. "You have to know that I love you. More than anything. And I know I'm going to mess up."

"I love you too. And I'll mess up too."

"Nah, baby." Cupping her face, he gently pressed his lips to hers. "You're perfect."

"Right," she chuckled, rolling her eyes despite the tears welling in them.

"But I promise I'll always try." He rested his forehead on hers. "I'm never going to give up on us."

She nodded as the first tear spilled over. "We're a team, Park. Craziness, chaos, and all, right?"

"Always, Kate." He kissed her again. "Always."

EPILOGUE

It had been four weeks since the surgery to shore up the tibial plateau in Kate's right leg with a titanium plate and a crap-ton of screws. Not to mention the work the surgeon had done to fix her torn meniscus.

Her left leg had fared better. Relatively speaking. While the meniscus in that leg had also been torn, it hadn't required surgery. So yeah. That was something.

She had always considered herself laid back. Well . . . *fairly* laid back, anyway. While she loved lists, planners, and all things organization, she also thought of herself as a go-with-the-flow kind of girl. Because frankly, her love for lists and planners and all things organization allowed her to pivot with purpose.

She'd also prided herself on being a patient person.

But over the last month, the last week in particular, she'd come to a new conclusion. She'd been wrong about herself. Terribly, terribly wrong.

Four long, grueling, non-weight-bearing weeks. Sure, the wheelchair was comfortable, and she was getting used to the walker. However, the mere thought of being in said wheelchair/walker combo for *another* four long, grueling, non-weight-bearing weeks was too much. It wasn't the pain that was the issue—she was off the hard stuff and down to a rotation of acetaminophen and ibuprofen.

The issue was her psyche.

Her mood was piss-poor. She knew full well she was being an irrational B, but she was going to crawl out of her freaking skin.

She loved Parker. She loved Raven. She loved Anna and Henry. She loved Blake, Jake, and Carmen. She loved everyone. But, holy crap, the hovering!

She just wanted to go to the bathroom without someone listening on the other side of the door. Was that too much to ask?

Parker had tricked out the downstairs bathroom with railings and assistance bars, so there was no way she could possibly fall. He'd even converted the office into their temporary bedroom so she wouldn't have to maneuver the stairs.

Then, for even more points, he'd gotten her a recliner that she didn't swim in—unlike the one he favored—and strategically placed it in the living room to provide her the optimal binge-watching angle. He'd even thought to get her movable trays for both sides of the recliner so all her stuff was easily accessible.

She grimaced. See! Ungrateful B.

"Penny for your thoughts?" Parker murmured, placing her lunch on the tray next to her. A cheesy, gooey tuna noodle casserole. A dish he detested with a passion, yet still made for her.

If she could bash herself over her head, she would. The man had done so much for her over the last month, from helping her shower and shave her legs to making whatever food she wanted to eat to holding and soothing her when she woke from a nightmare, and here she was, tucked snugly in her new, comfy recliner. Complaining.

The mayhem with Dave was still unresolved. While at the hospital, he'd needed emergency surgery for a brain bleed. There'd been severe complications, and he was still in the hospital in a coma. Despite that lingering anxiety, she was lucky. So dang lucky. She knew that. She really and truly did. But for the life of her, she couldn't shake her crap-tacular mood. She wanted to kick herself. But that would require use of her non-weight-bearing leg. Ugh.

"You want to get out of here for a while?"

Her gaze swung to his. Holy crap, was he serious? Since the hospital and craziness that was Dave, she'd left the house a total of three times. Each time had been for doctor appointments.

"Really?" She couldn't hold back a cringe; the hope—borderline desperation—in her voice was blatant to her own ears.

Parker moved the tray and knelt beside her. "I know it's been hard, baby. I know the last week has been especially tough and you've been . . . down."

She shook her head, her stomach knotting. "I've been a raging B, Park."

His lips tipped up and he stroked the side of her face. "I wouldn't exactly say 'raging'—"

"I would. Trust me. You don't know all the horrible, ungrateful things I've been thinking."

"Sorry." He leaned over and pressed a kiss to her head. "Still hard-pressed to call you a 'raging B,' horrible and ungrateful thoughts or not."

"You're too good to me," she murmured, finding her hands in her lap suddenly fascinating.

"Hey." He lifted her chin with a finger, and she had no choice but to meet his gaze. Pesky how he did that. "You'd do the same for me and you know it. Look, with Dave and then the hospital and surgery, it's been a whole hell of a lot. You've gotta cut yourself some slack."

Yeah, it had been a lot. Like *a lot* a lot. Like she should probably make an appointment to see her old therapist because she knew she shouldn't let her feelings fester. But still. A lot or not, it didn't give her the right to treat everyone who was helping her poorly. Even if it was in her own mind.

"How about this?" Parker began as he rose and took her plate of tuna noodle casserole away. She opened her mouth to protest, but he kept on talking. "Now that you have more strength, what do say we blow this joint?"

Her brows rose. "You were serious about getting out of here?"

"Absolutely." He gave her a quick once-over, and a smirk played at the edges of his lips. "You cool wearing what you're wearing when we go out?"

Glancing down, she chuckled. Recovery attire. Fuzzy socks, baggy black sweatpants with the right leg cut off at the knee, and an equally baggy T-shirt that was one of Parker's. "In the off chance we run into anyone we know," she glanced down again, "or *anyone*, for that matter, could you get me some normal socks and a long-sleeve shirt? Either the lilac one or the mint green one?"

"The soft shirts I like, right?" he asked over his shoulder as he made his way toward the stairs.

"Yup," she called out. "Thank you!" She smiled as she watched him leave the room. For one, the man looked as good from behind as he did from the front. For another, her stomach fluttered knowing that wonderful man knew her wardrobe, knew what she meant without words. Heck, knew *her*.

Within moments, Parker was back and handing her the lilac shirt. As she switched tops, he swapped out her socks.

Then the next twenty minutes were a juggle of walkers and wheelchairs and loading her into Parker's car.

Once settled and on their way, she let out a breath and glanced at the man next to her. "Thank you for doing this, Park."

He snagged her hand, brought it to his lips, then rested their joined hands on his thigh. "Any particular destination you have in mind?"

She shook her head. "Your house is beautiful and all, but right now, anywhere but there is good with me."

"Our house, baby," he said, his gaze on the traffic.

Her brow scrunched. "Come again?"

"You said *your* house. But, baby, it's not just my house. It's *our* house." He brought her hand to his lips again, then shot her a wink. Her heart squeezed in the best possible way. This sweet, sweet man . . .

"Since you don't have a particular destination in mind, are you up for an adventure?"

"Um . . . yes?" As much as she hated to admit it, she still tired easily. Each week was a definite improvement, but she was exhausted and ready for bed by eight most nights.

"Don't worry, I've got you. It's a low-key type of wheelchair-accessible adventure."

She squeezed his hand. "Well, in that case, count me in." She never should have doubted him.

As Parker drove through the city, he updated her on the latest news and gossip at the pub. He was giving her the play-by-play of Raven putting a douchey customer in his place by way of a verbal smackdown when Parker abruptly stopped mid-sentence.

A quick glance showed they were by the stadiums. "Uh, Parker . . . where are we going?"

His bottle-green eyes twinkled. "You trust me, baby?"

Just like that, her insides settled, the momentary wariness

gone. She grinned and leaned back in her seat. "One thousand percent, Park. Let the adventure begin."

They hung a left onto Edgar Martinez Drive, then took an immediate right into the T-Mobile Park parking garage. The *empty* parking garage, seeing as baseball season was over. Her eyes widened when a man lifted a hand to them in greeting, waved a card in front of the parking gate's sensor, and the bar raised.

As they approached, Parker lowered his window, and he gave the man a chin lift and a simple, "Thanks, man. Appreciate it."

Before Kate could question what they were doing, the car was parked in a handicap space on the Suite Level. Parker hung the red handicap placard on his mirror, then exited the car to pull her wheelchair from the trunk. When her door opened, he leaned in and kissed her lips. "Trust me, okay?"

She took a moment to stroke the side of his face, his stubble both scratchy and soft against her palm. "You know I do."

His eyes danced at her words, and she let out an exhale. Though her heart was about to beat out of her chest, she trusted this man with her life. But what was he up to?

Once settled in her wheelchair, Parker draped a soft fleece blanket over her lap, dropped a kiss on her forehead, then wheeled her over the skybridge to the stadium's Suite Level entrance, where a security guard held the door open for them.

Parker relayed his thanks to the man, while she could only stare silently, utterly puzzled as to what was going on. Then it was an elevator ride down, then through a maze of hallways and corridors in the innards of T-Mobile Park.

Thoroughly turned around and confused after what felt like a long, *long* time being wheeled around, Kate glanced up at him as they turned yet another corner. "So, would you say that this is the part of the adventure where you stop and ask for directions . . ."

Then her jaw dropped. The corner they'd just turned had brought them onto the field. Like onto the actual field where the Mariners played.

Holy moly, what was going on?

"Parker," she murmured as he pushed her along the edge of the field toward home plate. "What . . ."

Again, her words died. And again, her heart threatened to beat out of her chest. Because at home plate sat a little square table draped in a blue and green Mariners-colored tablecloth with a single chair next to it. Atop the table sat two champagne flutes and an ice bucket with a bottle containing the unmistakable yellow label of Veuve Clicquot popping out the top.

Her mouth opened and closed like a fish, no words forming, as he wheeled her to the table. Locking her brakes, Parker placed the lone chair next to her and grabbed the bottle of champagne from the ice.

Complete loss for words. All she could do was stare as he made quick work of the cork.

"I know the last few weeks have been tough on you, so I thought this would be a fun treat."

Her brows shot to her hairline. A fun treat? Was he out of his mind? A fun treat was getting froyo or going out for soup dumplings. This? Sitting at home plate with champagne in T-Mobile Park?

"Parker, this is *beyond* a treat. This is . . . astonishing. Unbelievable even." She glanced around the empty stadium, stupefied, and her stomach dropped. Guilt flooded her. "You have to know that I'm so sorry I've been in such a crappy mood. I know I've been horrible to be around and—"

"Baby, stop," he interrupted. He filled the two flutes with

champagne and placed the bottle back in the bucket. "Sure, you've been grumpy—"

"A raging B, Park. A raging B."

The corners of his lips tipped up. "*Grumpy* the last week or so. But I don't care. Don't ever think I don't want to be around you." Moving his chair, he sat facing her, leaned forward, and took both of her hands in his. "When you were missing, I'd never been more scared in my life. I almost lost you, Kate." He paused and cleared his throat, his eyes glistening with emotion. "So, if you want to complain and be in a bad mood? Then go for it, baby. Because I will take you complaining or in a bad mood any time. Because it means that you're with me."

The weight that had been strangling her heart loosened. Oh, this amazing man . . .

"I don't deserve you," she murmured, her gaze dropping to their joined hands.

"Baby, look at me."

She did. The love shining in his green eyes stole her breath.

"I love you, Kate. I know all of this has been hard on you, but I'm here beside you, and I'll do everything I can to help you get through this. We're a team, remember? And I'm pretty sure eight weeks of non-weight-bearing recovery is covered in that whole 'craziness, chaos, and all' bit."

Warmth filled her as he brought her hands to his lips and pressed the softest kisses onto each of her knuckles. Then, with a wink, he rose and moved his chair so he was again sitting next to her. "Here," he said, handing her a champagne flute. He then nodded toward the jumbotron in the outfield.

Taking a sip of the fruity, bubbly champagne, she nearly choked when the giant screen flickered to life in the empty stadium. A short montage of Mariners clips flashed on the screen.

Then her heart stopped.

Playing on the jumbotron was the Kiss Cam footage. *Their* Kiss Cam footage. Her heart thunked hard and butterflies fluttered wildly in her stomach as the clip of her and Parker filled the screen. She blinked back tears of happiness and wonder as she watched him kiss her all those weeks ago. Like magic, a peaceful calm filled her, down to the depths of her soul.

"How did you arrange all . . ." Her question trailed off on a gasp as she turned her attention from the giant screen to the man next to her.

To the man holding open a small box with a beautiful diamond ring nestled in its cushions.

"Will you marry me?"

The battle she'd been fighting against her tears was lost, and her heart shook with joy. Cupping his face in her hands, she pulled him toward her. "Craziness, chaos, and all," she murmured against his lips. "Yes, Parker. It would be my honor to marry you."

"I love you, Kate," he said, claiming her lips.

A cheer erupted, and they broke apart. Kate laughed, tears continuing to stream down her face as everyone she loved—Raven, Anna, Henry, Blake, Jake, Carmen, and the entire pub crew—strolled out of the Mariners bullpen clapping and cheering. "How in the world did you pull this off?"

He slung his arm over her shoulder and pressed a kiss to her temple. "A whole lot of luck," he chuckled, then shot her that lopsided smile that melted her insides. "Brace, baby. If you thought the hovering was bad before, I'm afraid it's gonna get a lot more intense."

She was pretty sure she wouldn't mind the hovering this time around. Because if the hovering entailed planning a wedding to this wonderful, gorgeous man? Then she was game.

"Ready for our crew?" he asked as the group hit the infield.

"With you?" He nodded. The grin splitting her face was starting to hurt. And she didn't care one bit. "Always, Parker. Always."

ENJOY THIS BOOK?

Thank you so much for reading Parker & Kate's story! If you enjoyed it, I'd love your help spreading the word. Reviews encourage other readers to try out a book. It may seem like a small thing, but they're so important to getting the word out & mean the world to every author.

If you could take a moment to leave a review or rating on Amazon, Goodreads, and/or BookBub, I would be forever grateful! Thank you! :)

ABOUT THE AUTHOR

Christina Sol is an award-winning author who writes what she loves to read—romance filled with heart, heat, and suspense.
When Christina's not writing, reading, or knitting, she's watching football or fueling her washi, sticker, and planner obsession.
Christina lives in the Pacific Northwest with her husband and two children.

CONNECT WITH CHRISTINA ONLINE
www.christinasol.com

instagram.com/christinasol.author
facebook.com/christinasol.author
bookbub.com/authors/christina-sol
tiktok.com/@thechristinasol

ACKNOWLEDGMENTS

First and foremost, to my dear readers: I know there are a million options out there to choose from, so from the bottom of my heart, thank you so much for choosing to spend your precious time reading Parker & Kate's story. I hope you enjoyed it and that it provided you an entertaining distraction.

Heather G: critique partner extraordinaire—thank you for everything!

Lynne P & Megan S: your feedback and honesty took this story to the next level—thank you!

Jen C & Danielle R: thank you both for beta reading! Your comments on this story meant SO much to me.

LJ at Mayhem Cover Creations: thank you—these covers are everything!

Todd, Lucy & Jackson: it has been chaos and craziness, but thank you for your patience and support. I love you guys.

To my family and friends: thank you SO much for all your encouragement and support! It truly means the world to me. :)